ACCLAIM FOR BE

THE STORY OF

"Beth Wiseman's *The Story of Love* had me turning the pages as quickly as I could read them. Her compelling unpredictable romance between two strong characters with complicated lives plays out beautifully, one unexpected turn after another. Beth has done it again."

—Patricia Davids, *USA TODAY* bestselling author of Amish romance

THE BOOKSELLER'S PROMISE

"*The Bookseller's Promise* beautifully illustrates the power of love, family bonds, and the good news of the gospel . . . A captivating story of discovering faith and finding hope in the midst of despair."

—Jennifer Beckstrand, author of The Matchmakers of Huckleberry Hill series

A SEASON OF CHANGE

"A beautiful story about love, forgiveness, and finding family in an unexpected place."

—Kathleen Fuller, *USA TODAY* bestselling author

AN UNLIKELY MATCH

"With multiple vibrant story lines, Wiseman's excellent tale will have readers anticipating the next. Any fan of Amish romance will love this."

—*Publishers Weekly*

"This was such a sweet story. I cheered on Evelyn and Jayce the whole way. Jayce is having issues with his difficult father, who's brought a Hollywood crew to Amish country to film a scene in a nearby cave. Evelyn has a strong, supportive family, so she feels for Jayce immediately. As they grow closer and help each other overcome fears and phobias, they know this can't last. But God, and two persnickety Amish sisters, Lizzie and Esther, have other plans. Can a Hollywood boy fall for an Amish girl and make it work? Find out. Read this delightful, heartwarming story!"

—Lenora Worth, author of *Their Amish Reunion*

"Beth Wiseman's *An Unlikely Match* will keep you turning the pages as you are pulled into this heartwarming and unpredictable Amish romance story about Evelyn and Jayce, two interesting and compelling characters. Beth doesn't disappoint keeping you guessing as to how this story will end."

—Molly Jebber, bestselling Amish inspirational historical romance author

A PICTURE OF LOVE

"This is a warm story of romance and second chances with some great characters that fans of the genre will love."

—*Parkersburg News & Sentinel*

"Beth Wiseman's *A Picture of Love* will delight readers of Amish fiction. Naomi and Amos's romance is a heartfelt story of love, forgiveness, and second chances. This book has everything readers love about a Beth Wiseman story—an authentic portrait of the Amish community, humor, the power of grace and hope and, above all, faith in God's Word and His promises."

—Amy Clipston, bestselling author of *The Coffee Corner*

A BEAUTIFUL ARRANGEMENT

"*A Beautiful Arrangement* has everything you want in an escape novel."

—*Amish Heartland*

"Wiseman's delightful third installment of the Amish Journey series centers on the struggles and unexpected joys of a marriage of convenience . . . Series devotees and newcomers alike will find this engrossing romance hard to put down."

—*Publishers Weekly*

"*A Beautiful Arrangement* has so much heart, you won't want to put it down until you've read the last page. I love second-chance love stories, and Lydia and Samuel's story is heartbreaking and sweet with unexpected twists and turns that make their journey to love all the more satisfying. Beth's fans will cherish this book."

—Jennifer Beckstrand, author of The Petersheim Brothers series

LISTENING TO LOVE

"Wiseman is at her best in this surprising tale of love and faith."

—*Publishers Weekly*

"I always find Beth Wiseman's books to be both tenderly romantic and thought provoking. She has a way of setting a scene that makes me feel like I'm part of an Amish community and visiting for supper. I loved the title of this book, the message about faith and God, and the heartfelt romance between Lucas and Natalie. *Listening to Love* has everything I love in a Beth Wiseman novel—a strong faith message, a touching romance, and a beautiful sense of place. Beth is such an incredibly gifted storyteller."

—Shelley Shepard Gray, bestselling author

"*Listening to Love* is vintage Beth Wiseman . . . Clear your calendar because you're going to want to read this one in a single sitting."

—Vannetta Chapman, author of
Shipshewana Amish Mystery series

HEARTS IN HARMONY

"This is a sweet story, not only of romance, but of older generations and younger generations coming together in friendship. It's a tearjerker as well as an uplifting story."

—*Parkersburg News & Sentinel*

"Beth Wiseman has penned a poignant story of friendship, faith, and love that is sure to touch readers' hearts."

—Kathleen Fuller, *USA TODAY* bestselling author

"Beth Wiseman's *Hearts in Harmony* is a lyrical hymn. Mary and Levi are heartwarming, lovable characters who instantly feel like dear friends. Once readers open this book, they won't put it down until they've reached the last page."

—Amy Clipston, bestselling author of *A Seat by the Hearth*

The

STORY *of*

LOVE

Other Books by Beth Wiseman

The
STORY *of*
LOVE

AN AMISH BOOKSTORE NOVEL

BETH WISEMAN

 ZONDERVAN®

ZONDERVAN

The Story of Love

Copyright © 2022 by Elizabeth Wiseman Mackey

Requests for information should be addressed to:

Zondervan, *3900 Sparks Dr. SE, Grand Rapids, Michigan 49546*

Library of Congress Cataloging-in-Publication Data

Names: Wiseman, Beth, 1962- author.
Title: The story of love / Beth Wiseman.
Description: Grand Rapids, Michigan : Zondervan, [2022] I Series: An Amish
 bookstore novel I Summary: "In the second novel of Beth Wiseman's new
 Amish Bookstore series, wounds from the past must be healed to make way
 for a promising future"-- Provided by publisher.
Identifiers: LCCN 2022016208 (print) I LCCN 2022016209 (ebook) I ISBN
 9780310365648 (paperback) I ISBN 9780310365679 (library binding) I ISBN
 9780310365655 (epub) I ISBN 9780310365662
Subjects: LCGFT: Novels.
Classification: LCC PS3623.I83 S76 2022 (print) I LCC PS3623.I83 (ebook)
 I DDC 813/.6--dc23/eng/20220407
LC record available at https://lccn.loc.gov/2022016208
LC ebook record available at https://lccn.loc.gov/2022016209

Zondervan titles may be purchased in bulk for educational, business, fundraising, or sales
promotional use. For information, please email SpecialMarkets@Zondervan.com.

Printed in the United States of America

22 23 24 25 26 LSC 10 9 8 7 6 5 4 3 2 1

To Blue. RIP, my furry friend.
You are forever in our hearts.

GLOSSARY

ab im kopp: crazy (lit: addled in the head)
ach: [exclamation]
boppli: baby
bruder: brother
daadi haus: small house on property for parents
danki: thanks
Die Kelt is farichderlich den winder: The cold is terrible this winter.
Deitsch: Dutch
dochder: daughter
Englisch: non-Amish folk/English language
fraa: wife
Gott: God
grossdaadi: grandfather
gut: good
kaffi: coffee
kinner: children
lieb: love
maedel: young woman
mamm: mom
mei: my

mudder: mother

nee: no

Ordnung: the unwritten rules of the Amish

rumschpringe: adolescent rite of passage (lit: jumping around)

schweschder: sister

schweeger: brother-in-law

sohn: son

Wie bischt: Hello/how are you

wunderbar: wonderful

ya: yes

PROLOGUE

Yvonne locked the door of her house in Houston for the final time, then slipped the key under the mat like she had promised the new owners—a young family with two small children.

She walked down the sidewalk but turned around and stared at the first and only house she'd ever purchased . . . and recently sold.

"Goodbye, house." There was a sob building in her throat, but she refused to cry. She was starting a new chapter in her life, in a new place far from the city she had always called home.

It was a life overhaul, but when her friends Eva and Jake had mentioned they were looking for someone to run their bookstore, Yvonne had jumped on the opportunity. The need for a change had been niggling at her for a while, but prior to the idea of managing the bookstore, she'd been undecided about what she wanted to do. At the time, the decision seemed easy. She loved books and being around people,

Eva and Jake were like family, and a move to the country would allow her to breathe in a slower lifestyle. Now that the move was here, her stomach quaked with a mixture of excitement and anxiety.

Sighing, she hoisted her purse up on her shoulder and walked to the new red SUV she'd bought, complete with four-wheel drive, which she'd been told she would need in southern Indiana. A moving truck was two days ahead of her, and by the time she arrived at her new rental house in Montgomery, her furniture and boxes should be there.

She had three red suitcases in the far back, some fragile items on the seat behind her, and several CDs and audiobooks in the console. It would take two to three days to drive to Montgomery, depending on the weather and if she got tired.

As she pulled out of the driveway, she took a deep breath, determined to keep at bay her anxiety over this big change and instead embrace the new adventure. It had been a year since she'd seen her friends Eva and Jake, but they had kept in contact via snail mail and the occasional phone call. Eva was seven months pregnant and on bed rest due to some early contractions, and Jake's father had taken ill, leaving Jake with sole responsibility for the entire farm. It wasn't a huge homestead, but it was almost more than one man could handle. Jake's father had already been of limited help on the property since he'd hurt his back in a tractor accident. Now, he was also fighting the early stages of pancreatic cancer. Jake was spread too thin running the bookstore, and he wanted to put his family's welfare first.

Yvonne's prior job, searching for rare books, had

required a lot of travel. It had been almost a year and a half since Trevor's death, and even though her grief had gotten easier over time, her fear of flying had not. Every time she got on a plane, she envisioned her fiancé's plane crashing. This had naturally limited her ability to fulfill her job duties.

Now she would be running an Amish bookstore in Montgomery, Indiana. It would be a cultural overhaul in a small town with folks driving around in buggies alongside cars. During her previous times there, she'd learned the Amish weren't as different as people often perceived. Becoming good friends with Jake and Eva had ended up serving her well in a lot of areas. They had helped her learn that a relationship with God could be life changing and introduced her to a world where community meant everything. Yvonne was looking forward to her new life, scary as it seemed sometimes.

Her Aunt Emma—the only relative she was close to who lived nearby—was going to miss her, and Yvonne would feel the void, too, especially since her aunt had raised her. They had promised to visit often, and their last meal together had been Thanksgiving, just the two of them, a few days ago. There had been some tears, but Aunt Emma was happy Yvonne was venturing off on a new journey, something her aunt had thought she needed since Trevor died.

If all of this change wasn't enough, Yvonne would now have to face Abraham Byler—an Amish man who had traded in his suspenders and buggy for a job as a policeman—for the first time in a year. He'd taken a liking to Yvonne at Eva and Jake's wedding and had even written to her in Houston several times. The letters had never been very long but always sweet. He would ask how she was doing, wish her well, and often include a prayer before closing with *"Blessings to you, Abraham."* Yvonne had been drawn to Abraham at the wedding, too, and even gone on a walk with him. She'd been surprised by how easily they had connected, and their conversation hadn't felt like just small talk. But she'd felt guilty about being attracted to him only five months after Trevor's death, so she hadn't written him back, and his letters stopped coming three months ago.

Maybe, after a year and a half, it was time to jump back into the dating game. Abraham seemed like a kind man— who happened to be incredibly handsome. A tall guy with dark hair and dreamy blue eyes. Her stomach flipped when she thought about the possibility of going out with him, even though she was nervous about having to face him. Surely Eva or Jake had told him she was moving to Montgomery. They were pretty good friends.

Yvonne smiled. Change was in the air, and she prayed hard that this would be a good move for her.

CHAPTER 1

Yvonne stood behind the counter at the bookstore as Jake stroked his beard and stared at a list of notes he had written down. When he looked up, she smiled. "What?" he asked, grinning.

"I'm still getting used to that beard." She mimicked his hand by rubbing her chin. "But it totally works for you." Amish men remained clean-shaven until they were married. Then they never trimmed or cut their facial hair again, except above their lip. No mustaches were allowed.

He chuckled. "Eva says it's scratchy."

His forehead creased with concern. "Are you sure you feel comfortable enough to be here on your own? I can stay a little longer if you want me to."

She shook her head. "Nope, I'm good. You've got a sick father and a bedridden wife. Take care of your family, and I'll see you later for dinner. And remember that I'm bringing pizzas." Jake had spent three days training her, and in the evenings she'd joined him and Eva for dinner at their house—"supper," as they called the evening meal. Jake's mother had been doing most of the cooking since Eva was supposed to rest most of the day. Tonight, Yvonne wanted to treat them. She'd told Eva she would bring enough pizza for Jake's parents too. Eva had told her once that pizza was an indulgence and that they all loved it.

"I will call you if I have any questions or problems." Most of the Amish people in the area, except for some of the elders, had cell phones to be used for business or emergencies, Eva had told her.

"*Ya*, okay, then." Jake smiled. "We're happy to have you here, and the timing was perfect for you to take the job."

"I'm glad to be here too." She motioned toward the door. "Now go. I'll take good care of the place."

He hesitated but finally moved toward the door. "*Danki*, Yvonne," he said over his shoulder. The bell jingled as he exited the building.

Yvonne pulled her sweater snug around her. There was a nice fire going in the wood-burning stove not far from where she stood, but a blast of cool air had snuck in when Jake opened the door. She glanced up at the skylights, reminding herself there was no electricity in the entire store. It didn't present any real problems, except she missed having a microwave. There was a propane burner on the kitchen counter in the back room, but it wasn't the same as quickly zapping a meal. And the manual credit-card machine was a hindrance.

Still, she was grateful to be here in this new environment. It was only ten o'clock on a Tuesday, and so far, there hadn't been any customers, so she decided to peruse the shelves. She loved books—the way they smelled, how they felt in your hands.

She gingerly ran her hand along some titles Jake had just unpacked and put on the shelf. She'd already studied the inventory they had in stock. There was a nice assortment of fiction and nonfiction. Jake had told her all of the books were "clean reads," but he did carry romance, mysteries, and thrillers along with an assortment of biographies, Bibles, and other religious books. Jake had also told her that his customers were Amish and *Englisch*—their term for non-Amish people.

Yvonne glanced over her shoulder when the bell on the door jingled and a lovely woman about her age walked in. She was tall and thin with rich, glowing auburn hair that hung in graceful curves just past her shoulders. She was wearing a stylish brown pantsuit with tan stilettos. Yvonne eyed her own blue jeans, casual white blouse, and black sweater. She had quickly adapted to a more laidback style since she'd arrived in the country. This woman didn't strike her as a local.

"Hello. Can I help you find anything?" Yvonne walked toward her. "Or do you just want to look around?"

The woman eyed Yvonne up and down, only the hint of a smile on her face. "You must be the new person Jake hired?" She raised a sculpted eyebrow.

"Yes, I'm Yvonne Wilson." She extended her hand, and the woman hesitated but eventually made contact, barely. It was one of those tentative handshakes where only her fingers participated.

"I'm Brianna Stone. And I think I'll just browse if that's okay." She spoke softly, a delicacy that matched everything about her. Yvonne wondered what she did for a living.

Yvonne waved an arm around. "Sure. Of course." She paused. "By the way, I love the name Brianna. I always thought that if I ever had a daughter, I would consider that as a name for her."

"Thanks." Brianna strolled toward the gift section. The woman walked like a model on a runway—with grace, her head held high, and an abundance of confidence. She was truly stunning.

Yvonne stepped behind the counter and sat down on the stool as she eyed her clothes again. She might need to step up her game if she planned to date again.

Brianna chose a spot in the gift section of the store where she could catch glimpses of Yvonne as discreetly as possible. The woman was pretty, she supposed. Short, with shoulder-length brown hair, hazel eyes, and a friendly smile.

So, she is my competition. Brianna had only been dating Abraham Byler for three months, but several people had already told her he'd had a huge crush—for lack of a better word—on a friend of Jake and Eva's. He'd apparently even written to her in Houston after they'd spent time together at Jake and Eva's wedding. When she'd casually asked Abraham about it one evening, he'd just shrugged and said, "Yeah, we kind of connected, but I never heard back from her." Brianna had heard regret in his voice, which hadn't really bothered her until she learned that the woman had moved to Montgomery.

Her relationship with Abraham was just starting to get serious, and she didn't need any distractions. Montgomery was a small town with few eligible bachelors. Abraham was a catch for sure, and Brianna had always had a thing for handsome men in uniform.

As she eyed Yvonne again, she surmised that "cute" was the best way to describe her. Not gorgeous but appealing enough to warrant competition. Surely Abraham wouldn't still have interest in a woman he hadn't seen in a year and only spent a few hours with and who'd never returned his phone calls or letters.

Just the same, Brianna wanted Yvonne to know that Abraham was off-limits, and it seemed best to establish that fact early on. She picked up two five-by-seven picture frames with tasteful crystal-like hearts in each corner, then walked toward Yvonne and set them on the counter.

"Those are some of my favorites," Yvonne said as Brianna dug around in her purse, finally pulling out the envelope she'd been searching for.

"Yes, they're lovely." She took out two identical photos from the envelope. "I just want to make sure this picture fits. I'm pretty sure it's a five-by-seven." As she placed the picture atop the frame, she lifted her eyes to Yvonne, not wanting to miss her reaction.

"Is that . . ." Yvonne turned one of the pictures around, then picked it up as she blinked her eyes a few times. "That's Abraham Byler." Her eyes widened.

"Yes." Brianna smiled. "It's one of my favorite photos

of us. We were at dinner in Bloomington, and I asked the waitress to take a picture of us. It was our three-month anniversary—three months that we've been dating." She knew the answer to her next question but wanted to hear what Yvonne would say. "Do you know Abraham?"

Yvonne set the photo down. "Um . . . no, not really. I mean, we met a few times, but I don't really know him."

"He's an amazing man, so kind and thoughtful. On our first date, he brought me a dozen yellow roses and told me how beautiful I looked." She kept her eyes on Yvonne as a momentary look of discomfort revealed itself in the woman's expression. "And then we slipped naturally into a relationship and have been going out ever since."

Yvonne chewed her bottom lip for a few seconds, then attempted to smile. "That's wonderful. He seemed like a super nice guy the few times I was around him."

"He's great." Brianna handed Yvonne her credit card. "Tonight, he's coming to my place, and I'm cooking him dinner. I'm going to give him this framed picture of us to keep at his place. And I'll have one at my house."

Yvonne was having a hard time hiding her disappointment that Abraham was dating someone, but she forced herself to stop gnawing on her lip and ran Brianna's card through the antique credit-card machine. She should have expected this, and she shouldn't be surprised that he'd chosen someone as beautiful as Brianna to go out with. But Yvonne wished more than ever that she would have at least written

Abraham back. It would have been the polite thing to do, no matter her feelings at the time.

She'd been afraid to face him for the first time, but maybe she didn't need to be since dating him was now off the table. It was silly of her to think he wouldn't have found someone. Brianna had said they'd been dating for three months, right about the time Abraham's letters stopped coming.

Yvonne wrapped the frames with tissue paper as Brianna slipped the photos back into the envelope, then carefully put it in her purse. After Yvonne slipped the items into a bag, she handed it to Brianna. "I'm sure he'll love the framed picture."

"Yeah, I think he will. I know I'll love having one at my place."

She took her credit card back and put it in her wallet, which Yvonne noticed was a Louis Vuitton that matched her purse by the same designer. Those bags cost upward of twenty-five hundred dollars, a fact that made Yvonne more curious than ever about what Brianna did for a living. She obviously didn't come from a simple upbringing like Abraham. Or maybe she did but now had a job that afforded her such luxuries. Yvonne thought she'd done well in her career before, but she could have never bought a Louis Vuitton.

"Nice to meet you," Brianna said in her soft voice as she gave a quick wave before she turned to head toward the door.

"You too." Yvonne watched her walk down the sidewalk and get into her Mercedes. What was this seemingly sophisticated woman doing in a small town like Montgomery? Her curiosity was piqued since, based on her limited knowledge of Abraham, he and Brianna appeared a bit mismatched. Then Yvonne recalled her own attire when she'd blown into town a year and a half ago. She'd probably given off the same impression at the time.

She recalled the walk she'd taken with Abraham the day of Jake and Eva's wedding. Abraham had sensed that Yvonne needed to get away from the hustle and bustle as Amish ladies scurried everywhere, putting food out for the reception. Being at a wedding had rebirthed her grief, and talking about it with Abraham had come easily. She'd found herself sharing about Trevor more than she'd meant to, but Abraham had seemed to genuinely care about her loss. When he'd asked if he could write to her when she left, she'd told him yes. Looking back, she'd been afraid she might actually fall for Abraham. It had felt like it would be a betrayal to Trevor if she corresponded with Abraham.

Yvonne attempted to wrap up her thoughts about Abraham and bask in this new opportunity, but she was frazzled. To distract herself, she scribbled herself a note to remember to pick up the pizzas later, then made a list of things she wanted to accomplish today. Staying busy had a way of keeping random thoughts at bay.

Yvonne arrived with four large pizzas that evening. "There's a plain cheese one, a pepperoni, a meat-lover's, and a supreme," she said as she set the boxes on the table. Eva was already sitting on a kitchen chair. Her friend joined the family for meals, but Yvonne always excused herself quickly after they ate so Eva could get back in bed.

"This is so nice of you." Eva eyed the boxes, then looked up at Yvonne. "*Danki* so much for doing this."

Yvonne chuckled. "Are you kidding me? This is the least I can do for all the meals you've shared with me since I got here. I appreciate all your mom's fabulous cooking." She pointed to the pizza boxes. "Should I take them a pizza at the *daadi haus*?" It was two of the few words Yvonne knew in Pennsylvania Dutch, referring to the smaller house on the property where parents or grandparents usually retired to when it was time for one of their children to marry and start a family. Jake was the obvious choice to remain in the main house since he was an only child.

"*Mamm* said she'd be over later to pick up some pizza," Jake said as he loaded a slice from each pie onto his plate. "She said to thank you. *Mei* parents love pizza as much as Eva and I do."

After they all had food on their plates, they bowed their heads in silent prayer.

"So, how did it go at the store today on your first day by yourself?" Jake asked.

Yvonne finished chewing before dabbing her mouth with a napkin. "There weren't many people, but I remember you said that's typical for a Tuesday. Everything went fine, though. A few ladies from Illinois came in and bought quite a bit." She was trying to ease into a conversation about Abraham. They hadn't brought up his name since she'd arrived. "And I met Abraham Byler's girlfriend, Brianna."

Jake and Eva exchanged looks before Jake cleared his

throat. "Uh, *ya*, they've been dating about three months. We don't know much about her. I've talked to Abe, so I know he's been spending a lot of time with her, but we haven't met Brianna."

"Before I had to stay in bed most of the day—which I'm so tired of—a couple of ladies at a Sister's Day were talking about his new girlfriend. Abe's family is still here, and since he grew up Amish, everyone knows who he is."

"She didn't seem like his type." Yvonne regretted the judgmental comment right away.

Jake grinned. "*Ya*, I think he was a little smitten with you, but he understood that it hadn't been that long since your fiancé passed."

"But you said he wrote you letters and even tried to call, right?" Eva shifted her weight in her chair, flinching a little. "This *boppli* moves around a lot."

"She's just eager to get here." Yvonne smiled. "Yes, I believe it to be a girl even though you don't know that for sure. And, yes, Abraham did try to correspond with me." She shrugged. "I just felt it was too soon to have a close male friend, but I should have written him back. I feel bad about that."

They ate quietly for a few minutes.

"Does he know I'm living here now?" Yvonne tried to sound casual and didn't make eye contact with Jake or Eva.

"*Ya*, he does. I don't know how serious things are with him and Brianna." Jake waggled his brows at Yvonne. "Want me to find out?"

Yvonne felt herself blushing. "No. Don't do that. I don't want to wreck anything he has going on with Brianna, although I don't think that's possible anyway. The woman is knockout gorgeous, which is fitting since he is such a good-looking man."

"Looks aren't everything." Eva grinned, then turned to Jake. "I just happened to have lucked out and married the most handsome man on the planet, who also has a huge heart."

Jake blew her a kiss. "Back atcha, *mei* beautiful *fraa*."

Yvonne smiled. Jake and Eva were cute together. And they had Yvonne starting to think she wanted someone special in her life too. But it didn't look like it was going to be Abraham Byler.

CHAPTER 2

Abraham sat on Brianna's couch, sinking into the plush cushions colored in hues of blue and turquoise. Brianna had placed a wrapped package on her glass coffee table, which actually seemed too tall for a coffee table and had long, winding silver legs. Everything about Brianna's house was modern and looked like it could be featured in a magazine—a stark contrast to the farmhouse Abraham had redone a couple of years ago. When he sat on his couch at home, he could put his socked feet on top of the coffee table. Not here. Nor did he think he would even if the table were lower. It just felt more formal here.

"I got you something today." Brianna sat down beside him, smiling. "Open it."

"And what did I do to deserve this?" Abraham angled around the radio attached to the belt that held up his blue jeans, the volume turned down as low as it would go. He was off duty but on call and hoping it would be a quiet night as he reached for the package wrapped in blue paper. It matched the living room, which was decorated in blue and white, along with her kitchen. Shiny white floors flowed throughout. Her bedroom was also decorated in the same colors, with a bedspread covered in large blue-and-white flowers. Not that he had ever been in her bed. Maybe it was his Amish upbringing, but he wanted to reserve that sacred act for marriage.

Brianna seemed to have other ideas about that sometimes and could be hard to resist. She was beautiful, generous almost to a fault, and one of the smartest people he'd ever known. She was a certified public accountant and worked from home, but he was still unclear why she'd packed up her life in New York and moved to the small town of Montgomery. She was evasive every time he brought up the subject. As a cop, he'd had the thought to run a background check on her, but he'd immediately quashed that idea. It was wrong on a lot of levels, including an abuse of his job. He was dating the woman, not investigating her, and an unwillingness to discuss her background didn't make her a criminal.

"It's just a little something." Brianna folded her hands in her lap as she waited for him to unwrap the gift.

He swallowed hard when he saw the photo of them inside a pretty frame with hearts in each corner. His first thought was that it seemed too soon for such a gift. But Brianna was clearly waiting for a response. "It's pretty." He forced a smile. "Thank you."

She snuggled up to him and kissed him on the cheek. "Now, when we're not together, you'll have a picture of us at your place." She pointed to a hutch against the wall. "See, I have a photo of us too."

After nodding to acknowledge her identical frame and picture, he said, "Thank you," again. "I appreciate the gift and . . ." He breathed in the scent of something heavenly coming from the kitchen. Everything about Brianna's place was lavish and made him uncomfortable, but her cooking skills were top-notch. "What's that I smell cooking?"

"It's a *tartiflette,* which is a fancy word for a cheese-and-potato bake. It's French. I think you'll like it." She leaned around and kissed him on the mouth, the aroma of her floral perfume filling his nostrils and tempting him to follow her lead, but he gently eased her away.

"I'm starving," he said and smiled before he gave her a quick peck.

She stood, motioning for him to do the same. "The table is set, and I have a fresh pitcher of sweet tea ready for you."

Abraham followed her into the kitchen, which was almost as big as his living room. He inhaled again as his stomach growled, then helped her finish prepping the food. In minutes, the main dish, a salad, and bread sat waiting on the white table. As usual, Brianna had a glass of red wine by her plate. Abraham reached across the table for her hand and thanked God for the food and an abundance of blessings.

"Amen," they both said. He wasn't sure where Brianna's faith stood, but she had participated in prayer ever since he had offered to say the blessing before their first meal together.

The food was incredible, and he'd told her so at least three times when she finally cleared her throat and said, "I went into Jake Lantz's bookstore today. That's where I got the frames."

Abraham nodded as he reached for another slice of bread. It wasn't like his mother made, but it was from a local bakery and pretty tasty. "They're good people, Jake and Eva. I heard she's on bed rest until the baby is born. And Jake's father is ill. Last I heard he was going to hire someone to run the bookstore." Abraham had been anxious about Yvonne's arrival ever since Jake told him she would be moving to Indiana.

"He did." Brianna was soft-spoken most of the time, but her voice rose a little louder now. "A woman named Yvonne who moved here from Texas."

Abraham couldn't recall mentioning Yvonne to Brianna, but it was a small town, and she could have heard the news from anyone. Or maybe Yvonne had told her.

"Do you know her?" Brianna raised an eyebrow.

Abraham knew better than to react with much excitement even though he was instantly elated on the inside. He hadn't known Yvonne was already here. He also didn't know exactly how much Brianna knew about his prior interactions with Yvonne, limited as they were.

He nodded, finished chewing. "I met her a couple of times." *And I've never stopped thinking about her.* "But I don't really know her." He recalled the letters he'd sent her and how she never wrote back or answered his call. He'd been disappointed at the time, but he understood. It had been too soon for her to acknowledge an attraction between them. He was sure she'd felt it too; they had just clicked naturally. But the timing was off.

And now she was living here, and the timing felt off again.

"She seemed very nice." Brianna beamed, and Abraham wondered if the two women would become friends, which felt odd for some reason. "Didn't you say that new officer you introduced me to is single and looking to meet someone? Maybe you should connect the two of them."

"Bruce? Yeah, he's looking to meet someone, but I don't think they'd be a good fit." Abraham didn't like the idea of anyone he knew dating Yvonne. He had been so enchanted with her at the time, he didn't think he'd like seeing her involved with one of his friends or associates.

"Why not?" Brianna had set her fork down and seemed genuinely interested. Or jealous. There were a few people in town who knew Abraham had written to Yvonne. Again, he wondered how much Brianna knew.

He shrugged. "I don't know either one very well, but I can't really picture them together."

"Hmm . . ." Yvonne wiped her mouth with her napkin. Abraham waited for more, but she was quiet. They both were until the static of his radio broke the silence.

Abraham responded to the call before he looked across the table at Brianna. "I'm so sorry."

She sighed. "I know. I know. You've got to go. Duty calls." She stood when he did, then walked around the corner of the table and kissed him passionately. "I'll be up late if you want to come back after you go take care of the bad guys."

He sighed. "Maureen and Will Robertson aren't exactly bad guys, but they act like it when they fight. This is the

20

third domestic-violence call that's come in on them." He kissed her before he moved toward the door, stopping with his hand on the knob and turning to face her as she approached him. "That was a wonderful dinner. Thank you."

"Of course." She gazed into his eyes. "Remember, I'm here if you want to come back."

"I'll call you," he said before giving her one final kiss and dashing out the door.

There wasn't much crime in Montgomery. Mostly domestic issues, the occasional robbery, and too many car and buggy accidents. At least that's how it had been since he joined the force well over a decade ago. Leaving his Amish upbringing had been a tough call and particularly hard on his family since he'd spent nineteen years living the Amish ways. But since he hadn't been baptized, he was free to make that choice without being shunned.

Now, at thirty-seven, he usually didn't have any regrets. Sometimes he missed the closeness of the community. He was still welcomed among them, but he was looking in from the outside now. He'd prayed hard about it for a lot of years, but even as a teenager, his decision not to be baptized had been backed up by the fact that he'd always thought he would eventually choose a lifestyle that didn't include the Amish ways. A friend's legal mishap had sparked his decision to leave, and it only gained fuel as he got older.

When he'd joined the police force, members of the community had been shocked since the Amish were passive, and being a cop crossed that line repeatedly. But even though he'd overhauled his life, he'd held tightly to his Christian faith. And over the years his family and friends had grown at least more accustomed to his career.

When he showed up at Maureen and Will Robertson's house, Maureen was on the porch holding her cell phone and crying. Even in the dim light, Abraham could see her swollen eye, which would eventually turn black—like the other times. She had a cut on her lip.

"Are you ready to press charges now?" He handed Maureen a handkerchief to press against her mouth, which was bleeding.

"He doesn't mean to get like this. I know he had a bad day at work, and I probably shouldn't have called 911." Maureen hung her head. She was a young gal, early twenties. Abraham had told her before that she needed to break this pattern unless she wanted to live this way the rest of her life.

"But you did call." Abraham moved past her. "Will! Get out here," he yelled over Maureen's shoulder.

Will was older than Maureen by over a decade. He was Abraham's age, and they'd lived here all their lives. As kids, they hadn't gone to school together since Abraham had attended school only through the eighth grade, as required in his district. Later, he'd pursued his education to get into law enforcement. But he remembered Will had been a bully even when they were younger, and as an adult he'd always seemed to hook up with younger, naïve women. The only reason Abraham knew Maureen was because of these frequent phone calls.

"I just want to take back the call." Maureen sniffled with the handkerchief still pressed to her mouth. "I'm not pressing any charges."

Abraham turned his attention to Will as the man stumbled onto the front porch. "Hear that? No charges," Will slurred.

"Maureen, this isn't going to stop until you do something." Abraham put a hand on his holster when Will pushed her out of the way and moved toward him. He'd never had to pull his weapon, and he hoped he never had to, but he was trained to be prepared.

"She ain't pressing any charges, so get off my property." Will staggered closer, then turned to Maureen. "Go on back in the house, sweetie."

Abraham shook his head. Legally, he could take Will in, but it would all be for nothing. Maureen was too afraid of Will to press charges. Even if Abraham did go ahead and arrest Will, it would probably make things worse for Maureen when he got out of jail.

"You're a bully, Will. Always have been, and I guess that will never change." He pointed a finger at him. "But I'll be hoping for Maureen's sake that she wises up and gives you the boot."

Abraham turned to leave, and before he'd gotten back in his patrol car, Will had gone inside and slammed the door. Abraham sat for a few minutes and prayed for the couple, especially for Maureen. After he prayed, he decided to go home instead of back to Brianna's. Hearing Yvonne was in town—to stay—had rocked his world a little, which made him feel both exhilarated and guilty. Brianna was great, and he was lucky to be with her. But he couldn't forget the short time he'd spent with Yvonne. There was something about her that had kept him up nights.

Wednesday morning, Yvonne flipped through a catalog of books. Jake had asked her to pick out a few authors that he didn't typically stock—to try something new—but to keep it clean. She'd found four new authors that she thought would make good additions to his inventory. She was still browsing when her first customer of the day walked in the door.

She could feel the blush in her face before either of them said anything. "Hi, Abraham." He looked exactly as she remembered, except even more handsome and somehow taller.

"I heard you were in town." He slowly approached the counter. "Nice to see you again."

Yvonne sighed. "It's nice to see you too. I'm sorry I didn't return your letters or call. I was, um . . . in a bad place at the time."

"It's okay. Really. I understand." He edged closer to the counter. "You seem to be doing well. Do you like living here so far?"

"Well, it's only been a few days, but I'm definitely enjoying the slower pace. And everyone has been really nice." She took a deep breath. "I met your girlfriend, Brianna, yesterday. She's absolutely gorgeous."

Now it was Abraham whose face reddened. "Yeah, we've been seeing each other about three months."

"That's what she said." Yvonne nervously tucked her hair behind her ears. "What does she do for a living, if you don't mind me asking? She dressed as if she had a professional job, and it's such a small town, and . . ." She shrugged. "I was just wondering."

Abraham walked even closer to the counter, near enough that Yvonne caught a whiff of his cologne, which took her back to the day they'd shared a walk at Jake and Eva's wedding.

"She's a certified public account, a CPA, and she works from home." He chuckled a little. "She dresses like that every time she leaves the house. I always tell her it's a lot more casual here than in New York."

Yvonne thought about Trevor and how much he'd loved his trips to the Big Apple. Even though it had been a year and a half since her fiancé had died, there were still triggers that brought back memories.

"Well, she's lovely." She paused, tipped her head to one side. "What made her move here from New York?" Cringing, she added, "I hope I'm not being too nosy. I mean, I made the move from Houston. Similar situation, I guess. But I would think that moving here from New York would be even more of a culture shock. Did she live in New York City?"

Abraham nodded. "*Ya,* she did. And to tell you the truth, I'm not sure exactly why she packed up and left." He scratched his clean-shaven chin. "She never wants to talk about it, so I haven't pushed too much."

Yvonne smiled. "I can still hear your Amish accent when you say certain words."

"I get that a lot. I spoke the dialect for so long, I guess part of it will always be with me. Kind of like the religion itself, it still lingers in my heart."

"On our walk all that time ago, you said that an injustice was done to a friend of yours when you were young, and that's why you chose to pursue a field in law enforcement." He'd told her that an Amish boy had been unfairly jailed and ridiculed and that he'd wanted to be a voice for his people. "Do you ever regret leaving your roots?"

"Well, I didn't go very far." He grinned, which caused Yvonne's stomach to flip. Abraham was definitely more handsome than she'd remembered. "I purposely stayed here in Montgomery as kind of a voice for the Amish folks. And my family is here." He scratched his cheek. "As for regrets? Yeah, sometimes I have regrets, but they are few and far between."

He seemed intentional with his use of "yeah" instead of "*ya*." Yvonne wondered what his regrets were, but she didn't want to be too pushy. She was already asking a lot of questions.

An awkward silence ensued. Yvonne tugged on her earlobe. "Well, is there anything I can help you with today? Looking for anything special?"

Abraham should probably lie right now, but he hadn't been brought up that way. "No. I just came to say hello and to wish you well in this new venture." She blushed a little. "I'm sure Jake was thrilled that you were willing to make the move. The poor guy has been running himself ragged trying to keep up with the bookstore and the farm. His dad isn't able to help at all, and of course Eva can't do much right now either."

"I know. I feel bad for them, and I plan to do some cooking—frozen meals they can just heat up. Jake's mother has been doing most of the cooking, and they fed me several nights. I took pizza for everyone last night, but maybe over the weekend I can prepare some meals in between unpacking."

"I wouldn't worry about it too much if you don't have time to cook for them. Members of the community have been taking them lots of food. His mother enjoys cooking, so she probably insisted on cooking for you upon your arrival."

Abraham was having a hard time taking his eyes off her or making a move to leave. Her brown hair was still just above her shoulders, and her hazel eyes and sweeping lashes always captured him. He'd been wildly attracted to her from the first time he saw her, here in the bookstore, even though the circumstances could have been better. Someone had broken in, and Abraham had responded to the call.

She grinned, which sent his senses reeling. "I'm quite sure everyone in this community cooks better than I do. I've never had a meal here that I didn't love—and I'm a pretty picky eater. But I'll find ways to help Eva and Jake."

He waved an arm around the store. "It looks like you already have by accepting Jake's job offer."

She laughed, which he'd never heard before, and joy shone in her eyes. Perhaps time really did heal, and her grief was becoming more distant.

"He didn't exactly *offer* me the job. I kinda begged. I was desperate for a change. But I do think he was glad to have someone he knows, and who loves books, to run the store."

"Someone he trusts too." Abraham felt warmth flow through him in her presence. It had been that way before and had resurfaced just seeing her.

Brianna. A pang of guilt punched him in the gut. "I guess I should go. I just wanted to stop by and wish you well."

"I'm glad you did."

He stared at her and knew he'd analyze those four words the rest of the day. Did she mean to sound as sultry as she did? Had he imagined it?

Abraham gave a quick wave and turned to leave. As the bell on the door jingled behind him, he walked the short distance to his patrol car. What was it about Yvonne Wilson that caused his heart to flutter? And how was he going to make it stop? Montgomery was a small town, and they were going to run into each other. The problem was twofold: Abraham didn't want the heady sensation to stop, but he had a girlfriend. He wasn't going to do anything to hurt Brianna. She'd been great.

Brianna stayed far enough off the dirt side road, her car parked behind a cluster of trees, that Abraham couldn't see her. She didn't like being this person—a spy on her boyfriend—but she'd had a sick feeling in the pit of her stomach the night before that Abraham might go see Yvonne. And her boyfriend—a term that now felt threatened—hadn't even waited twenty-four hours before making contact with his former infatuation.

She waited until he pulled out of the bookstore parking

lot and was on the main road before she called him. The call went straight to voice mail. "Hey, you." She tried to sound chipper even though her emotions were going in another direction. "I just called to say good morning and to wish you a good day." She decided not to ask him to call her, to wait and see if he would, even just to return the good-day wishes.

After she'd sat in her car thinking for a few minutes, she finally started it up and left her hiding place. She was drawn like a magnet to the bookstore, desperate to tell Yvonne Wilson to keep her claws away from Abraham, but that was crazy behavior, and she wasn't going there. Instead, she carried on with her plans for the day: to drive to Bloomington for a day of spa treatments—massage, pedicure, and manicure. The hour-long drive would give her time to think. She didn't want to make the same mistakes she'd made in New York with Mitch.

When her cell phone rang, Abraham's name flashed across the screen on her console, and she pushed the button on her steering wheel to answer. Her clenched stomach relaxed. He'd called her back within only a few minutes.

"Hi, there." She did her best to sound casual and unaffected by his actions this morning.

"Sorry I missed your call. I'm going to do my best to have a good day even though it's going to be a long day. We've got a training session tonight, a mandatory thing. They've brought in some guy from Indianapolis who specializes in when to draw your gun and when not to. It sounds repetitive, like other training sessions."

"Aw, that sounds like we won't be able to see each other

tonight." She wondered briefly if he was telling the truth but reminded herself that Abraham didn't condone lying, no matter what. He'd said so more than once.

They'd been spending most of their evenings together even though Abraham wouldn't spend the night. Brianna had done everything to seduce him into her bed, but she'd finally given up and promised herself she would respect his boundaries, no matter how archaic they were.

"I'm afraid not. Sorry about that. But I wanted to call and tell you to have a good day. Hope you enjoy your 'day of maintenance,' as you call it." He chuckled, which was nice to hear. Everything sounded normal.

"Thank you, and I'm planning to make it a good day. How can I go wrong with a little pampering?" She paused. "So, how's your morning been so far? Any calls?" Biting her bottom lip, she waited to see if he would tell her he'd been to the bookstore.

"Nope. No calls yet today. And that's fine by me."

She waited to see if he would offer up more. When he didn't, she asked, "So what have you been up to then? Just riding around and keeping the community safe?" It was an effort to keep up this cheerful attitude when her chest felt so tight.

"That's it. Just driving around and making sure the people in Montgomery are safe." He didn't sound like a man who was hiding something. She was going to have to ask him a direct question.

"Well, I know I feel safe just knowing you're out there. So, no stops at the bakery this morning or anywhere else?"

"No, I ate a little something before I left home, so I

didn't stop for donuts." He laughed. "Cops and donuts. Seems to be the running joke."

Brianna tightened her grip on the steering wheel. He wasn't lying, but he wasn't offering up information about stopping at the bookstore. She was going to give it one more shot. "Well, I know when it's slow in the morning, you like to stop and visit with people or get some breakfast."

"Just cruising the streets. But I'll check in with you later to see how your spa day went."

Her heart pounded against her chest like a base drum. Still not lying but definitely covering up the fact that he'd gone to see Yvonne this morning. She was going to need to keep a close eye on his whereabouts, which was exhausting. But she wasn't going to lose Abraham. She couldn't. She was in love with him even if she hadn't told him yet.

CHAPTER 3

Abraham had managed to wiggle out of Brianna's interrogation, but he wondered why she was questioning him so heavily about his whereabouts. He didn't owe her an explanation for every person he visited. That was his rationalization even though guilt gnawed away at him for not telling her he'd gone to see Yvonne at the bookstore.

Why didn't I tell her?

He knew why. His attraction to Yvonne hadn't diminished. In all fairness to Brianna, he probably needed to stay clear of Yvonne. The last thing he needed was complications in his life.

He hadn't introduced Brianna to his family yet. She had promised friends in New York that she would spend Thanksgiving with them, so he had dodged that bullet, but he would have to invite her for Christmas. He tried to envision his Old Order Amish parents, two brothers, their wives, and kids . . . and Brianna, driving an expensive car, wearing flashy jewelry, donning fancy clothes, and representing everything his family didn't approve of. But Abraham had also been taught that you don't judge a person on the outside. He hoped his parents would keep that in mind when they met his girlfriend.

The first time he'd taken Brianna to his restored farmhouse, she'd said it was cute and cozy but might need a woman's touch. If that included modernizing his place and painting everything in bright colors, he wasn't having it. He liked the history his old house represented and had decorated it modestly to stay in touch with that time period and the way he was brought up. It wasn't a big issue since Brianna always wanted him to go to her house, and they were way too early into their relationship to consider future living arrangements. Besides, he cared a lot for Brianna, but seeing Yvonne made him question how deep his feelings ran for his girlfriend.

Abraham responded when a call came in—domestic dispute. He took a deep breath but let it out and relaxed when the address wasn't Maureen and Will's.

Yvonne wrapped up her day by finishing with the inventory Jake had started. A few customers had come into the store. No stellar sales but Jake said Wednesdays were slow too. Basically, he'd said that the store did 80 percent of its business on Friday and Saturday. Yvonne had already picked out a stack of books to read whenever things were caught up. Jake had encouraged her to do that even though she'd argued at first, citing he wasn't paying her to read books. But she had buried her head in a good story when it was slow today. Keeping her mind occupied was her way to avoid overthinking her visit with Abraham.

He crept into her thoughts on the way home, though. Seeing him and knowing he was taken had stung more than she would have expected.

She eventually shook free of her thoughts about Abraham and focused on the evening she had planned. She had a house full of boxes to unpack. She'd already told Jake she wasn't coming for dinner—supper, she reminded herself. Tonight, it would be warm jammies while unpacking in front of the fireplace and listening to Christmas music. It was much colder here than in Texas, and it was supposed to dip below freezing tonight. She hoped to find the box with her Christmas decorations so she could get into the spirit of the season.

Thirty minutes later, she turned onto the road that led to the small farmhouse she'd rented. It was newly restored, and the owners had said if she liked the house and five acres, they could talk about her buying the place down the line. This was the first time Yvonne hadn't had neighbors. In Houston, she'd either lived in an apartment, condo, or neighborhood where the houses were right next to each other. She loved this place—being able to see the stars on a clear night and take in the sounds and smells of crackling wood in the fireplace. The coyotes had unnerved her at first, but Jake said they were a lot farther away than they sounded and that she'd likely never lay eyes on one.

But she gasped when she pulled up to her house.

On the front porch sat a huge black-and-white dog. No resemblance to a coyote, but it might as well have been one. She'd always been terrified of dogs, especially large ones, since she'd been bitten by a neighbor's dog when she was six or seven.

This animal looked hungry. His ribs protruded, and his fur was matted in clumps all over his salt-and-pepper body. She honked her horn several times thinking that would scare the dog away, but he didn't budge.

After she rolled down her window, she leaned her head out. "Go away! Go!" She waved an arm in a motion for him to take off, but the animal just lay down, his paws in front of him. Then he laid his head down between his front legs. He looked like he was praying, which brought Yvonne around to that idea. *Please, God, get this dog off my porch.*

When that didn't happen, she opened the car door but stayed safely behind it. "Go, now! Go away!" The dog didn't move. "I can't sleep in my car!" she yelled, which didn't generate any response.

She climbed back into her car and laid on the horn, repeatedly. It was starting to get dark, and sure enough, she heard coyotes in the distance. This dog was ruining the night she'd had planned.

She honked over and over and over again . . . until she heard a car approaching from behind her. Jake and Eva had said she would be perfectly safe out here. Now, she wasn't sure what she was more afraid of—the stranger behind her or the dog keeping her from getting into her house.

Trembling, she stepped out of the car and slowly turned

around. It was a patrol car that had pulled up behind her. A man stepped out and walked toward her.

"Abraham? What are you doing here?" She gave her head a quick shake.

His mouth fell open, and he looked equally as shocked as she was. "I didn't know you were living in the Reynolds' old place. I mean, I knew they had fixed it up with plans to rent it, but . . ." He ran a hand through his hair. "Wow. Smaller world than I'd thought."

"What are you doing here?" Yvonne's heart thudded as she asked the question again.

"I was getting ready to go into a training session, and we got a call from a lady who doesn't live too far from here. She said someone was blowing their car horn continuously, and she was worried something was wrong. I offered to take the call, mostly to get out of the training session." He grinned.

"I didn't think I had any neighbors." She sighed as her pulse began to return to normal.

"Not close by," he said. "But the sound of a car horn travels. Are you okay?"

She shook her head. "No." Then she pointed to the scraggly animal on the porch. "That dog won't move so I can get into my house."

He took a few steps toward the porch, calling over his shoulder, "Did he growl at you when you tried to go inside?"

"I didn't get past where I'm at right now." She still stood safely behind her car door.

Abraham squatted down and held out his hand. "Hey, fella. You friendly?"

The dog didn't rise from his prayer position.

"Is he a dangerous breed?" Yvonne considered all dogs a threat and cringed when Abraham stood and took a couple more steps toward the animal.

"He looks like a blue heeler, but he's definitely a mixed breed. Heelers don't get to this size on their own. If this fellow wasn't half starved, he'd probably weigh about eighty pounds, if you consider the size of his paws and length."

"Are they vicious dogs?" Yvonne pulled her sweater tighter around herself as her teeth chattered. It was almost completely dark now, but a lamppost in the yard generated a little light.

"All dogs *can* be vicious. It depends how they're raised. Heelers are typically incredibly loyal and protective. They're also cattle dogs, used to herd cows." He took several more steps. "Hey, fellow."

The animal still didn't move.

"He looks like he might be sick. Or she. Hard to tell with *it* laying down. Or maybe just hungry." Abraham kept his eye on the dog. "Do you have any snacks or anything in your purse?"

"Let me check." Yvonne reached into the car for her purse and began digging around. She rushed back to a standing position and held up the only thing she could find. "I have a package of peanut-butter crackers."

Abraham walked backward until he was close enough to take the crackers from her. He opened the package and moved forward again, holding out one of the treats. "You hungry, fellow?" He tossed the snack onto the porch. As it landed near the dog's paws, the animal lunged off the porch in one leap, then disappeared into the night. Abraham jumped back and stumbled from the dog's sudden movement, but he caught his balance.

Yvonne rushed to him. She put a hand on his arm. "Are you okay?"

"*Ya*, I'm fine."

There it was again, that reminder that Abraham hadn't always been non-Amish.

"Do you think he'll come back?" She lowered her arm to her side.

He shrugged. "I don't know. Probably not."

Yvonne went back to the car to get her purse, then fumbled for the key to the house. "Well, the least I can do is offer you some hot cocoa, coffee, tea . . . something. It's all a mess. I'm still unpacking."

He touched a finger to his chin. "Hmm . . . Rush back for my training session that I did not want to go to? Or have coffee with you? I think I'll choose the latter."

Yvonne smiled as her teeth chattered and she put the key in the lock.

"Do you have plenty of firewood? It's going to freeze later tonight. These older houses aren't usually insulated very well."

She pushed the door open and stepped aside so he could enter. "Yes, Jake had a bunch chopped up for me. There's some in the little storage shed, and I have some by the fireplace."

Abraham rubbed his hands together. "Want me to start a fire?"

"That would be great. Just step around the boxes, and I'll make us some coffee." Yvonne paused. "Or would you prefer hot chocolate? Some people don't drink coffee at night. Although I'm not one of them. But I have both."

"I'm a cop. We drink coffee pretty much around the clock since our shifts are always changing, so that sounds great."

Yvonne wound around a stack of boxes and into the kitchen. Most of the kitchen was in order, so she easily started a pot of coffee and returned shortly with two cups. "It's black, but I have milk and sugar if you want some." She set both cups atop her coffee table, which she'd managed to maneuver in front of the couch the night before.

"Black is fine," Abraham said as he stoked the small fire until a decent blaze attached to the dry wood.

"I'm afraid it's a special brand of coffee I like that has a pecan flavor. It's not for everyone." She took a sip of hers before she sat on the couch.

Abraham left the fire, reached for his cup, and brought it to his mouth. "Wow. It's different, but I like it." He took a seat on the couch, but he didn't sit too close.

"Thank you so much. I guess from now on, if I have a problem, I know I just have to honk my horn a bunch of times, and someone will come." She grinned at him as she realized they had stepped back into a comfortable conversation, just the way they had a year ago. Their conversation that morning had been awkward, but it was beginning to feel like no time had passed since they'd last chatted together.

"Or you can call my cell phone." He paused. "Do you have decent cell service out here?"

"Well, not really decent. I go between two bars and

no bars." She shrugged. "But I like this place more than anything I looked at. And there aren't many houses in Montgomery for rent."

"What's your cell number? I'll call your phone so you'll have my number." He glanced at her. "You know, in case the dog comes back or something."

Yvonne told him the number, and she heard her phone ringing in her purse in the kitchen. "Done," he said.

"I guess most people would have tried to befriend the dog, but I got bitten by a big dog when I was little, and I've been scared of dogs ever since." She twisted to face him on the couch, tucking one foot underneath her as she took a sip of coffee.

He shook his head. "No, you were right not to approach him." He grinned. "I'll guess we'll call him a *him* even though we don't know." He cupped his hands around the mug. "Yeah, I like this coffee."

"It's not exactly what I drank at home, but it's close enough." She stared at him until he looked at her, then forced her eyes away from his. "I'm sorry to take you from your training session." She looked back at him and smiled.

"Yeah, bad you." He chuckled as he shook his head. "It was just another higher-up officer giving yet another presentation on when and when not to draw your weapon. I've never had to pull out my gun. There's just not a lot of crime around here."

Yvonne sighed. "I have to get used to the quiet. In Houston, there were always sirens, horns honking, and noise. Here, it's so tranquil. And I love it, but . . ." She cringed a little. "Those coyotes are a little unnerving."

"They'll never come close to the house. You'll probably never see one."

"That's what Jake said. So instead, I have a wild dog who decided to camp out on my porch." She set her cup down on the coffee table. "Listen, I know you said it was fine, but I really am sorry that I didn't answer the phone or return your letters. I was just in such a bad place for such a long time, and . . ." She finally locked eyes with him. "But I hope we can be friends." Yvonne would have hoped for more, but she had no plans to interfere in his and Brianna's relationship.

"It really is okay. I liked you." He smiled as his face turned a little red. "Still do. But I should have given you some time, and I shouldn't have written more than one letter when you didn't answer. So, yes, I'd like to be friends too."

"A person can never have too many friends." She felt a warmth in her cheeks, but she was unsure where to go with the conversation, considering Abraham's relationship status. They were quiet for a while, so she decided to change the subject so things didn't become awkward. "Do you ever miss it, being Amish? I know you said that you have regrets sometimes, but do you miss the whole package, the lifestyle?" She waited, since he seemed to be pondering her question.

Abraham couldn't take his eyes from her. She mesmerized him. And she surprised him. Brianna would have never asked him such a question. Brianna had said more than once that she didn't understand how the Amish lived the way they did and that it was hard for her to imagine him ever being "one of them." He knew he was comparing the two women.

"*Ya*, I do miss it sometimes. Especially when I'm around my family." He paused as he recalled his life before. "Don't get me wrong—my family treats me the same way they always have. We're all close. I have two brothers. But I also know it broke their hearts when I decided not to get baptized into the community. It was even harder for them to understand why I wanted to be a cop, especially since the Amish are passive people. I miss the Amish church services and the fellowship afterward. I go to a nondenominational church just outside of Montgomery, but it's different." He chuckled. "I still go to barn raisings, though, and no one argues about having an extra person helping out, Amish or not. It gives me that sense of belonging, even if it's just for a day or two."

"When I first came to Montgomery, it was in search of a book that a client wanted." She paused, took a sip of coffee. "That's what I used to do—find rare books for people." She waved her hand dismissively. "Anyway, that's how I met Jake and Eva. It was a rocky beginning, since Jake had a book that I desperately wanted to buy for a client, and he had no desire to sell it. But the book—along with Jake and Eva—changed my life. I guess you could say that it was a combined effort from the book and Jake and Eva that helped me develop a relationship with God that I hadn't had before. I ended up being friends with them too."

"God works things out in His time frame." Abraham smiled.

"Yes, He does." She nodded. "When I arrived here, I'd never really been around Amish people before. It was intriguing and confusing, but the more time I spent around Eva, Jake, their families, and other members of the community, the more I began to understand the allure of living such a simple life."

"How so?" Abraham's eyes gleamed with genuine interest.

Yvonne leaned her shoulder against the couch and brought her other leg underneath her. "Things are slower, for one thing. I mean, people work hard, but everyone isn't rushing around at warp speed trying to get somewhere. And I like the fact that there's not competition between the women. I mean, everyone wears the same thing, so no one is trying to outdress the other. Money doesn't seem to be a huge issue either."

Abraham chuckled. "Don't forget, the Amish folks are human. And, believe me, there is plenty of competition. Women compete for a man's affection the same way men do, just like those outside of the district. But . . ." He laughed again. "I think the women mostly take pride in their cooking. Everyone wants to be the best at it. And it's not just the women. I once heard an Amish man boldly dare anyone to grow a bigger watermelon than he had." He shrugged. "There's pride and competition. Maybe not as much as in the outside world, but it's there."

She sighed. "I suppose so, but everyone is so nice." She raised an eyebrow. "It's not like that everywhere. I've traveled quite a bit."

Abraham basked in the warmth of the crackling fire,

the pecan coffee, and Yvonne's company. He didn't want to leave, but he couldn't think of a reason to stay once he'd finished his drink.

"It's going to take me a while to get everything unpacked, but tonight I was hoping to find the box that had my Christmas decorations." Her eyes scanned her living room. Containers lined the walls, while others sat in the middle of the floor.

"Is the box marked?" *Bingo. A reason not to leave yet.* "I could help you look for it."

She shook her head. "No, you don't have to do that."

His heart sank as disappointment set in that she wasn't eager for him to stay.

"Unless, of course, you need another reason to get out of that training class?" She playfully lifted her eyebrows up and down.

Is she flirting? "Gee . . . let me think on it." After rolling his eyes, unable to keep the grin from his face, he stood. "Where do we start?" He eyed the dozens of boxes, secretly wishing it would take hours to find her Christmas decorations.

After Yvonne lifted herself from the couch, she raised her shoulders, her hands palms up, and said, "I have no idea."

"We might need more coffee." He picked his cup up and took the final sip.

"Follow me." She motioned for him to join her in the kitchen, where he leaned against the counter while she refilled both of their cups. While they stood there, his phone buzzed in his pocket. Probably work, wondering what was taking so long.

"Excuse me." He pulled out the phone and saw Brianna's name on the screen, and the same guilty pang shot through him again. He silenced the phone and put it back into his pocket.

What am I doing?

CHAPTER 4

B rianna chastised herself for calling Abraham's phone four times. Each call had gone to his voice mail after a couple of rings, which was odd. His training session wouldn't last until nine o'clock. At least, she didn't think so.

She paced her kitchen, clutching a glass of red wine and fuming on the inside. Finally, she took a deep breath, sat down at the kitchen table, and forced herself to calm down. All this insecurity took her back to New York, to Mitch. Six months into their relationship, she had caught him cheating on her. The memories were more like an open wound than a scar, even though they'd broken up six months ago, and for three of those months since, she'd been in a relationship with Abraham.

Drumming her free hand on the table, she drank the last of her wine. This was how things began going badly with Mitch. He'd stopped taking her calls. Brianna wanted to believe this was different, that Abraham would never cheat on her, but his failure to admit he'd been to the bookstore to see Yvonne had set in motion an irrational bout of jealousy.

Sighing, she picked up her phone and called Abraham again, only to have the call ring a couple of times again before it went to voice mail.

After she poured herself another glass of wine, she paced some more, determined not to be this person—jealous, untrusting, and rattled. Prior to today, Abraham had never given her a reason not to trust him. He had to still be in his training session. He'd never said how long it was supposed to last, so she was overreacting. She decided to get into her night clothes, sure he would call her later.

Abraham eyed the small Christmas tree that stood no taller than four feet. Mostly, he gazed at Yvonne and knew he should have left two hours ago. But she'd quickly found the decorations in a box, and they had assembled the artificial tree and placed it on the end table they'd moved to one side of the couch. He wasn't feeling very good about himself after silencing Brianna's third call, but she would have left a voice mail if something was wrong. And he was having a good time. He'd never put up a Christmas tree before, even a small one like Yvonne's. She'd been so animated and fun to be around that he just hadn't been able to pull himself away, even to return his girlfriend's call.

"I can't believe you've never had a tree before." She picked up a red ornament that had slid off one of the fake branches and rehung it. "I know the Amish don't put up

Christmas trees, but when you left the faith, you never wanted one at your house?"

Abraham shrugged. "Old habits die hard, I guess. *Mei mamm* always decorated the house. We had tinsel on the fireplace mantel, red candles, and other ornamental things displayed. And she wrapped presents and stacked them in various parts of the house, mostly in the living room. I guess I just kept that part of my upbringing and only put up a few decorations."

Her eyes glowed as she folded her hands in front of her. "I love Christmas, even though it was kind of weird when I was growing up. I wasn't brought up in a Christian home. I was raised by my aunt and uncle, who weren't religious people, but we always had a Christmas tree and enjoyed the festivities during this time of year. We never observed the holiday the way it was meant to be, though. But I carried on the tradition by putting up a Christmas tree after I moved out on my own. I still didn't understand the reason for the season, though, until I met Jake and Eva."

Pausing, she held his gaze. "Trevor and his family were believers, and I was so grateful for that after he died—that he had given his life to Jesus a long time ago. But last year was hard for several reasons. It was my first Christmas without Trevor, and it was my first *real* Christmas. I wanted to celebrate the fact that I understood what Christ had done for us. But Trevor wasn't there to experience that with me. He would have loved the fact that I was cherishing the true meaning of the holiday. Plus, I just missed him so much. So, it was a double whammy for me."

She took a deep breath as her eyes began to twinkle.

"But I'm much better this year, and I plan to embrace the season and this new phase in my life." She growled a little as she stared at her Christmas tree for a few seconds. Her expression caused Abraham to grin. "But that thing"—she pointed to the tree—"is putting a damper on the holiday spirit. It was okay in my house in Houston. I didn't really have much room there. But this old farmhouse in the country is bigger and seems to be screaming for a real tree—a really big one!"

She bounced up on her toes. She'd kicked her shoes off earlier in the evening and had been wearing a pair of bright-pink socks all night, and she'd changed into a pair of black sweatpants and a baggy black T-shirt. He'd never seen Brianna wear anything like that, but it totally worked on Yvonne. *Adorable* was the word that came to mind.

With that unspoken compliment, his thoughts returned to Brianna, which caused his stomach to lurch.

"I should probably go." It was after nine o'clock. He'd texted a fellow officer earlier and told him everything was fine but that he wouldn't be back at the training session. He smiled as he pointed to Yvonne's small Christmas tree. "As cute as that is, I agree. I think you should have a big Christmas tree that you really want."

She laughed. "I'm not sure it would fit on top of my SUV, and the size I have in mind definitely wouldn't fit inside the vehicle." Shrugging, she said, "Once I put up all of my other decorations and get unpacked, I'm sure I'll feel festive."

Abraham told his feet to move toward the door, but they were rooted to the wood floors. After a few awkward moments of silence, he cleared his throat. "Thanks for the coffee and for getting me out of my class this evening."

She took a few steps toward him. "I'm the one who should be thanking you. You saved me from that scary dog and helped me put up my tree." She smiled. "But if it got you out of a class you didn't want to be in, then I guess it's a win for both of us."

He gave a quick wave before he turned to leave. She followed him to the door, sidestepped him, and held it open. "It was fun tonight," she said as he stood there ogling her like a teenager.

Abraham nodded as his conscience kicked into gear. "Call me if you need help with that dog again." Then he turned and left, knowing he had enjoyed the visit more than he should have.

She waved from the porch as he got into his patrol car. He returned the gesture, backed out, and headed down the road.

Abraham tried not to use his phone in the car, so he waited until he got home to call Brianna. It was almost ten, but she was a night owl.

"I was starting to think you'd been taken hostage or something," she said when she answered. Abraham wasn't sure if he imagined the snappy tone in her voice or if he was just feeling guilty and paranoid.

"I'm sorry." He didn't want to lie, but any sort of explanation that would satisfy Brianna would be an untruth, so he decided to move in a different direction. "I'm going to make it up to you tomorrow night. I'll leave a little early, take you to dinner, then we can watch that movie you've been wanting to see on TV."

"Yes! That sounds wonderful." The bubbliness in her voice was obvious, and Abraham knew he'd made the right decision to jump on something he knew she'd enjoy. "Pick you up at six?" He intentionally yawned and hoped she wouldn't question him further.

"That sounds wonderful. So . . . how was the training class?"

He squeezed his eyes closed and searched for the truth since he had barely been at the meeting any time at all. "Boring." He yawned for real this time.

"And long," she said, followed by a sigh.

"Uh, yeah." He was quiet for a few seconds. "So, I'm going to shower and get to bed. But I'll be looking forward to seeing you tomorrow night."

As he hung up the phone, he realized he'd just lied to her after all. The only person he was looking forward to seeing again was Yvonne.

He crawled into bed an hour later with his stomach growling. Yvonne had put out some crackers and cheese but admitted she hadn't done much grocery shopping yet. He'd felt full and content at the time, just being with her and snacking. Mostly being with her.

Now, as he stared out the window into the darkness on a clear night, he caught a shooting star zipping across the black sky—a sign to make a wish. Oddly, he didn't know what to wish for, so instead he closed his eyes and prayed.

Yvonne drew in a deep breath. She could still smell the

lingering scent of Abraham's cologne as she eyed her little Christmas tree, lit with tiny white lights and red and white ornaments.

After she changed into a pair of warm pajamas, she stoked the fire, sat on the couch, and leaned her head back. What an amazing night it had been. She was so comfortable around Abraham, and they'd easily fallen into sync the way they'd done the few times they'd been around each other before. Under different circumstances, she would be hoping he'd ask her out. But Yvonne wasn't going to compete against someone as gorgeous as Brianna nor did she want to. Abraham and Brianna had an established relationship, and Yvonne wasn't going to get in the way of that. As much as she'd like to be friends with Abraham, she knew she needed to distance herself. She was wildly attracted to him, and not just physically. His personality was fun-loving and playful, qualities she liked in a man. But she would have to file this night away as an enjoyable evening with a guy she likely wouldn't be friends with—of her own choosing.

She felt regret the moment she had that thought, and after a couple of lengthy yawns, she took herself to bed.

Sleep didn't come easily. She tossed and turned for at least an hour, but when she woke up the next morning, she smiled with recollections of her time with Abraham the night before. Rubbing her eyes, she sat up, yawned, and reminded herself that he belonged to someone else.

She dressed quickly, barely applied makeup, and grabbed an energy bar on her way out. After she'd locked the door and heaved her purse up onto her shoulder, she stopped dead in her tracks about two steps onto the porch. The mangy, matted dog sat about five feet from where she was standing. As she gasped, her breath seized in her throat before she held it. She took a careful step back when the dog moved, but all it did was lay down and rest its head on his paws like he'd done the night before.

Slowly, she reached into her purse to find her phone, but changed her mind. She couldn't call for help, especially Abraham, over a dog.

"This is my house." She squinted her eyes at the dog as her chest tightened. "You need to go home. Wherever that is, you need to go."

The dog's pointed dark ears came to attention. In the light of day, his dark colors comingled with white looked almost dark blue. Blue heeler, she recalled Abraham saying, probably mixed with another breed. She could see the animal's ribs in patches where there was barely any hair, and what fur he did have resembled a worn rug that someone had braided.

She peeled the wrapper from the energy bar, then set it down. "I'm going to walk to my car now. Please don't follow me or bite me."

Moving slowly, she edged her way down the porch steps, then picked up speed as she shuffled through the frosty grass to her car. Abraham had been correct about the temperatures dipping last night. It wasn't until she was safely inside her vehicle that she began to shiver and cranked up the heat. She'd forgotten her coat, but as she eyed the dog, who hadn't moved, she chose not to go back inside.

She said a quick prayer that the animal wouldn't be

there when she returned this evening, then pushed the button on her steering wheel when her phone rang.

"Is everything okay?" she asked. Every time Eva called, Yvonne wondered if she was having the baby. The bed rest was to prevent an early delivery, but she'd known more than one person to have their baby before the due date, even when taking it easy the way Eva was doing.

"*Ya*, I guess." Eva sighed. "Technically, I should only be using the phone for emergencies. But my boredom feels like an emergency. I don't want this *boppli* coming yet, but I sure do want this *boppli* to get here, if that even makes sense."

Yvonne smiled. "It makes sense, and it won't be that much longer. I know you're ready for her to get here."

Eva chuckled. "You are *so* sure it's a girl."

"Yep. I am." Yvonne turned the heat up in the car.

"I can hear your teeth chattering."

"Yeah, I forgot my coat. And I didn't want to go back inside the house. I had a hard enough time getting out." Yvonne told her about the dog—and about Abraham coming over.

"Hmm . . . interesting."

Yvonne began to shake her head. "No, don't go there. He has a girlfriend, remember? And I saw her. She's a knockout."

"So are you," Eva quickly said. "And looks surely aren't everything."

"I know. But Abraham is such a nice guy, and I wouldn't do anything to cause problems between him and his girlfriend. I wouldn't want to do that to anyone." Even though she didn't believe she'd stand a chance against someone like Brianna. Yvonne was usually a confident person, but Brianna had movie-star looks. She reminded herself it didn't matter, that she had no intentions of making a play for Abraham.

"*Ach*, well, I better go. I hear Jake coming into the house, probably to check on me for the third time this morning since he's been working outside." She sighed. "He's a nervous Nellie about this *boppli*."

Yvonne smiled. She could remember her aunt saying that phrase sometimes—*nervous Nellie*. "He's just excited. I'm going to finally get some real groceries after I leave the bookstore today. I was embarrassed to tell Abraham that all I had were energy bars, some cheese and crackers, and coffee. I need some real food. Is there anything you need me to pick up for you?"

"*Nee*, between *mei* mother-in-law and others bringing food, I can't think of a thing. We have enough casseroles to last a week. Jake put some in the freezer."

Well, it didn't sound like Yvonne needed to do any cooking for Jake and Eva. "Okay, I'll be by to see you in a couple of days. I'm going to get food and try to finish unpacking. But make another one of these emergency calls if you need anything."

Eva chuckled. "*Ya*, will do. *Danki*."

By the time they'd ended the call, Yvonne was at the bookstore. If it was another slow day, she was going to grab a book off her pile and escape for a while, like Jake suggested. She needed to steer her thoughts away from Abraham.

Abraham knocked on Brianna's door ten minutes before six, carrying a bouquet of yellow roses. He'd brought her flowers a couple of times before, but this evening it was a silent offering to ease the guilt he'd felt about ignoring Brianna's calls and not being completely truthful about his whereabouts last night.

She opened the door and let out a small squeal. "Flowers!" She took the roses when he held them out, then gave him a dainty hug, the way she did when she didn't want to wrinkle her clothes or mess up her makeup. "Come in."

Abraham stepped over the threshold and onto the glistening tile. Brianna had bought an older home in Montgomery, but you'd never know it. Everything had been updated and modernized. The bold colors still blinded him a little every time he entered.

"You look beautiful," he said as he eyed her black slacks and fitted blue sweater. With her black high heels, she was almost as tall as he was. Her auburn hair lay in soft curls just past her shoulders. She was a beautiful woman . . . but it didn't stop his thoughts from drifting to Yvonne almost instantly—the way she wore her baggy T-shirt, sweatpants, and those cute pink socks.

"And you are incredibly handsome." Brianna sauntered up to him and kissed him softly on the mouth. Abraham knew his dark-blue jeans, long-sleeved white shirt, and black cowboy boots didn't really measure up to Brianna's attire. It never did.

Grinning, he slipped off his black leather jacket and laid it on the back of her couch. "Are you hungry? I thought we'd try a new steak place just outside of town, if that's okay with you?"

"Sure. I'm fine with anything." She smiled as she headed toward the blue high-back chair where her purse hung, along with a black coat draped across the back.

Abraham knew she wasn't "fine with anything." She didn't like buffets, which always ruled out Gasthof Village and Stoll's Lakeview Restaurant, two of his favorite places. But tonight was her night. He owed her that. "I just need to use your bathroom before we go."

"You know where it's at," she said, smiling as she slipped an arm into her coat.

Abraham made his way down the hall, and without his jacket on, he noticed he had a spot on his white shirt. After studying it for a few moments in the bathroom mirror, he looked around for something to try to wipe it off. He hated to use one of Brianna's blue hand towels with the white ruffles on the edge. He opened a cabinet and took out a washrag, wet it, and after a little effort cleared the spot.

When he finally made his way back to the living room, Brianna stood with her coat on and purse slung over her shoulder.

Abraham held up the rag. "I had a spot on my shirt, so I used this to clean it. I have no idea what it was." He pointed to the wet spot about the size of a golf ball and chuckled. "Hopefully it will be gone by the time we get to the restaurant." Gesturing to the rag, he asked, "Do you want me to put this somewhere?"

"I'll take it." She used one finger and her thumb to take it from him, then carried it to her laundry room.

Abraham slipped into his coat and habitually reached for his phone in the right pocket. But it wasn't there. He quickly thrust his hand into his left pocket and took out his cell phone and stared at it. *I never put my phone in my left pocket.*

He was still holding the device when Brianna emerged. It was hard not to ask her if she had looked at his phone for some reason, but if she hadn't, what an awful accusation that would be.

"Oh, I knocked your coat off the back of the couch by accident. Your phone fell out, so I slipped it back into one of the pockets."

Relief swept over him as he nodded and returned the phone to its usual place in the right pocket of his coat. "You ready?"

She nodded, and they left for the restaurant. Brianna was unusually quiet on the way.

CHAPTER 5

It was around six thirty that evening when Yvonne pulled up to her house with a carful of groceries. She'd left the porch light on since it would be dark by the time she returned from shopping. The soft rays, combined with the lamp in the yard, illuminated the dog sprawled out on the porch as if he owned the place. He looked bigger with his four legs stretched out, even though his ribs were more visible. The energy bar was gone.

Yvonne drummed her fingers on the steering wheel and sighed. The dog lifted his head, yawned, then lay back down. She could see now that her visitor was a male, and he also didn't have much of a tail. Yvonne wondered if it had been clipped at birth. She'd heard of that, and if so, the dog must have had an owner, but it would have been a very long time ago based on his appearance.

She stepped out of the car on shaky legs, retrieved as many bags as she could from the back seat, then with key in hand headed toward the house and took slow steps up to the porch. Her legs shook even more when the dog lifted himself to a standing position. But the little bit of tail he wiggled back and forth she took as a good sign.

The animal stood perfectly still the entire time Yvonne went back and forth with groceries.

After she had everything in the house, she closed the door and locked it, then unloaded two hundred dollars' worth of food. When she was done, she peeked out the window. The dog had sat down, and his tongue was hanging out of his mouth.

She filled up a large plastic bowl with water, eased the door open, and set it right outside before she quickly slammed the door shut. Her unwanted guest went directly to the bowl and drank every last drop, then looked up at her with droopy eyes as she stared at him through the window near the door. She filled the bowl two more times, then opened two large cans of shredded chicken and dumped them into another bowl. She might be afraid of dogs, but she wasn't going to stand by and let one starve to death.

After the dog ate the chicken, she opened two more cans and, without even stepping onto the porch, leaned over and dumped them into the bowl. She watched again through the window and shook her head.

"You can't live here." The dog's pointed black ears twitched as if he heard her. "Go home."

She knew in her heart that this fellow didn't have a home. Maybe she could find someone who needed a farm dog. Abraham had said blue heelers were herders. Tomorrow, she'd start asking around if anyone wanted a dog and was willing to nurse him back to health.

Abraham. She sat on her couch, slipped out of her tennis shoes, eased her feet up on the coffee table, and wondered what he was doing.

Brianna tapped her foot nervously under the table at the restaurant and fought the urge to chew on her fingernail. Her insides were tied in knots. In the car, and now, she'd wanted to scream at Abraham and tell him how dare he call Yvonne the night before when he'd ignored her calls. But she needed to stow the emotions that were gnawing at her insides. When she'd confronted Mitch about calls to another woman, he had denied a relationship but also changed his password on his cell phone. Brianna needed to handle this better. Yvonne hadn't been here long enough for anything to really get started between her and Abraham, so she'd just have to make sure things didn't heat up between them.

"The salmon is great." She gazed across the table at Abraham, focusing on his dreamy blue eyes. He was a catch, no doubt. One she had no plans to let get away. "How's your steak?"

He finished chewing, then dabbed at his mouth with a napkin. "It's good. Medium rare, just the way I like it. Perfect."

Brianna smiled. "Good. I'm glad."

She and Abraham had briefly shared with each other about their romantic histories. Brianna had left a busload of information out of her side of the conversation. She'd had more relationships than she cared to admit to Abraham. Especially when he said he'd only dated three women, and he'd only been serious with one. When she'd questioned him about it, asked what happened, he'd said he was holding out for the right person, and that over time he'd realized Nina wasn't the one. He'd told her it was an awful breakup, but he'd also said that Nina didn't live in Montgomery anymore. She'd moved to Georgia where she had family. And after doing some digging, Brianna learned that the two other women Abraham had dated were happily married with children.

Brianna wasn't sure if she wanted children. But she was thirty-four, and she'd have a baby for Abraham if it meant holding on to him. He had said more than once that he wanted a large family. Brianna would give him one baby after they were married, but she had no plans to raise a bunch of kids. She cringed when she thought about what pregnancy did to the body, often leaving horrendous stretch marks.

"The dessert menu looked tempting." Abraham had finished everything on his plate. He raised his eyebrows up and down, grinning.

Brianna was still working on her salmon and sweet potatoes and picking at her salad. The food was decent, but her nerves were shot. It was killing her not to question Abraham about calling Yvonne. He'd stopped to see the woman yesterday, too, and Brianna had certainly given him ample opportunity to tell her. And he hadn't.

She bit her lip, knowing she would need to stay alert and

keep an eye on this situation. Yvonne was not going to yank the rug out from under her. Brianna had spent three months with Abraham. If only she could get Abraham into bed, she knew she could close the deal, but he was old-fashioned, presumably due to his Amish upbringing. Brianna had thought it was kind of cute at first, but they were grown adults, and she had ways to get him to change his mind. He was a man, after all. Maybe the time had come to pull a few tricks out of her bag.

Abraham was tempted to sweep Brianna into his arms and carry her to bed as they made out like teenagers on her front porch following the meal. Brianna pressed against him, igniting all the right senses, and Abraham worried he was going to slip one day and go against his beliefs.

"I gotta go," he said, breathless, but her mouth was on his again, and he feared the feel of her body against his was driving him to a point of no return. He eased his hands from her face and gently latched onto her shoulders and put some distance between them.

She lowered her head as her lip trembled like she might cry. He cradled her chin with one hand and lifted her eyes to his. "Brianna . . ." He gazed into her moist eyes and took a deep breath. "You are absolutely gorgeous, and I love spending time with you, but . . . we've talked about this before. I don't want to be intimate in the way that you're suggesting. I know my feelings must seem outdated by today's standards, but it's just how I feel, and I'm sorry." He'd told himself a hundred times that he wasn't Amish, that he didn't have to abide by the rules of that faith. But like it or not, his beliefs were ingrained in him, and he remained convinced that sex before marriage was wrong in the eyes of God. "We've talked about this," he said again softly as he took his hand from her chin, then tucked strands of her auburn hair behind her ears.

"I just want to show you how much I love you." She gently brushed her lips against his, fanning her fingers through his hair.

Abraham had stopped breathing. *Whoa.* They'd only been dating three months, and in his mind, they were no-where near using the *L* word. He cared for Brianna a great deal, but he couldn't in good conscience tell her he loved her. He liked her a lot, but love was something he took seri-ously. He had loved Nina, but in the end, they still weren't right for each other.

He didn't know what to say, but allowing her to keep kissing him gave him an out, at least for the moment. So he went with it—until things heated up to the boiling point again. This time, he was firmer when he put his hands on her arms and stepped back.

"I've got an early shift in the morning. I had a great time tonight, but I really need to leave."

Her lower lip curled into a pout. "Okay," she said qui-etly as she avoided looking at him. She was surely disap-pointed that he hadn't returned the sentiment, and he hoped things wouldn't be awkward between them.

"I'll call you tomorrow, okay?" He kissed her tenderly, and she nodded.

"I'm sorry." She dabbed at her eye with her finger as she blinked back tears. "I just . . ." Then she covered her face with her hands. "I'm moving too quickly with you." She lowered her hands, her face streaked with tears as the moonlight lit her beautiful face. "And I don't mean to. I've just never met anyone like you, and you already mean so much to me."

Abraham hung his head, then looked up at her and eased her into his arms. "Please don't cry." He cupped the back of her head and kissed her forehead, feeling like a cad. "Everything is okay."

"Are you sure?" She buried her face in his chest, and he gently coaxed her away and waited until she looked at him.

"I'm sure. I guess I just need to take things at a little slower pace, that's all." Sighing, he shook his head, then grinned, hoping to make her feel better. "But you don't make that very easy."

She smiled a little. "I'll behave."

Abraham kissed her one more time before he went to his car. It was a short drive home, and he had to pass by the road that led to Yvonne's house. As he yawned, he wondered what she was doing, if she was curled up on the couch wearing her pink socks with a crackling fire going and her tiny Christmas tree lit up. It made him smile to think about her, which felt wrong in a lot of ways.

But an hour later when his phone rang and Yvonne's name flashed across the screen, he couldn't answer it fast enough.

"Did I wake you up?" she asked after he answered.

"No. I had just gotten into bed. Is everything okay?" His heart raced at the sound of her voice.

"Well, I guess." She paused. "That dog has decided to make my front porch his home. He was there when I left for the bookstore, and he was there when I got home. I had gone to get groceries, so I forced myself to walk by him repeatedly as I unloaded them."

"Did he ever get aggressive?" Abraham turned on the lamp by his bed, then fluffed his pillows. He was wide awake now.

"No. He wagged the little bit of tail he has, so I took that as a good sign. Then I gave him some water. He drank three bowls of it. After that, I gave him some canned chicken."

"Sounds like he's your dog now." Abraham chuckled.

"Uh . . . no. Not at all." She laughed. "But I do want to find a home for him, and since you are out and about, I was going to ask you to spread the word. Maybe you know a farmer who needs a good herding dog? I asked Jake to ask around also."

Abraham thought for a few moments. "I can't think of anyone off the top of my head, but I'll ask around." He cleared his throat. "So, did you get unpacked, get some food?"

"I feel so bad that I didn't have anything to offer you but cheese and crackers. And not much else got unpacked, but I'm loaded up with food now."

"Best cheese and crackers I've ever had."

She giggled. "Yeah, right."

Abraham wasn't ready to hang up with her, but after neither of them spoke, she said, "Well, I'll let you go. I have to think about what I'm going to feed that *dog* in the morning."

"Maybe that *dog* needs a name?"

"Ha! No. That would mean I'm keeping him, and I'm not." She said the last part through a yawn. "I'll let you get to sleep. Have a good day tomorrow."

"You too."

He clicked off the light and stared into the darkness. He pictured Yvonne the way he had before, all cozy in her living room. Just the sound of her voice filled him with a warmth that surprised him. Quickly, his thoughts shifted to Brianna. He felt like he needed to cool things down with her, and he asked himself if it had anything to do with Yvonne. He told himself it didn't. Brianna was just moving too fast for him. *Love* was a word he'd only used once in his life with regard to someone he was in a relationship with, and it had taken him over a year to do so.

Brianna tossed and turned, and when she looked at the clock, it was nearly midnight.

I messed up.

She shouldn't have told Abraham that she loved him. It was too soon, and it wasn't something you could take back. Seducing him wasn't working either. She was coming on too strong, and she should pull back a little . . . but not too much. There didn't need to be too much wiggle room where Yvonne could creep into the picture.

But every time she thought about Abraham calling or going to visit that woman, it sent fury spiraling through her. It also bothered her that Abraham had no interest in trying to set up Yvonne with the new guy, Bruce, that he worked with.

She jumped when her cell phone rang. *Who is calling at midnight?* A wave of panic shot through her. Had someone gotten hurt, been in an accident? She reached for her phone and watched it ringing as she bit her bottom lip over the name the screen displayed. No way she was answering. Mitch would leave a message, and he'd probably be yelling since that's what he did. She'd never known a man who hollered as much as Mitch. Their breakup had been a mess. Enough so that Brianna had felt the need to relocate to another state.

When her phone signaled that he'd left a voice mail, she placed the phone back on her nightstand. She would listen to his message tomorrow. Or maybe never. Anything he had to say would only upset her. And she was pretty sure she knew why he was calling. He was a heartless man and a cheater. It was his fault that she was so insecure about Abraham, and she shouldn't be. In her heart she knew Abraham would never go behind her back with another woman.

She felt comfort in that thought as she finally drifted to sleep.

Yvonne looked out the window the next morning, sighed, then opened a couple of cans of tuna. She was already out of chicken. If she didn't find a home for this loitering animal, she was going to need to buy some dog food.

This time, she stepped farther out onto the porch, and

the dog slowly moved toward her. Her heart raced as she set the bowl down. "I'm out of chicken. Tuna will have to do this morning."

The animal sat down, eyed his breakfast, then looked up at her with sad eyes.

"Did someone not take care of you? Are you just displaced from your owners?" Maybe she should put up a *Dog Found* sign. Even though the dog had clearly found her, not the other way around.

Slowly she put out her hand, half expecting the animal to bite it off. But her mangy houseguest sniffed her fingers, then gave her knuckles a quick lick, as if thanking her for the food. She surprised herself by not reacting harshly to his touch.

"You're welcome," she said softly as she took her hand back and left for the bookstore.

Today was a big day, and Jake would probably already be there when she arrived. The bookstore was receiving a plaque that designated the building as an historic site, and someone from City Hall was coming to present the honor to Jake.

"I wish Eva could be here too." Jake stood near the wood-burning stove that was stationed in the bookstore for use during the winter. He'd had a nice fire already going when Yvonne walked in.

She stowed her purse behind the counter and joined him by the stove, holding her hands near the open flame. "I know. I wish she could be here too. Is she feeling okay?"

Jake nodded. "*Ya*, she feels okay, but she's bored and tired of being in bed the majority of the day."

"I can understand that." She took off her sweater and draped it over her arm. "Hey, did you give any thought to who might want a dog? That unkempt, homeless, half-starved animal is still camped out on my porch." She shivered. "I'm not crazy about dogs. They scare me. He's a big fellow." She paused. "But not aggressive or anything." Shrugging, she added, "Abraham is going to check around too."

"I'm still thinking on it." He paused, raised an eyebrow, and smirked. "Abraham? I didn't know you two were in communication."

"He stopped by the store to say hi. And then when I couldn't get the dog off my porch, I kept honking my horn, trying to scare him away, which didn't work." She rolled her eyes. "Some faraway neighbor phoned it in—all the honking—and Abraham was the one to respond to the call."

"You definitely left an impression on him. He brought up your name several times after the wedding and told me about your walk, saying you just sort of clicked." Jake grinned.

Yvonne sighed. "Whatever. We're just friends."

"Okay." Jake smiled broader. "If you say so."

"Don't worry about my lack of a love life. I'm just now ready to start dating, and it feels daunting. I was with Trevor for so long . . ." She trailed off, then stuffed her sweater where her purse now sat. "What time is that guy supposed to be here?"

"He said around nine." Jake glanced around. "The place looks great."

"All I've done is finish the inventory and clean. I feel

overpaid. You need to give me a project." She sat on the stool behind the counter, sighing again. "And you need to find a home for my dog."

"Um . . . You just said '*my* dog.'" He snickered as he looped his thumbs beneath his suspenders.

"Only until *you* find him a new home." Deciding the counter was too far from the woodstove, Yvonne reached for her sweater again and draped it over her shoulders. "I was warm by that fire, but it's a bit chilly over here." She scratched her chin. "Exactly how cold does it get here in the winter?"

"It gets down to zero, but that isn't likely to happen until January and February, our coldest months. It's supposed to freeze again tonight, but it will warm up tomorrow. It will do that on and off through December."

"You have Christmas decorations for the store, right? I know you don't put up a tree, but decorating is something I could take care of when it's slow. Spruce things up for Christmas."

"*Ya*, there's a box or two in the basement. I'll get them for you after the official leaves."

Yvonne pointed out the large window that ran nearly the length of the store in the front. "That must be him." An older gentleman stepped out of a black pickup truck, then used a cane to help himself get to the door. Jake walked to the entrance and held the door open.

"Hello, Jake. I'm so happy that this is finally happening." The older fellow smiled, then turned to Yvonne.

Jake motioned to Yvonne. "This is the woman I was telling you about on the phone—Yvonne. She's mostly running the bookstore now so I can take care of the farm, and as I explained, *mei fraa* is having to rest prior to giving birth."

The man extended his hand across the counter. "Nice to meet you, Yvonne. I'm Walter Meadows." He looked over his shoulder. "Jake, I couldn't handle the cane and the plaque. It's on the front seat of my truck, if you wouldn't mind fetching it."

Jake rushed out the door.

"And how are you enjoying Montgomery so far?" Walter had kind hazel eyes with enough feathering lines to indicate a long life stretching across his face like a well-traveled roadmap.

"I like it very much." She considered asking him if he wanted a dog, but the man seemed to have enough trouble getting around himself.

"This looks great," Jake said as he came back inside carrying the plaque. He held it up to show Yvonne.

"I love it," she said.

Mr. Meadows glanced out the window. "The fellow from the newspaper is supposed to be here to take a picture, and I know you won't want to be in it, but since your new employee isn't Amish, perhaps she'd do the honors?"

Jake nodded. "*Ya*, that will work."

Yvonne gulped. She'd woken up late and hadn't even bothered with any makeup. "Uh . . ."

"You're okay with that, aren't you, Yvonne?" Jake's voice held a thread of worry in it.

"Um, sure." She didn't know many people here anyway. Although she momentarily thought about Abraham seeing the photo.

A guy around Yvonne's age walked in a few minutes later with a camera bag swung over his shoulder. He had thick black glasses, hair shaved so short he almost looked bald, and a red-and-white checkered shirt on. He reminded Yvonne of someone back in the fifties. And after he'd snapped a few pictures of Yvonne accepting the plaque from Mr. Meadows, he was gone like a flash.

"That boy is always in a hurry, and I'm not sure why that is." Mr. Meadows chuckled. "There's not that much news around here."

He gazed around the store with a faraway look in his eyes. "My grandfather used to tell me stories about this place, of back when he was a boy before your grandfather purchased the building and turned it into a bookstore."

"*Ya, mei grossdaadi* said it used to be a general store." Jake smiled. "He had stories too."

Walter raised his eyebrows. "You found the hidden treasure yet?" He laughed, and so did Jake.

"*Nee*, I couldn't bring myself to start busting out walls based on a rumor, and neither could *mei grossdaadi*." Jake shook his head. "I guess it will just stay a rumor."

Walter went on to talk about other things, but Yvonne couldn't wait for him to leave, and once he was out the door, she turned to Jake with eyes widened. "Hidden treasure? You're kidding me? Why haven't you ever mentioned it?"

Jake shrugged. "Because it's probably just nonsense."

Yvonne stared at him for a long while, her adrenaline spiking. "Jake. I'm the girl who used to chase down rare books. I love this kind of stuff. As bad as I wanted and needed a change, I miss that part of my old job—the chase, looking for something rare or mysterious." She paused. "I don't miss flying, and I don't miss the hustle and bustle of the city, but you have to admit that the possibility of a buried treasure is a little exciting." She rubbed her hands together and raised her eyebrows. "So, what's the story?"

"*Ach*, wow. I can see you're going to buy into this, but you have to promise not to tear down any walls." He laughed.

Yvonne lifted her chin and frowned. "Okay, no tearing down walls. So, what's the deal?"

"According to *mei grossdaadi* and others, the old man who ran the general store in this building was a bit *ab im kopp*—off in the head. So, no one really took his ramblings seriously. But, *supposedly* . . . he was in possession of a rare coin collection worth hundreds of thousands of dollars, and he boasted that he'd hidden it in these walls."

Yvonne gasped before she brought a hand to her mouth, then lowered it. "Wow. How cool is that?"

Jake shook his head. "This building has been renovated more than once, and no one found anything." He chuckled. "I can see the wheels spinning in your head. You said you needed a project." Shrugging, he grinned. "If I were you, I'd choose putting up Christmas decorations over trying to find a coin collection that probably doesn't exist."

Yvonne wiggled her mouth back and forth. "Hmm . . . You're probably right. But what a lucky guy you are to have so many interesting little factoids about this place. A rare book that your grandfather told you not to ever sell . . . and now this."

"*This* has been around forever, and no one really believes it. Don't lose any sleep over it."

Yvonne thought for a few moments, picturing herself tearing down everything but the wall framing in this place, only to find nothing. "Yeah, you're probably right."

But still intriguing.

CHAPTER 6

Yvonne stepped out of her car, put her hands on her hips, and sighed. "Somehow, I knew you'd still be here." She walked around to the hatch on her SUV, opened it, and took out a twenty-pound bag of dog food.

"This is temporary." She nodded to the bag of food she held with both arms. "Just until we find you a home."

She dropped the bag of food just inside the door, then slipped out of the boots she'd worn today, before scurrying in her socks to get a fire going. As Abraham had mentioned, the old farmhouse, despite central air and heat, didn't seem to have much insulation. As she worked to get the fire going using a fire starter, Jake's story about the coins was still on her mind. She'd thought about it all the way home, but ultimately, she knew she had to leave it alone. It wasn't her building to dig around in to find some rumored rare coins. And she had to agree with Jake. It wasn't worth doing any structural damage to the building when renovations in the past hadn't unmasked any hidden treasures. But she still couldn't help but wonder if there was any truth to the rumor.

After she'd fed the dog—which sounded funny in her mind—she ate, showered, climbed into bed, and snuggled into the covers, her teeth chattering. It was way too early to go to sleep, but it was the warmest place in the house, beneath several warm blankets. Tomorrow, she would buy an electric heater for her bedroom.

She recalled Jake saying it was going to freeze again tonight. Groaning, she forced herself out of bed and dug through a box in the corner of her bedroom that had blankets in it, then with an armload, stomped toward the front door and unlocked it. After she'd turned on the porchlight, she stepped onto the porch.

No dog. She set the pile of blankets in the area the animal had been staying, wondering if she should whistle for him. She realized she didn't know much about taking care of a dog. Why hadn't she at least gotten a cardboard box or something to protect the animal from the cold weather? He'd obviously left to find somewhere warm to sleep.

She should have felt good about that. The dog was gone.

She went back inside, locked the door, then shuffled back to her bedroom, refusing to worry about a dog that wasn't even hers. Her mind was deep into a good book when her phone buzzed on the nightstand.

Abraham.

"I may have found a home for your dog, but I see he isn't here," he said after she answered.

Yvonne bolted upright in bed. "Are you *here*?"

"Yep. I have something for you."

Yvonne glanced down at her polka-dot green-and-red Christmas pajamas that should have been tossed several Christmases ago. "Uh . . . sorry, I was in bed. Not asleep. I, uh . . ."

"Are you sure I didn't wake you up? I can come back another—"

"No, no." She was on her feet now. "Give me two minutes."

After she threw on some clothes, she noticed she was wearing the same sweats and baggy T-shirt she'd had on the last time Abraham was there. She skidded into the bathroom, almost falling, and stared at her no-makeup face, then grumbled as she rushed to the door.

"Sorry!" She ran a hand through her messy strands. "I don't usually go to bed this early, but I've been into a good book, and it stays so cold in the house, and . . ." She shrugged.

He was out of uniform, wearing jeans and a black jacket over a white shirt, and driving a pickup truck. She peered over his shoulder, and between the moonlight and the lamp in the yard, she could see something in the bed of the truck. "What's that?"

"I brought you a housewarming present." He held a hand up. "Be right back."

Yvonne couldn't contain a gasp of surprise when she saw what he was dragging behind him. "Oh, wow," she said softly. As he pulled the enormous Christmas tree across the yard, she said, "What have you done?" Her heart was smiling, feeling warm and tingly that he would do such a thing.

He stopped right before the first step that led up to

the porch. "Too big?" He grinned from ear to ear. Yvonne wanted to hug him, but all she could do was shake her head and smile.

"Step aside, then." He winked at her as he hauled the tree up the steps and she held the door open. He manhandled the tree to the far corner—which was the perfect place for it—leaving a trail of pine needles along the way, along with the aroma of the season.

"That thing must have cost a fortune, and I insist on paying you for it." Yvonne stared at the tree, which was easily over eight feet tall. Thankfully, the old farmhouse had ten-foot ceilings.

Abraham chuckled. "Pay me? I'd never *buy* a Christmas tree. This came from my property. Freshly cut by yours truly."

Yvonne closed her eyes and breathed in the piney scent. "It smells like Christmas." When she opened her eyes, Abraham was smiling.

"I'm glad you like it." He scratched his head. "Where's your dog?"

She sighed. "He's not *my* dog, but I have no idea. Do you think maybe he went somewhere to be warm since it's going to freeze tonight? Do animals have a sixth sense about that sort of thing?"

Abraham shrugged. "I don't know. Maybe. Are the blankets on the porch for the dog?"

"Yeah. Kind of lame, I guess. I don't know how much that would protect him from the elements." Yvonne eyed her tree again. "Wow. I just can't thank you enough for this." She wondered what had prompted him to give her such a wonderful gift. Maybe he was just a nice guy—to everyone. She wasn't going to make more of it than it was.

After she cleared her throat and her thoughts, she said, "Who did you find that would take the dog?"

"A farmer down the road from me." He stood by the fire, which had dwindled. "Are you intentionally letting this die down, or do you want me to add a couple of logs?"

"You can add a couple of logs. That would be great. I didn't keep up with it after I climbed into bed." She folded her arms across her chest and rubbed her shoulders. "This house must really not have much insulation."

"These old farmhouses usually don't. I had to add some when I bought my place." He stoked the fire until orange sparks began to shimmer upward, then pointed at the tree. "Do you have a stand for it?"

"No, but I'll get one tomorrow." She pressed her hands together and lifted up on her toes. "I love it. Thank you so much. Um . . . Do you want some coffee, or cocoa, or something?"

Again, she was inviting him into her life, despite her resolve to keep him at a distance. But she couldn't seem to help herself.

Abraham glanced at the clock on Yvonne's mantel. It was only seven thirty, and he wanted to stay, to sit with Yvonne, sip on something warm, and enjoy the fire. Mostly he just wanted to be in her company.

"I-I better go, but thanks for the offer." He'd told

Brianna he wouldn't be seeing her tonight, but spending too much time with Yvonne didn't feel right, even though there was nothing else he wanted more. Brianna was coming on a little too strong, and he needed to cool things down until he could decipher his feelings. They had been exclusively dating each other, even though they hadn't established the terms of their relationship. Well, *Abraham* hadn't established the terms of their relationship, but Brianna's use of the *L* word seemed to indicate that *she* had, and the sentiment had thrown him for a loop. He cared for Brianna and enjoyed spending time with her, but he was nowhere close to telling her he loved her.

And then there was his attraction to Yvonne, which grew every time he was near her. He felt comfortable around Yvonne in a way that he wasn't with Brianna, in ways he couldn't clearly identify. It still felt a little dishonorable even to be here, but seeing Yvonne's face when he brought in the Christmas tree had lessened the guilt. Besides, they were just friends.

"Sure, of course. I'm sure you're probably heading to Brianna's." Yvonne avoided his eyes as she spoke, which sparked a curiosity. Did she want him to stay?

"Actually, no. I have an early shift tomorrow morning." It was what he'd told Brianna too. It was true, but it was also his way of putting a little distance between them.

"Well, I can't thank you enough for this beautiful gift. I'll get a stand and more decorations tomorrow." Her eyes twinkled as she admired the enormous pine, and Abraham was glad he'd taken the time to cut down the tree for her. Her little imitation with the twinkling lights on the table dulled by comparison. He wished he could help her decorate, especially since he'd never put ornaments on a tree, or even had one before.

"Enjoy," he said before he spun around to leave. She followed him to the door, and he turned to face her. "It's fun to watch you so excited about Christmas."

She sighed. "This move, my new job . . . It's all been a big change for the better, and I want to truly embrace the Christmas spirit." She paused as her eyes briefly locked with his. "Try to, at least."

Abraham watched her expression change as her gaze drifted somewhere over his shoulder, seemingly lost in thought. He should go, but his need to offer words of encouragement hung on the tip of his tongue, a longing to let her know he understood how conflicted she must feel. "It probably seems bittersweet to be celebrating the true meaning of Christmas for the first time but without the man you love." Right away, he wondered if he had overstepped since he couldn't read her expression. But his pulse settled when she offered him a small, shy smile.

"I'll see him again." Her eyes met with his again. "And I'm making new friends to share the holidays with."

As a blush filled her cheeks, Abraham wondered if he was making more of her comment than he should.

"You can never have too many friends," he said, thinking it sounded lame, but it was better than blurting out how much he wanted to stay. "I guess I better go." He forced himself to step onto the porch, then glanced at the pile of blankets. "Still no dog. I guess he's hunkered down for the night somewhere. Call me if he comes back, and

I'll come pick him up since I found someone who will take him."

"Will do."

Abraham thought about Yvonne all the way home: the way she smelled, how cute she looked in sweatpants and a T-shirt, and how badly he had wanted to stay. More and more, he was thinking that maybe he needed to end things with Brianna. What was the point in slowing things down? He was beginning to think that time wasn't going to make him fall in love with her, especially if he was this attracted to Yvonne. Maybe it would be kinder to just make a clean break.

He didn't call her when he got home.

Brianna stared at her phone and forced herself not to call Abraham. *I can do this.* Even though it irritated her to no end that he hadn't called. There was a time when he'd called her every day as soon as he got off work. But, if she didn't want to push him away, she was going to need to practice patience.

She pulled out a chair at her kitchen table and sat down with her glass of wine, setting it next to her phone before she eyed a stack of paperwork she'd placed on the table. Her work wouldn't pick up until after the holidays, when her clients would bombard her with all the documents she needed to do their tax returns by the April-fifteenth deadline. But she still had a few projects that needed her attention. She picked up the file on the top of the pile, placed it in front of her, and read the notes she'd made, but she couldn't concentrate. She wanted Abraham to call. And she still hadn't listened to Mitch's voice mail.

Sighing, she decided to get it over with . . . after she guzzled the rest of the wine in her glass. It would be a nasty voice mail that she probably deserved, but at the time she'd sent Mitch his little gift, she'd been fuming mad at him. She didn't even live in the state anymore, yet he'd filed a restraining order against her. She pressed Play to hear his voice mail.

"Brianna, you are the sickest person I have ever known. And I suggest you read the fine print on the restraining order. You are not *supposed to contact me in any way, and your little gift is the most disgusting thing I've ever seen. Who does that, Brianna? Who sends someone a box of dog poop?"*

Brianna paused the message, squeezed her eyes closed, and cringed. Her vengeful act had been too much, and she'd known it the moment she'd sent the package. But it was too late to undo what she'd done.

She made a few mental notes: *Think before you act. Think before you tell someone you love them after only three months. Exhibit patience.* She took a deep breath before resuming the voice mail.

"You need some help. Some serious help. And I really hope you get it. But either way, do not contact me at all— not via email, snail mail, telephone, or text. Stay out of my life and away from me and Samantha."

Anger rippled down Brianna's spine just hearing that woman's name. She pushed Delete on the voice mail, then set her phone down and drummed her fingers on the table. It was taking everything she had not to call Abraham.

Yvonne finished the book she'd been reading, then slipped into her furry robe and a pair of oversize fuzzy white slippers with red bows on top. Her teeth chattered as she walked through the living room to the kitchen. Even though the heat pumped with its best effort, the fire had died down, and she could feel the frigid air seeping in from places that were obviously not in plain view.

It was too late to be getting a snack—nearly midnight—but it didn't stop her from opening the pantry and perusing the contents. When she didn't find anything that struck her as appetizing, she walked to the window and peeked out. The dog was back, curled up on the blankets . . . and shivering. She stared at him for a long while. What if he was destructive or did his business inside the house? Or turned violent like the dog that had bitten her when she was a child?

It was a risk she was going to take. She opened the door, and it was definitely freezing outside. Dewy drops of moisture had frozen atop the brownish grass in the yard, and Yvonne's teeth chattered even more on the porch. The dog opened its eyes and lifted its head.

"If I let you in the house"—she eyed his knotted fur and visible ribs, which tugged at her heart even more—"are you going to behave? As in not tear anything up or go crazy and bite me?"

The animal lowered his head back to prayer position,

but he kept his eyes on Yvonne. She patted her knee. "Come on. It's too cold out here."

The dog didn't get up. She tried to coax him inside a couple more times, but he didn't move. "Okay, well, I tried."

She was opening the door to go back inside when the dog stood and slowly walked to her side. The animal looked at her but quickly cowered and lowered his head.

"You're as scared of me as I was of you, aren't you?" She reached out to touch his head, but he inched out of her reach at first, then slowly brought his nose closer and licked her hand. "Let's go inside," she said softly before she scooped up the blankets and the dog followed her in. She locked the door, and the animal lay down on the blankets facing the door and resumed his prayer position.

Yvonne hoped he stayed there all night and didn't try to get on the couch. He was filthy.

She pointed a finger at him. "Be good, okay?"

The dog yawned, then closed his eyes. Yvonne went back to bed, passing her Christmas tree propped against the wall, dimly lit by the smoldering orange embers in the fireplace. She smiled before she snuggled into bed, a warm feeling falling over her before she fell asleep.

Abraham had responded to two calls by ten o'clock Saturday morning after starting his shift at 5:00 a.m. One was a trespasser, which Abraham never saw upon arrival or after looking around. The other was a traffic accident, and luckily there were no serious injuries, only a possible broken arm that sent the driver in an ambulance to the hospital.

He was on the road near his brother's farm, so he decided to pay his older sibling a visit while things were slow. Leroy waved from the slanted tin roof when Abraham stepped out of his car.

"You're as *ab im kopp* as ever!" Abraham hollered to his brother in the familiar dialect, which always felt good.

"Who are you calling crazy, *bruder*?" Leroy lowered himself, then slid down the roof to where he had a ladder propped against the house. Abraham remembered how they used to slide down the roof for fun and land on the trampoline . . . until their youngest brother, Daniel, missed his mark and broke his leg. Their mother had put an end to that form of entertainment.

Leroy stepped down the ladder and landed with a thud on the grass, already dried out from the overnight freeze. The sun was bright, and there wasn't a cloud in the sky. Abraham had shed his jacket an hour ago.

"How is crime fighting going?" Leroy held up a finger. "Or, better yet, tell me about the beautiful redhead. How is Brianna doing?" His brother waggled his eyebrows, grinning.

Abraham's brothers were married to beautiful Amish women. But anyone who saw Brianna was instantly hypnotized by her unique beauty: shiny auburn hair, long legs, and a killer smile with the whitest teeth he'd ever seen. He'd tried to picture his girlfriend without makeup—something he'd never seen—and living life as an Amish woman. It only made him chuckle.

"There isn't much crime fighting going on this morning, and Brianna is just fine." Abraham fell into step with his brother when Leroy started toward the barn.

Leroy put a hand on Abraham's shoulder, turning to him with a smile. "It's *gut* to see you."

Abraham nodded. Leroy always said it was good to see him, even if it had only been a week or two, or even a few days, since their last visit. His elder brother was always cheerful, the first person to offer up a smile, to lend a hand to help a neighbor. And he was a doting husband and father, much more actively involved in childrearing than their father had been. Abraham had always admired him and wanted to be just like him. All that had changed after his friend's trouble, when Abraham decided to leave the faith, crushing his family at the time.

"When you gonna bring that gal around?" Leroy nudged him as they stood over their father's workbench, which was technically Leroy's now since their parents had moved into the smaller *daadi haus* on the property.

"She'll be here Christmas, remember?" Abraham cringed at the thought, as he'd done before when he thought about introducing Brianna to his family. The only reason Leroy knew her was because they'd briefly run into him at Walmart a month ago. He recalled his predictions about his parents, who would be kind and gracious but secretly disapproving of a woman as fancy as Brianna, even though Abraham wasn't Amish anymore. His brothers would spend a lot of time staring at her. Everyone did. And his sisters-in-law would likely not say much, in part because she was an outsider, but also because she was

THE STORY OF LOVE

beautiful and they'd probably catch their husbands staring at her.

In the beginning of their relationship, Abraham had been proud to have her on his arm. He was the envy of the men in town and all who saw them together. Lately, though, she'd begun to feel a little weighty on his arm. Her use of the *L* word so early into their relationship felt like pressure for him to reciprocate. If she hadn't told him she loved him, would they have continued on without the heaviness he carried in his chest now?

"*Mamm*, Anna, and Catheryn are already planning the meal." Leroy chuckled. His wife, Anna, and their younger brother's wife, Catheryn, were very close to his and Leroy's mother. Again, he tried to picture Brianna in that group and couldn't get a visual.

"It will be *wunderbar*, as it is every year," Abraham said as his brother dug around in a box of roofing nails.

"You miss it, don't you?" Leroy smiled in a sad way. "Our way of life."

"Sometimes." He missed it more than he cared to admit, but it was too late to go back to the life he'd chosen to leave. He'd been out in the world too long. Even if "the world" was still just Montgomery, Indiana.

It had started out to be the best of both worlds—fulfilling his calling to be a police officer and being near his family. But time had a way of making him feel a little more detached from his loved ones, and that was the hardest part. Even though they were in touch, Abraham's life was completely different from theirs. Despite the overall peacefulness of the community, Abraham had seen things that the average Amish person wouldn't be exposed to. He'd respected his badge and done what was necessary in situations that warranted it. If a person resisted arrest, it was Abraham's job to wrestle the guy into handcuffs and cart him to jail. He'd been a witness in court concerning several car accidents, some of which had had victims who died. Occasionally, drifters wandered in and stirred up trouble, prompting Abraham to handle the situation accordingly—not passively, the way he'd been brought up to behave no matter the circumstances. He recalled the strangers who had wandered into town and burglarized the bookstore the first time he'd met Yvonne.

Static caught his attention, and he reached for the radio clipped to his belt just as the dispatcher spoke. "Domestic dispute . . ." He recognized the address. Maureen and Will. Another part of his job that had led him even further away from his roots. Not to say the Amish didn't have relationship issues. They did. But most of the time the problems were resolved peacefully, without involving the law.

Sighing, he said, "I gotta go."

"Duty calls," Leroy said as he lifted his hand from the box of nails.

"It will be a waste of time. Do you remember Will Robertson from when we were younger?"

"*Ya*, I do." Leroy frowned, something he rarely did. "I see him every now and then. Seems like he's still a bully and not very nice to his wife. I saw him at the hardware store dragging her around by her arm and calling her names I'd never say aloud."

"This is my third call to their house in the past month,

the latest one just a few days ago. But there have been plenty of other times someone has called in on them."

Abraham responded to the call and told dispatch he was on his way, then continued his train of thought with Leroy. "Maureen's had a black eye and other visible signs of abuse, but she refuses to press charges, which I don't really understand. Unless she's just afraid of making things worse for herself." He gave a quick wave as he headed for the barn exit.

"*Gut* to see you," Leroy repeated. "Come when you can stay a while."

He looked over his shoulder and smiled. "I will."

By the time Abraham arrived at Maureen and Will's house, two neighbors stood in the yard, both women.

"He's threatening to kill her," said one of the women, an older lady. "And I'm pretty sure he's going to if she doesn't leave him."

The other lady, also older, just shook her head.

Abraham pounded on the door. The yelling stopped, although he could hear Maureen whimpering. Will would likely come out blasting nasty comments, then Maureen would refuse to put an end to this.

But when Will opened the door with a gun pointed at Maureen's temple, Abraham's stomach lurched and his chest tightened. Will's face was a glowering mask of rage, his nostrils flared with fury. Maureen's eye was still yellow from her last run-in with her husband, and her stance was one of resignation, limp in his arms as tears trailed down her cheeks.

"Whatcha gonna do, Mr. Amish Man?" Will taunted

him, his face bursting with bubbly red anger. The stench of alcohol filled the space around them.

"Will, put the gun down." Abraham glanced over his shoulder at the two women. "Go home!"

The ladies scurried off, one of them crying.

"This ain't your business, Abraham. This is between me and my wife."

Abraham's hand trembled where it rested atop his weapon. He'd always known this moment might come, but now that it was here, he had to force himself to calm down. Pulling a firearm on Will might get Maureen killed.

"Will, put the gun down," he said again as he struggled to keep his voice from shaking. "Let's sit down and talk about this."

As the gun bore down against Maureen's head, Will twisted it like he was screwing it into her temple, and she cried out in agony. Will then lifted the pistol and shot into the sky, bringing forth screams of terror from Maureen. As she flailed in his grip, he began to lower the gun again.

Instantly, Abraham drew his own weapon, his mind racing through all the possible scenarios he'd been drilled on. In the end there was only one solution. His only hope of quickly disarming Will and getting Maureen out of danger was to shoot Will in the arm.

Which he did, just as Will fired off another shot as well.

CHAPTER 7

Yvonne had spent the morning dusting, straightening books, and organizing the gift section when there weren't any customers. It was slow for a Saturday, but she supposed the rain might have kept folks inside. As she ventured down each aisle, she thought about the rare coins and where they might be hidden—if they existed. Jake didn't believe they did, but it made for fun speculations.

She had let out her furry houseguest at seven this morning. The animal didn't appear to have moved all night long, staying just inside the door in the living room. After she'd fed him, he had taken his place on the porch, relaxing into his praying position.

Today, after work, she would buy Christmas decorations for her tree, along with a stand. Then she'd spend a quiet night listening to holiday music, decorating her tree, and maybe even finishing her unpacking. She glanced at the clock on her phone. It was only three. Two more hours to go. Usually, she wasn't antsy about leaving work, but her Christmas tree was calling to be decorated.

She would miss spending the holidays with Aunt Emma, but her aunt had been invited to spend Christmas with relatives in California whom she hadn't seen in years. Even though it would be their first time not to be together for the holidays, Yvonne wouldn't begrudge her aunt an opportunity to reconnect with family members.

She was sure Jake and Eva would invite her for Christmas, but the Amish did things differently. No lavish gifts, which was fine, and no tree. But they also celebrated for two days. That sounded like a perk, but then she recalled Eva saying that the day after the twenty-fifth was usually spent visiting shut-ins and delivering meals.

She closed the book she'd been reading and smiled as she pictured her beautiful Christmas tree, then thought again how Abraham had brought it for her. As much as she would love to invite him over to see the tree after it was decorated, it wasn't a good idea. She sensed her attraction to him might be mutual—a thought that sent her insides swirling. But her emotions could do nothing but spin like a vinyl record stuck in the same place. No matter her attraction to Abraham, he wasn't available. *He has a girlfriend*, she reminded herself again.

A loud clap of thunder made her jump and look toward the window. Through the heavy downfall outside the glass, she saw a van pull into the parking lot. Four Amish women popped open umbrellas and rushed toward the store. As they stepped over the threshold, they spoke to one another in Pennsylvania Dutch before one of the ladies turned to Yvonne.

"Where should we put these umbrellas? I'm sorry we're dripping on your floor."

Yvonne came around the corner and waved a dismissive hand. "No worries. I have a place for them." Jake kept a large tin bucket in the corner, and she'd seen him stow umbrellas there before.

After she'd taken all the umbrellas, she said, "Anything I can help you find, or just browsing?"

The woman who'd spoken before answered, "We're just looking today. *Danki.* I mean thank you."

She tucked her head and joined the other three ladies on the aisle where the children's books were shelved. Yvonne had noticed that some of the Amish women were friendlier than others. A few seemed leery of an outsider. Jake had said it would take a while for some of the Amish folks to warm up to her, but he'd also said it wouldn't affect the local Amish shopping at the bookstore. Yvonne hoped he was right.

"Let me know if you need help." Yvonne sat on the stool where she'd been stationed when she wasn't dusting, organizing, and imagining hidden treasure buried somewhere within the walls.

Then, out of nowhere, one of the women covered her face with her hands and began to weep. Yvonne bit her bottom lip, not wanting to interfere, but decided she could offer some assistance. She wound around the corner of the counter and walked toward the ladies.

"I don't mean to bother you, but can I get you a glass of water or some tissues?" Yvonne suspected all the women were around her age, early to midthirties.

The woman crying took in a deep breath and bit her lip, but she was still visibly upset; tears gathered in the corners of her eyes, and her face was flushed. Another of the ladies spoke up.

"She's very upset. Her brother-in-law was in a shooting accident earlier today. He's all right, but the entire ordeal has everyone shook up." The woman wagged her head. "We just don't have much of that kind of thing here in our community."

"That's terrible. I'm so sorry." Yvonne waited, but no one said anything more. "I'm going to get a glass of water."

She turned to leave, but on her way to the back room, she heard one of the women say "Abraham" amidst the Pennsylvania Dutch they spoke. There were probably a dozen Abrahams in this area, or more, but Yvonne did an about-face.

"I'm sorry, but did you say 'Abraham'?" If there was a rare shooting, it seemed plausible that it might have involved a police officer. "Was it Abraham Byler?" The possibility tore at her insides.

"*Ya*." The crying woman sniffled. "That's *mei schweeger—mei* brother-in-law—and he was shot this morning trying to break up a fight between an *Englisch* man and his *fraa*."

Yvonne gasped before she brought a hand to her mouth. "Is he okay?" Her heart thudded against her chest. "Is he in the hospital?"

"*Ya*, he will be okay, but he was shot in the arm. He should be able to leave the hospital tomorrow, we hope." The woman sniffed again, then dabbed at her eyes with a tissue one of the other ladies had given her. "Do you know Abraham?"

"Um, yes. I mean, not well . . . but, yes, we're friends." Her heartbeat slowed a little after hearing he would be okay.

One of the other ladies cleared her throat. "You are the woman from Texas, *ya*? Jake had mentioned that he was hiring you to run the bookstore." The women exchanged brief glances before refocusing on Yvonne.

"Yes, I'm friends with Jake and Eva. I met Abraham during my last visit here—once here when there was a break-in and then again at Jake and Eva's wedding."

The women nodded knowingly, as if this wasn't particularly newsworthy but provided a brief distraction from the shooting.

An awkward silence followed until Yvonne asked, "Could you tell me which hospital and if it would be okay for me to visit him?"

Abraham's sister-in-law had stopped crying. "*Ya, ya.* He's at the hospital in Bedford, and as far as I know, he can have visitors outside of family."

"Okay. Thank you." Yvonne pointed over her shoulder. "Should I go get a glass of water for you?"

"*Nee*, I'm all right. Thank you, though." The woman paused to blot her eyes again. "I'm sorry for this, for crying. Our family is very close, and we've always known that Abraham was in danger with his job, but I don't think we ever thought something like this might happen—for him to get shot."

"No worries at all. We all cry sometimes." Yvonne offered up a weak smile. "Please, look around. And if you need anything, or change your mind about that glass of water, just let me know."

The women nodded before they began to make their way down the aisle.

Yvonne went back to her spot behind the counter and stared at her cell phone. Five o'clock wasn't going to get here soon enough.

Brianna stood on one side of Abraham's bed while his parents stood on the other side. Abraham had introduced them, and they'd politely said hello, but that was it. This wasn't the best of circumstances for her to meet Abraham's parents, who had been in his room when she arrived. She was hoping they'd leave soon since she knew better than to show any signs of affection in front of them, and she longed to kiss the man she loved.

Finally, his father said they should go, instructing Abraham to call them if he needed anything, saying he would leave his mobile phone turned on.

"Very nice to meet you both." Brianna smiled.

They both nodded before turning to go. After the door closed behind them, Brianna pulled a chair close to the bed, then kissed Abraham on the mouth, gently lingering, before she sat. "I've been waiting to do that since I got here." She reached for his left hand and squeezed. His upper right arm, near his shoulder, was bandaged, and his arm sat in a sling. "Thank God you are all right. Are you in pain?"

"*Nee.*" He sighed. "Sorry. I mean no. I was speaking

with my parents in Pennsylvania Dutch before you got here, and sometimes it just sticks."

Brianna had heard him speaking with Amish people in their native dialect before, although she didn't like not being able to understand what was being said. "I was so scared when you called, but it gave me a great deal of comfort to hear your voice and know you were okay." She stared into his beautiful blue eyes. "It's terrible that you were shot, just horrible, but according to what the nurses said in the hallway, you are a hero."

"I don't feel like a hero. I shattered Will's wrist. He may lose his hand." Abraham looked away from her. She gently cupped his chin and eased his eyes back to hers.

"Look at me, Abraham. The man had a gun to his wife's head. You saved her life. And for that, you are a hero." She leaned down and kissed him again. "You were already my hero anyway."

"He wouldn't have killed her. I could have talked him into putting down the gun, but I was caught off guard when he fired a shot into the air." He shook his head.

"Well, look at it this way. You saved her life in another way. Now he can't beat on her because he will be in jail, and I would think he'll be charged with attempted murder since he shot you."

He gave a half shrug with his left shoulder. "I don't know. Probably."

"And tomorrow, when you are released, you need to come stay with me, so you'll have someone to take care of you." She hated that he'd been shot, but by tomorrow night, they would at least be sleeping in the same bed together.

Abraham had no plans to stay at Brianna's house, but he felt too drugged to argue about it right now. He'd told the nurses to stop giving him pain meds, that he didn't need them, but the staff was insistent he should have drugs to avoid the pain coming on and the risk of elevated blood pressure.

"Thank you for coming," he said sleepily. "I called you from the ambulance. I didn't want you to hear from someone else."

"And I love you for that."

There was that *L* word again.

She leaned over and kissed him again. "I'm not going to stay long because I can tell you're tired and need to rest."

He nodded in appreciation, also feeling sick to his stomach about this entire thing. He could still recall the way the gun felt in his hand when he fired at Will's arm, just after Will's wild shot into the air. Even after tons of shooting practice, it felt entirely different to shoot a person. His recollection of Will's face in that moment might haunt him forever. Pure torment with a heavy dose of anger as Will aimed the gun at Abraham. Luckily, Maureen had dropped to the ground, and Abraham had been blessed to only be shot in the arm. He'd still been able to wrestle the gun from what was left of Will's hand.

Thinking about it made him want to throw up.

Brianna stood and brushed his hair back from his forehead. "Do you need anything before I go? Or is there anything I can bring you in the morning?"

"No, but thank you. I'm probably just going to sleep." He worried if peaceful slumber would ever come, today or in the future.

There was a soft knock at the door, and Abraham managed a weak, "Come in."

"Am I interrupting? Is this a bad time?" Yvonne poked only her head into the room.

Abraham's eyes widened. He no longer wanted to doze off, even though he wasn't sure he could fight it for long. "Hey, Yvonne."

She turned to Brianna. "Hi. Should I come back another time?"

"Absolutely not." Brianna motioned for Yvonne to come in, then sat in the chair by the bed. "Our patient is worn out and tired, so you might want to make it a short visit."

Abraham almost said he could speak for himself, but Brianna was right. He was fading fast.

"Of course." Yvonne took a few steps closer and put a hand on his good arm, but she didn't leave it there long enough. "One of your sisters-in-law came into the bookstore earlier with some other ladies. I'm sorry, I didn't even get their names . . . but she told me what happened. Abraham, I am so sorry."

"The doctor said I'm going to heal just fine, but I'll be on desk duty for a while, and somewhere down the line, I'll have to endure a trial. I suspect that's a long way off." He smiled, couldn't help it. "Thank you for coming, but you didn't have to do that."

"I know." She looked at Brianna and smiled. "I know you're in good hands, but I just wanted to stop in for a minute. It's the least I can do since you brought me that awesome Christmas tree."

Abraham's eyes darted to Brianna, who stiffened instantly. He opened his mouth to explain, but Yvonne had already started to speak to Brianna.

"I had a stray dog show up at my place, and Abraham thinks he might have found a home for it." She waved a hand. "Anyway, he saw my pitiful little Charlie Brown Christmas tree and brought me one that he cut down. I'm so grateful."

"Abraham is very thoughtful." Brianna plastered on a smile, but Abraham wasn't sure it was genuine. He had seen subtle hints over the past three months that Brianna might be a little jealous sometimes. He could already foresee the questions coming from her later.

"Aw, sweetie." Brianna stood, then leaned down and kissed him. "I know how exhausted you are." She smiled at Yvonne. "We should probably go and let him get some rest."

"Sure. You're right." Yvonne briefly touched his arm again. "I'll be praying for you, for a speedy recovery."

Brianna thought her insides might explode. Exactly how much conversation and visits had her boyfriend and Yvonne had? She was going to need to ramp up her game.

"I'll text or call you later, babe." Brianna started slowly to the door.

Yvonne gave a quick wave, and once they were in the hallway, they fell into step.

"It's terrible that this happened to such a nice guy." Yvonne sighed.

"I know. He's so good to everyone. I mean, he barely knows you, yet he still wanted to make sure you had a nice Christmas tree." Brianna gave a casual shrug as she smiled. "He's just like that to everyone."

"The world needs more like him, for sure." Yvonne pushed the Down button for the elevator.

"Well, I'll make sure he is well taken care of when he's released." The door opened and they both stepped inside. "He'll be staying with me starting tomorrow. I work from home, so it's easiest for me to take care of him."

"That's great. How long will he be staying with you?" Yvonne stepped aside when the elevator door opened to the lobby, then followed Brianna out.

After they were side by side again, Brianna answered. "He'll be staying with me indefinitely. It really doesn't make sense for us to live in two different houses when we spend so much time together. I mean, we haven't made any formal plans to live together, but I foresee that on the horizon very soon. For now, he'll stay with me for as long as he needs to until we discuss more permanent arrangements."

Yvonne knew when a woman was staking a claim on a man, and Brianna was certainly leaving no doubt in Yvonne's mind that Abraham was off the market. Yvonne hadn't realized things were that serious with Abraham and his girlfriend. But there was no mistaking the look on Brianna's face when Yvonne mentioned the Christmas tree and that Abraham had been at her house. It was obvious Brianna hadn't known. She wished she could take it back, but the damage was done. She hadn't intentionally meant to throw Abraham under the bus, but she also wondered why he didn't tell his girlfriend about the time he spent with her. Was Brianna the jealous type? Did Abraham harbor feelings for Yvonne that he was exploring, which made him feel guilty? Or was Yvonne's mind running around in circles again?

"Well, it's great that he has you to take care of him. And when he is feeling better, will you remind him about the dog?" She sighed. "I'm not really a dog person, and Abraham said he would pick it up and take it to its new owner. Obviously, things have changed and he's going to need some recovery time, but if you can just ask him to call or text me the name of the man, I'll contact him directly about the dog." Yvonne fought a sinking feeling in the pit of her stomach, but it was probably best that she didn't cling to any ideas about seeing Abraham, even as a friend.

Even though she almost convinced herself that she needed to put some distance between them, she'd wanted nothing more than to stay with him longer just now.

"Of course. I'll remind him." Brianna slowed her stride. "I'm parked that way."

"I'm in the opposite direction. It was nice to see you again, although I wish it hadn't been under these circumstances." Yvonne smiled.

"Lovely to see you too." Brianna gave a quick wave. "Bye, now."

Yvonne made the fifty-minute drive from Bedford back to Montgomery. When she stepped out of the car, she just smiled. "You might as well come in," she said as she unlocked the door.

The dog moseyed to her side and crossed the threshold with her, instantly taking his position right by the door.

Yvonne stared at her tree. She hadn't felt like stopping for ornaments and a stand after leaving the hospital. It had felt so special that Abraham had brought her the gift—initially. But maybe he'd cut lots of trees and given them away. Brianna said he was just that type of guy. Either way, she would wait to hear from him about the dog but otherwise stay away. Consciously or not, she worried she might interfere with him and Brianna, and she wasn't that kind of woman.

But when she saw a text from Abraham, her spirits lifted as quickly as her prior thoughts flew out the window. She read it as her heart fluttered more than it should.

Thank you for stopping by. It was nice to see you.

She thought about what to write back. She wanted to be genuine but not flirty. Abraham was about to be living with a woman. A serious commitment.

As I said, I will be praying for you to have a speedy recovery.

She waited.

Thank you. I'll be eager to see that Christmas tree when you have it all decorated.

Was he being nice? Friendly? Or flirting?

She wasn't sure. So she didn't respond.

CHAPTER 8

Abraham waited as long as he could for Yvonne to respond, but he couldn't keep his eyes open, and the nurse had been right to keep the pain meds coming. Now that the anesthesia had worn off, his shoulder was starting to hurt. But he wanted to prompt Yvonne one more time.

Have a great evening. Listen to Christmas music.

Fifteen minutes later, still no answer, and he couldn't fight sleep anymore. And that's what he wanted: to sleep and forget about this entire day. Everyone would remind him that he'd done the right thing, but it felt wrong to Abraham, and he knew he would question his choice for a long time. Violence was never the way to go, and he should have worked harder to keep Will calm and have a peaceful resolution. Instead, he'd shot a man and ended up wounded himself.

It felt like only five minutes later when he woke up and saw breakfast on his bedside tray. His head held dreamy remnants of nurses coming in and out during the night, but it was a blur. And before he'd even had a sip of coffee, Brianna walked into the room.

"What time is it?" he asked wearily as she eased up to the bed.

"Around eight. How are you feeling?" Brianna reached behind her for the chair and scooted it next to the bed. She looked gorgeous, as always, wearing black slacks and a turquoise-colored blouse. She had a black scarf around her neck, and her auburn hair was pulled into a twist. She looked elegant. Her green eyes sparkled against her ivory skin. Sometimes she reminded Abraham of a porcelain doll. Fragile, but perfect. He was a lucky man that someone like Brianna had taken an interest in him. Maybe he should be more accepting of her feelings instead of allowing her use of the *L* word to frighten him. But he didn't think real love should be scary.

"Okay, I guess." He flinched when he shifted his weight. "For a guy who has been shot."

She rolled her lip into a pout, which was cute. "I hate that this happened to you. But if it makes you feel any better, I stopped at the nurse's station on my way to your room, and the nurse said they are already working on your release papers. She said you remained stable through the night, so the doctor agreed to sign off for you to go home." She paused. "But you have to have someone with you, at least for a few days, so I'll be taking you to my place."

Abraham considered his options. Neither his parents nor his brothers had room for him at their places, even though he was sure they'd have kids bunk up and share a room if he needed the space. But he didn't want to inconvenience anyone. He was sure his mother would offer to stay with him at his house, where he'd be most comfortable, but his mother would be anything but comfortable. She'd be out of sorts with the electricity, modern appliances, and everything that would serve as a reminder one of her children had chosen the outside world. Abraham didn't want to put her through that. He was reasonably close to his parents, but he mostly visited them at their house, as opposed to them coming out to his place.

After he weighed his options, he locked eyes with Brianna. "Can we please stay at my place? I think I'll recover better in my own bed." He'd rather be alone, but having Brianna at his house was better than the sterility of her house. He didn't think he'd ever feel at home there.

She pouted again. "In that old farmhouse? Are you sure?"

Abraham considered how luxurious his parents considered his house to be, a broad comparison to how Brianna viewed his home. "Brianna, I can take care of myself. I . . ." He couldn't tell her he loved her because he didn't. Maybe he would someday, but not now. "I appreciate you. And I'm grateful that you are willing to take care of me, but I'll be okay. I know my house isn't your favorite."

"Don't be silly. I like your farmplace. It's just different from what I'm used to, but we will stay there. You can't go home alone. I'll stay until you feel better. I can make sure you take your meds on time, prepare your meals, and see that you get plenty of rest."

He moved in bed and moaned a little, which didn't make him feel very manly, but his arm ached from his shoulder and down past his elbow. If there was any sort of silver lining, Brianna was a good cook. "Okay. It should only be for a day or two."

———

Brianna wasn't crazy about staying at Abraham's place. It was filled with antique furniture and smelled old. But she wanted to be close to him, to nurture him back to good health, and to show him what a good wife she could be. Being under the same roof would provide them with a whole new level of intimacy.

"I'll stay as long as you need me." She stood, leaned over the bed, and kissed him softly before she sat again. "You need to eat." Nodding to the tray on his bedside table, she said, "It doesn't look like you've even touched your coffee. Are you hungry?"

"Not really." He flinched as he shifted his weight in the bed. "But I'll take that coffee."

She handed him the cup, then frowned at his breakfast offerings and shook her head. "I promise you will have three home-cooked meals and nothing like whatever is on that tray."

He smiled. "You know how much I love your cooking."

"Thank you." She basked in the compliment before she crinkled her nose. "It smells like antiseptic in here."

Abraham nodded before he took a sip of coffee.

Brianna couldn't wait until they were together at his house. She would make him realize how much he needed her and wanted to be with her forever.

After Abraham had a few more sips of his coffee and had a chance to wake up a little more, he reached for his cell phone. He was disappointed Yvonne hadn't responded to his texts, but his mother had left a voice mail.

"I need to listen to this message. It's from my mom." He grinned. "I didn't know my mother knew how to leave a voice mail. She rarely uses a cell phone." He pushed the button and put the call on speaker.

"Abraham, please let me know how you are feeling and if you are still going home today. We lieb you and will be by to see you soon."

"Aw, that was nice," Brianna said, smiling.

Abraham took another drink of his coffee and hoped his parents wouldn't visit while Brianna was staying with him. That wouldn't go over well at all, but his mother had said they'd be by soon, so it was probably unavoidable. Abraham was already nervous about his girlfriend sleeping in his bed, but he couldn't ask her to sleep on the couch, and he couldn't give up his bed with his arm the way it was. He had two extra bedrooms, but one room was set up as an office, and the other room had workout equipment that he rarely used. It would only be for a day or two, though.

"Do you have food at your house?" Brianna asked. "Usually, it takes forever to get released from the hospital, even when they've started the paperwork. I was wondering if I should make a grocery run, take it to your house, then come pick you up?"

"I have about as much food as the average bachelor." Abraham grinned.

Brianna chuckled. "Uh-oh. That's not good. I'm going to go check with the nurse, and if I have enough time before they release you, I'll go shopping."

Abraham opened the drawer of his bedside table, happy to see his wallet was there. He fished out a hundred-dollar bill.

"Here." He handed the money to Brianna when she walked back into the room. "We're going to need food whether you get it now or later, and I want to pay for it."

"You don't have to do that." She hesitated, then took the money. "But I'll match that and throw in a hundred dollars too. That way we'll have plenty of food to last us."

Abraham tried to smile as he wondered exactly how long Brianna was planning to stay.

Brianna spent almost three hundred dollars on groceries, and when she pulled onto the gravel driveway at Abraham's farmhouse, she hoped he had room in his refrigerator for everything. She probably should have checked before she shopped, but she'd made a quick trip to her house to get clothes and toiletries.

After she dug around in her purse for the key to Abraham's house, she trudged up the porch steps. She'd made herself a copy of the key he had given her so it would be more convenient in the future. It took several tries to get her new key to open the old lock, but when it did, she was greeted by that musty old smell she disliked. Hopefully the wax burner and scented candles she'd bought would get rid of some of the old-house odor.

She went straight to his refrigerator, pleased that she'd bought staples such as butter and milk since Abraham's inventory was sparse. He had a pitcher of what appeared to be tea, a loaf of bread, a six-pack of Diet Coke with one bottle missing, and a few condiments.

It took several trips for her to get everything unloaded. When she was done, she called him. "I'm at your house, and I just got the groceries put away," she said after he answered. "Are you ready to come home?"

"Oh, I'm ready." He sighed. "But the nurse said they're still waiting on the doctor to sign the paperwork, so it might be a while."

"Okay. Well, if it's all right with you, I'll tidy up a bit here. Not that it's a mess or anything, but we'll want everything super clean when you come home. You have a lot of stitches, so we want to take care that you don't get an infection."

"Brianna, I don't want you cleaning my house. You don't have to do that."

She glanced around, and for a bachelor pad, it was fairly clean. "I don't mind. Should I change your sheets?"

"No, they're okay. I changed them right before this happened."

"All right. Don't worry about a thing. I'm going to start some chili in the slow cooker . . ." She paused. "Uh, do you have a slow cooker?"

"Yeah, in the bottom cabinet to the left of the stove."

"Okay. Now that cooler temperatures are here, it feels like time for chili. Does that sound good?"

"It sounds great. But don't go to any trouble."

"I'm not. It won't take me long to get it going, then I'll head back to the hospital."

After they'd ended the call, Brianna set out the ingredients for chili. She recalled her mother sharing the recipe with her, long before she'd quit speaking to her parents. Their last argument had been over something stupid—she remembered that much—but couldn't pinpoint the final straw that had severed the relationship.

She browned the meat, chopped onions, and once everything was on Low in the slow cooker, she took her toiletry bag to Abraham's bathroom. She unpacked her toothbrush, makeup, deodorant, and other essentials and placed them in the medicine cabinet above the sink. She'd opened his medicine cabinet during her first trip to his house since you could tell a lot about a person by inspecting their toiletries. Nothing suspect had jumped out at her; the cabinet had his deodorant, cologne, toothbrush, dental floss, and all the normal stuff. No pill bottles or anything weird.

Brianna recalled searching Mitch's bathroom. She hadn't found anything odd there either. Perhaps a man's toiletries didn't offer up much about the true person after all, since Mitch had turned out to be a lowlife cheater.

She moseyed down the hallway to Abraham's bedroom.

It looked like a man's bedroom, decorated in neutral colors. His bedspread was a tan quilt, and there was a large picture on the wall of two horses in a field. He had one dresser and nightstands on either side of the bed. Only one had a lamp on it, so she assumed that was the side he slept on. She went back to the bathroom and returned with lotion she liked to use at night and set it on the nightstand that didn't have anything on it.

There was a Bible on Abraham's bedside table, along with a box of tissues. If there was a downside to being in a relationship with Abraham, it was his overt religious beliefs. He spoke often about God, prayed a lot—always before meals, even in restaurants—and he went to church on Sundays. Brianna believed in a higher power, and she prayed, but she wasn't as into it as he was. Abraham had tried to have a conversation about religion, but Brianna was a master at avoiding discussions about topics she didn't totally understand.

She opened his small closet, which was packed with clothes. Everything she'd brought would get wrinkled if she moved his clothes over and hung hers. She retrieved her suitcase from where she'd left it in the living room, then rolled it down the hallway to the extra bedroom where he kept an exercise bike and workout bench. She'd brought enough clothes for at least two weeks, but she could get more later.

After she'd hung everything up, she stirred the chili and decided to do a full walk-through. She checked every drawer, cabinet, and closet. Despite Abraham's noble job and seemingly clean reputation, a woman couldn't be too careful these days. She smiled when she didn't find anything that would indicate he had any secrets.

But she knew he had at least one: that Yvonne woman, whom Brianna planned to keep a close eye on.

Yvonne spent most of her Sunday unpacking, and she eventually made a trip to Walmart and bought a tree stand and plenty of decorations. She'd chosen to go as traditional as possible and bought all red and green ornaments. She felt bad that she hadn't attended church today. Soon, she'd start visiting churches in the area and hoped to find one she liked. Back in Texas, she'd attended a nondenominational Christian church.

It was nearing dark by the time she finished prettying up her tree, and she was pleased with the results. She'd chosen twinkling white lights, and after she'd packed up her little fake tree, she kept the angel topper for her new tree. Breathing in the scent of pine, the Christmas spirit finally washing over her, she thought about Abraham and thanked God again that he hadn't been more seriously injured.

As she listened to the holiday music playing softly in the background, she eyed her tree, glistening with red and green balls, lights twinkling in the near darkness. She snapped a picture, and before she could change her mind, she sent it to Abraham with a text. *Thanks again. More prayers for a speedy recovery.* Then she turned toward her front door and took a picture of the dog sleeping quietly there. She sent the picture with another message. *I named him Blue.*

Less than a minute later, her phone chirped. *The tree looks beautiful. I hope you're feeling the Christmas spirit. Thanks for the prayers.*

Yvonne smiled.

Her phone announced another text. *Maybe you should just keep the dog. I mean, you named him, lol.*

She thought for a few seconds before she responded. *He does seem to like it here. Please tell the farmer that I'm keeping the dog after all . . . What can I say? He grew on me, lol.*

Yvonne wondered if the dog would have had a warm place to sleep if he went to live with the farmer. She doubted he would be allowed inside. And, she had to admit, there was something comforting about having another presence in her house.

She stared at her phone, but it was silent, so she went to add another log on the fire. When her phone went off again, she scurried in her socks back to the couch.

I like the name Blue.

Yvonne typed. *He looks kind of blue. It seemed to fit since he's a blue heeler. But I guess it's not too original.* She paused, thinking. *I hope you and Brianna have a good evening. She said you would be staying at her place indefinitely. Get well!*

She'd broken her own rule: to distance herself from Abraham. She shouldn't have sent the pictures. Slouching into her couch, she put her feet up on the coffee table, covered up with a heavy blanket, and wondered if she would find someone to spend winter evenings with.

Abraham's eyes widened. Brianna was still in the shower, and he felt like he was doing something wrong by texting

Yvonne. But . . . they were just friends. Now he needed to set Yvonne straight. He tried to prop himself up more in bed, but it was a failed effort.

Brianna is staying here a day or two while I recover, but I assure you she is not staying indefinitely. He hit Send. For whatever reason, it felt important to let Yvonne know that.

He startled when his phone buzzed.

Oh. Maybe I misunderstood Brianna. I got the impression you two were making plans to live together.

Abraham bristled as he took a deep breath. *Did she tell you that?*

Like I said, maybe I misunderstood. Have a good evening.

Abraham wanted to keep texting with her, but he heard the shower turn off. He set his phone on the nightstand, moaning a little. The doctor had told him that the bullet had hit a muscle and that he would likely have more discomfort from that than the incision. *Discomfort* was an understatement. He wondered if it was time for another pain pill.

Brianna walked into his bedroom, which felt weird. They spent most of their time at her place, and the few times she'd come to his house, they hadn't spent any time in the bedroom. She wore a long white terrycloth robe and blue slippers. It was impossible not to wonder what she was wearing under that robe, but he also noticed that she still had on all her makeup. He thought women usually took off their makeup at night.

She walked around to his side of the bed. "You have a pained expression on your face," she said. "Are you hurting?"

As much as he hated to admit it, Abraham nodded. "Yeah, is it time for another pain pill?"

"It will be in about thirty minutes, so I don't see any harm taking it now." She opened the bottle on the bedside table and dropped a pill into the palm of her hand, then picked up a glass of water. "Can you sit up a little?"

"I tried." He felt defeated, and he also wondered what Brianna had told Yvonne about their living arrangements. Or had Yvonne really misunderstood?

Brianna set the pill and water on the nightstand. "Let me help you."

Abraham followed her lead as she put her hand behind his back and helped him sit up a little. Then she fluffed his pillows and folded one in half to support him better. As she got him situated, her cleavage sat right in his face, and he saw she was wearing something red, and apparently flimsy, beneath her robe. Abraham swallowed hard. He was well aware how unusual it was for a man his age not to have succumbed to sex by the time he was thirty-seven. He had wanted to give in more times than he could count, especially when he had dated Nina. But, luckily for him, Nina had shared his same feelings about intimacy, wanting to wait until marriage. Brianna tempted him every chance she got, and now he supposed she would slip into bed wearing something to entice him even more. Although the injury wasn't going to allow him to do anything. He could barely move without searing pain running the length of his arm.

"I'm going to go brush my teeth. Is there anything you need?" Her voice was soft and filled with tenderness. He knew he should be grateful that she was here to take care of him, but being taken care of wasn't a role he enjoyed.

"No, I'm okay." He yawned. "I'm sure when this pill kicks in, I'll be asleep pretty quickly."

She kissed him gently on the forehead. "Okay. Be right back."

Abraham inched himself back down to a lying position. It was easier easing himself down than it was to sit up. He wondered what he would do when he had to go to the bathroom. Would he have to wake Brianna up to help him sit up and get out of bed? Dating for three months just didn't feel long enough to be in this intimate of a setting.

His eyes were heavy when she walked back into the room, but not too heavy to be completely taken in by what she was wearing. Her red negligee left nothing to the imagination, and she made a point to stand by the bed long enough for him to take in every curve.

"You look beautiful." It was true. But he wondered how red his face was and if she could see him blushing in the dimly lit room.

"Thank you." She pulled back the covers and eased her way into the bed, careful not to touch his wounded shoulder that was on her side. "I want you to wake me up if you need anything at all."

He nodded. "Thanks for helping me out."

"Of course." She carefully leaned over him, exposing herself even more, as she kissed him on the cheek. "You just rest so you can get well."

After nodding again, he felt himself starting to drift off.

Brianna saw the way Abraham looked at her tonight, and there was lust in his eyes. He would need to get better first, but she was sure she could coax him into intimacy. He'd practically been drooling. She waited until he was snoring gently before she slipped out of bed and tiptoed to his side. He'd kept his phone close to him constantly, and she remembered Mitch used to do that when he was in the throes of cheating on her. She disconnected the phone from the charging cord. It only had one bar. She'd need to remember to plug it back in.

She scanned his recent phone calls. Nothing out of the ordinary—his mother's voice mail, a call from each of his brothers, and one from his friend Jake. She pushed his Text icon, and her chest tightened when she saw Yvonne's name and several texts. After she read their conversation, she seethed. The worst part should have been that Yvonne told him she heard they were making plans to live together. But even worse was the hurt Brianna felt that Abraham had made it clear that wasn't the case. And he'd made it clear to *her*. Yvonne would continue to try to get her claws into Abraham if Brianna didn't get control of this situation.

Trembling, she tiptoed to the bathroom, closed the door, and turned on the light. She fumbled around for a few minutes, but she eventually got the SIM card out of Abraham's old cell phone. She'd asked him repeatedly why he didn't upgrade, but he said he liked the simplicity of his phone. He couldn't even access the internet on this old model.

She held the small SIM card in her hand. She couldn't flush it and risk waking him up, so for now, she slipped it under the bathroom mat.

When she got back to the bedroom, she plugged in the phone and quietly placed it back on the nightstand.

CHAPTER 9

Yvonne turned up the heat in the car as she pulled out of the bookstore parking lot. She'd had quite a few customers throughout the day. It had frozen over for the past several nights, but it warmed up during the days with full sunshine, and the crisp, sunny weather seemed to draw people out. It wasn't as warm during the day as she would have preferred, staying in the forties. As a born and raised Texan, anything below fifty degrees was cold and warranted a fire in the fireplace. She wondered how she would do in January and February, when she'd been told that temps could drop below zero and might not get above freezing for days at a time.

She was, however, looking forward to the first real snowfall. There had been a few flurries since her arrival, but she was eager to see everything blanketed in white, especially at Christmastime. Accumulation was rare in Texas—mostly a light dusting that barely covered the grass.

She was disappointed that she hadn't heard from Abraham in four days, not even to check on the dog. Blue had slowly gotten more comfortable, and he had made his way to a spot in front of the fireplace. He was filling out too. His protruding ribs weren't as prevalent, and he had a gentle nature. Her new dog needed a bath, though, and she was nervous about that. What if he didn't like bathing? Would he turn violent?

Her thoughts wound back to Abraham. The man was recovering from a gunshot wound, and Yvonne and her dog were probably the last thing on his mind.

A few minutes later, she knocked on Jake and Eva's door. If Jake's buggy hadn't been parked outside, she would have just opened the door and yelled to Eva, who was still on bed rest.

"Glad you're here. Eva is going stir-crazy," Jake said as soon as he opened the door, stepping aside to let her in. "Everything going okay at the bookstore?"

Yvonne went straight to the fireplace, pulled off her gloves, and held her palms near the sizzling warmth. "Yep. All is okay. And I found the box of Christmas decorations in the attic, so everything looks festive." She looked over her shoulder. "You must really trust me since you haven't been in all week."

He sighed. "I'm afraid to go. I keep picturing you tearing down walls and looking for buried treasure."

She playfully slapped him on the arm when he sidled up next to her, then laughed. "No. I believe you. Probably just a rumor. But there is something I wanted to ask you."

"Hurry up and ask him!" Eva hollered from the bedroom. "Then come see me!"

"Told ya." Jake pointed toward their downstairs bed-room as he lifted an eyebrow.

Yvonne covered her mouth so as not to laugh again.

"What do you want to ask me?"

"Do you ever have book signings at the store?" She rubbed her hands together in front of the fire.

"Not in a long time. Unless it's a popular author, they usually don't do well." He shrugged. "And even the weather can affect the turnout."

"Well, a fairly popular author called this morning and said he would be in the area next week. His name is Larry Boone."

Jake looped his thumbs beneath his suspenders. "Never heard of him."

"He writes children's books, and we carry his books. I thought it might be a nice way to draw people into the store and a chance for me to meet more of the locals. But I'd need to spread the word quickly since it's such short notice. What do you think? I told him I'd call him tomorrow or later this evening."

"It's fine with me. What are you going to do to spread the word?" Jake shifted his weight and rubbed his chin.

"Well, obviously I can't reach the Amish ladies via email, but—"

"I'll call them all! They have phones! It will give me something to do!" Eva practically screeched. "Now, please come see me before I go completely crazy."

"You better go," Jake said as he shook his head. "I know we don't want this *boppli* to come too early, but, *ach* . . ." He shook his head. "Let Eva help you, and just handle it however you want. But I doubt we have very many of his books in stock."

"Only three," Yvonne said as she started toward the bedroom. "But he said he has plenty to bring, and he's willing to sell them to us at the same cost we pay the distributors, and he'll also take whatever is left with him. So there's no risk for the store."

"Perfect." Jake waved. "I'm off to work on our well. I think the pump is going out."

Yvonne walked into the bedroom and couldn't help but grin when she saw Eva.

"Go ahead. It's okay. Laugh." Eva pouted, then sighed.

She had her feet propped up on four pillows, her hands on her stomach, and her cheeks were rounder than Yvonne had ever seen them.

"Your hair is so long." Yvonne gazed at the thick brown tresses that spread around her and lay past her waist. "You've always had a prayer covering on or your hair was in a knot beneath a scarf." She paused. "Wow. Your hair is gorgeous."

Eva sighed. "*Danki.* That's the only thing I have going for me right now." She rolled her eyes. "I'm fat and miserable."

Yvonne sat on the side of the bed. "Not fat. Pregnant." Even though the Amish were known for their lack of pridefulness or concern about their looks, she suspected most young women cared about their appearance.

"I haven't seen you in a while. Tell me how the bookstore is doing. And what about Abraham?"

Yvonne eased out of her jacket and set it in her lap. A propane heater was keeping Eva and Jake's room super cozy, which reminded Yvonne she needed a source of heat for her bedroom. "The bookstore is doing pretty good, and I guess you heard me ask Jake about having a book signing? And I heard there's a rumor of buried coins in the bookstore, but I promised Jake I wouldn't tear down any walls." She shrugged. "That's about it."

Eva took a deep breath. "I overheard about the book signing, and I have heard of that author. I don't know anything about him, but his books sell steadily, a few here and there, so maybe the store can draw a small crowd. I'll start making some phone calls and ask others to spread the word. *Mamms* are more likely to buy something for their *kinner* as opposed to themselves." She chuckled. "As for the secret treasure, I've always thought it was a possibility." She raised her eyebrows, grinning.

"Well, Jake and the man who brought the plaque laughed it off. I'm surprised to hear you say that." Yvonne paused. "As for Abraham, I stopped by the hospital to see him. His girlfriend was there, and he was tired, so I didn't stay long. But I wanted to stop because he's been so nice to me. He brought me a Christmas tree, and he was also trying to help me find a home for a stray dog that showed up at my place." She smiled. "Although I've decided to keep the dog."

"I really thought something might rekindle between you and Abraham when you moved here."

Yvonne shrugged. "We're friends, I guess. But he's been dating Brianna for three months, and apparently things are more serious than I thought." She tapped a finger to her chin. "I mean, I think they are. I'm not sure." She blew out a breath of frustration.

Eva frowned, looking a bit confused.

"Let me clarify. I thought he was dating Brianna and that all was well, so I didn't want to interfere. Brianna even told me when we left the hospital together that he would be staying with her during his recovery, which . . . as it turns out, she's staying with him. She also told me that living together was the next step, and it sounded like it was something they were planning. But when I texted Abraham—we've done that a few times, very innocent—he said Brianna would only be there a couple of days and that they had no plans to live together. But I haven't heard from him in four days."

"Hmm . . ." Eva inched herself to a more upright position. "I hope he didn't have some sort of relapse or end up back in the hospital, but I think we would have heard if that had happened. News travels fast around here."

Yvonne chewed on her bottom lip. "I probably shouldn't have done this, but I actually called the hospital yesterday to see if he was a patient, and he's not."

Eva smiled. "You really like him, don't you?"

Yvonne held up her first finger and sat taller. "Only as a friend."

"But if he wasn't involved with Brianna?"

Yvonne lowered her arm. "If he was free and single, yes I would want to go out with him. And, it's worth mentioning, I got asked out several times in Texas, but I wasn't ready to date anyone. I compared everyone to Trevor, even a year later. Abraham is the first person that I have felt ready to go out with. And, wouldn't you know it, he's taken."

Eva groaned. "*Ya*, and I wish you could have gotten here sooner, before he had a girlfriend, because the two of you seem like such a good fit. But maybe three months ago would have still been too soon?"

Yvonne thought back to when the letters had stopped coming. "I probably should have written him back."

"You weren't ready." Eva shrugged.

"I could have just sent a courteous response, but at the time, it felt like a betrayal to Trevor."

They were quiet for a few moments.

"Our people are encouraged to remarry quickly following the death of a spouse. I know you and Trevor weren't married yet, but you were engaged, so similar circumstances." She paused. "If anything happened to Jake, though, I can't imagine dating someone else right away. I would need time, like you. And it takes as long as it takes. Unfortunately, the timing didn't cooperate with you and Abraham."

"I'm not sure it's as much about the timing as it is about the person. Don't get me wrong, I will love Trevor forever and cherish our memories, but honestly . . . it wasn't just the timing. I never felt like I wanted to pursue anything with another man until I actually *saw* Abraham again. If I had written him back, maybe that door would have stayed cracked."

"God always has a plan, and everything happens in His time frame."

Yvonne wrestled with her regret for a couple of seconds. "It is what it is, I guess." She paused. "Anyway. Enough of that. Is there anything you need?"

"*Ya.* For time to jump ahead about six weeks and the *boppli* to be born."

Yvonne laughed. "Besides that? And how are you keeping yourself entertained?"

Eva rambled on about how she couldn't do one more crossword puzzle, that she'd read several books . . .

Yvonne tried to stay in tune with what her friend was saying, but her mind drifted, the way it had been lately, as she wondered what Abraham was up to.

Abraham skipped his seven o'clock dose of pain meds Thursday evening. There was a constant ache in his shoulder, and occasionally his entire arm throbbed, but he'd felt drugged ever since he came home from the hospital. Even as an Amish kid in his *rumschpringe*, he'd never tried any type of recreational drugs, and he wasn't fond of the wooziness this medication caused. It had been necessary the first couple of days, but the pain was more manageable now, and he needed a clear head. Somehow, he had to tell Brianna to go home—without hurting her feelings. A day or two had turned into almost a week.

His parents had visited once, but he'd been so drugged up that he barely remembered them coming into his bedroom. Although the look on his mother's face had somehow stuck with him. *Disappointment.* She'd surely seen Brianna's lotion and other personal items on the other bedside table.

Without a phone, he was out of touch. With everyone. He'd found that first morning that his phone had died, and nothing he tried had gotten it working again. He'd used Brianna's phone to check in with work, but there were others he wanted to talk to, and he didn't have their phone numbers memorized. Highest on that list was Yvonne.

"What are you doing out of bed?" Brianna sashayed into the kitchen where he was sitting in a pair of jeans and button-up plaid shirt that had taken forever to get into. She was in her long white robe, and whatever was underneath was probably designed to taunt him. "Did you take your pain meds?"

"No. I don't need them anymore." He did, but he would endure the pain so he could get through this conversation without feeling loopy.

She slid into a chair across from him and pressed her lips together. "Are you sure?"

He nodded. "Yes."

After eyeing him for a couple of seconds, she asked, "Why are you dressed in jeans and a shirt?"

Abraham had been lounging in sweatpants and an old flannel shirt the past few days. "I needed to make sure I could get a pair of regular pants on. I'm going back to work tomorrow."

"I thought you were going to wait a few more days, until Monday, maybe." She folded her arms across her chest and leaned back in her chair. "If you go back too soon, you could have a setback."

"I'll be on desk duty. I'm ready to get out of this house." He also needed to get a new phone. Brianna had offered to get him one, but he had convinced her that he wanted to choose one on his own. He was sure she would pick out the latest and greatest with more features than he cared to learn.

He breathed in the scent of something heavenly keeping warm in the oven. "I'm going to miss your cooking when you're gone. The house has smelled good the whole time you've been here. And I can't thank you enough for taking care of me and feeding me."

The heavy lashes that shadowed her cheeks flew up, and she sat taller. "This sounds like I'm being dismissed, like you are ready for me to go."

I am. He ran his good hand through his hair as he contemplated the best way to handle things. "Brianna, I'm not ready to live with anyone." He'd already seen the amount of clothes she'd hung up in the extra bedroom, and she'd unpacked her toiletries in the bathroom. "I'm grateful that you've been here, but I hope I didn't lead you to believe that I was ready to take the next step in our relationship." He wasn't sure he ever would be. "And I'd like to be married before I live with anyone. I know that might seem outdated, but it's how I feel."

Her green eyes clawed at him like talons, but she harnessed her anger quickly, and her features softened. Thank goodness since she'd looked a little scary.

"I understand," she said softly as she lowered her head.

"Please don't be upset." He reached across the table and held out his hand until she put her fingers in his. "You know how much I care about you. But I need to take things at my own pace."

She nodded. "Okay." She finally looked up at him. "Are you breaking up with me?"

"No, no, no." He squeezed her hand. Maybe it would have been kinder to say yes since he didn't see this relationship taking the next step. But it seemed cruel when she'd just spent so much time taking care of him. "We just go back to the way things were," he said.

Following a distinct hardening of her gorgeous green eyes, she said, "Shall I pack up and go now?"

He was tempted to say yes to this, also, so he could get a good night's sleep—without the pain meds, hopefully, and without her rubbing up against him all night. Twice, he'd almost given in, but he would have regretted it.

"No, it's too late and already dark outside. You can go tomorrow morning, and I'll help you carry things out as best I can. I still have one good arm." He winked at her and grinned, hoping to lighten the tension filling the space around them.

She eased her hand from his and smiled. "I'll be gone in the morning."

Then she pushed back her chair, stood, and stomped off to the bedroom.

It hadn't gone well, but at least he'd have his house back to himself tomorrow.

CHAPTER 10

There had never been a man Brianna hadn't managed to seduce when she'd put her mind to it, but Abraham wasn't having any part of anything sexual. He had even asked her to please move over in the bed last night. She knew she was beautiful. She'd been told so her entire life. But Abraham was different, almost prudish. He wasn't Amish anymore, so she wasn't sure why he clung so steadfastly to abstinence. Perhaps that was part of his allure, but she'd recently begun to wonder if his resistance was solely based on his beliefs or if that woman had something to do with it. *Yvonne.*

As she and Abraham loaded up her things the next morning, there was an air of finality to it. Nothing she could quite put her finger on, but she had a niggling in her gut that Abraham was going to try to cool things down . . . and before they'd really heated up. She should never have told him she loved him. In her heart, she was sure she needed to give him space now, or she might really lose him.

"I know you'll be busy at work getting caught up on paperwork," she said as they worked together to get the last of her things in her car. "But please take the pain meds if you need them. And I'm a phone call away if there is anything I can do for you."

She closed the trunk and turned to him, waiting to see if he would initiate a kiss since it seemed like she was the one who usually made the first move.

He leaned in close and kissed her with all the passion she longed for, leaving her with a sense of hope that he wasn't trying to end things after all.

"I'll call you soon," he said. "You're right. I'll be busy. Even small-town cops have paperwork, and I'm sure there is a bunch waiting on me."

"No worries. Just whenever you have time." She bit her lip since she wanted to tell him how much she loved him, but she just smiled and got in her car.

A sense of relief washed over Abraham, but his insides twisted with guilt. Brianna had been very good to him. He decided to be optimistic that things might work out, but even as he had the thought, Yvonne's face skipped into his mind. And because of that, he didn't feel like he was being fair to Brianna.

He had two things on his agenda this morning before he went to the station. He decided to tackle the hardest one first.

Maureen and Will's house sat in an older neighborhood on the outskirts of Montgomery. When he parked his pickup in their driveway, he sat there for a few minutes. He'd been right to shoot Will. The man had held a gun to Maureen's head, then randomly fired off a shot in the air before he managed to shoot Abraham. Abraham had been justified in his actions, and the chief had told him just that. So why did the disturbing event play out in his mind over and over until his stomach clenched with pain?

A wave of apprehension swept over him as he stepped out of his truck and walked to the door. He knocked, waited a good while, and was about to leave when Maureen opened the door. Abraham was pretty sure this was the first time in the ten or so years they'd been married that Maureen didn't have a black eye or some other injury. He only saw them when someone called the police about their fighting.

"What are you doing here?" Maureen spat the words at him with a venomous tone.

She looked like the woman she used to be before she'd married Will. Her blonde hair was pulled back in a ponytail, and she had makeup on and gold hoop earrings. He wanted to tell her she looked nice, but that felt inappropriate.

"I came to check on you." Abraham was in uniform and his arm still in a sling as Maureen glared at him, her lips thinned with anger.

"If you're trying to ease your conscience, Abe, you can forget all about that. You ruined our lives! Will is being charged with attempted murder of a police officer, and bail is set so high he's stuck in jail!" She stomped a foot. "You've known us forever. How could you do this?"

Abraham had thought about what he would say, and he'd expected this type of response from Maureen. He probably shouldn't have come, but he had to. "Maureen, don't you feel the slightest bit relieved that Will is in jail, that you can have some time to yourself without having to worry about Will hitting you?"

She folded her arms across her chest and raised her chin, her lip trembling. "You *knew* Will would have put the gun down eventually. You *knew* he wouldn't hurt me. You just don't like him. You were waiting for an opportunity for something like this to happen."

He nodded to his arm. "I didn't exactly come out of this unscathed. Will shot me."

"After you shot him. All he did was fire in the air. He wouldn't have hurt anyone." Maureen's eyes bore into him like a wild animal about to pounce. "You're a no-good piece of . . ."

Abraham stood with his head lowered and absorbed every expletive she threw at him. No amount of trying to justify what he did was going to change Maureen's opinion. Maybe Will would have eventually put down the gun. But maybe not. What if Abraham had killed him? His chief had been correct that Abraham had handled the situation exactly as he'd been taught. But everything he'd learned prior to becoming a police officer stood in direct conflict with his actions, which left him feeling lost. He'd become a cop, in part, to make sure that the Amish were treated fairly. Like anyone who was different, sometimes there was prejudice against the Plain folk, like there had been with his friend all those years ago. Several *Englisch* boys had taunted Joshua about his clothes, way of life, and the way he talked. They'd taken turns pushing him and goading him. His friend had finally snapped and used his fists to fight back, which landed one of the boys in the hospital. Joshua had won a trip to jail. Nothing happened to the bullies.

Abraham had believed he could help with other injustices—mostly minor, since nothing really major ever happened in Montgomery. Now he was questioning everything about who he thought he wanted to be.

"Are you even hearing me, Abe?" Maureen spit when she spoke this time, hurling her words at him like jagged rocks.

"Yep. I just wanted to see if you were okay, and I see that you are." He took a deep breath, having gotten what he expected: a good verbal lashing. He'd be hailed as a hero at work. Deep down, he wasn't sure about that. Enduring Maureen's fury was his own self-punishment for a situation that gnawed at his insides whether his actions were proclaimed right or wrong by his superiors.

He turned and left. Maureen continued to shout vulgarities at him until he was in his truck and gone.

The next visit on his list would be more pleasant.

By the time he got to the bookstore, his heart rate had returned to normal. It was likely to spike again when he saw Yvonne, but for an entirely different reason.

When he walked in, she was chatting with Esther and Lizzie, the widows who ran the Peony Inn bed-and-breakfast. All three women looked at him when he walked in, but Lizzie was the one who approached him. She was a tiny thing who always had a lot to say. Abraham had heard plenty of stories about the more outspoken sister. She'd been known to kick their old renter—a grumpy fellow named Gus who had passed—in the shin, for one thing. Abraham braced himself for whatever Lizzie might say.

"You shot someone." Lizzie adjusted her prayer covering before she thrust both hands to her hips, her small black purse dangling from her wrist. "That mean old Will Robertson."

"Yes." He wasn't surprised Lizzie had gotten to the point right away, but hearing the words stung. He glanced at Yvonne, who sent him a sympathetic look, which he welcomed, especially since she had no way of knowing how upset he was about the whole thing.

"I know it was self-defense, and that things are different in the *Englisch* world, but you used to be one of us, and I don't like this news one bit." Lizzie moved her dentures around in her mouth, something she always did.

Esther, the quieter of the two women, sidled up to her sister while Yvonne hung back.

"Lizzie, leave the boy alone. He was doing his job, and he's been through a traumatic ordeal." She turned to Abraham. "We were just discussing some details with Yvonne about a book signing she will be having, but we are leaving now." She latched on to Lizzie's arm and dragged her toward the door.

Abraham wondered how many of the Amish would feel the way Lizzie did. He still felt tied to his roots, no matter his choices. It had been gracious of Esther to change the subject, but he was sure the shooting would continue to be brought up by others.

After they were gone, Yvonne rushed toward him. "I'm glad to see that you're okay. After I didn't hear from you, I finally called your phone last night, but it went straight to voice mail."

It warmed his heart that she had been worried. "My phone quit working. One of the other officers went and got me a new one, and it should be there when I get to the station."

A shadow of alarm touched her face. "You're already going back to work?"

"*Ya*, just desk duty, though." He shifted his weight. It felt good and bad to have his uniform back on again. "I, uh . . . just wondered how things were working out with your new dog. I let the farmer I told you about know that you decided to keep him."

She smiled, which was the best thing that had happened to Abraham so far today.

"I bought him a dog bed, and he sleeps in front of the fireplace. He's really a sweet fellow, and it just feels good to have another body in the house." She chuckled. "Even if it isn't a human body."

Abraham glanced around the bookstore at the Christmas decorations. "Wow. It looks great in here, very festive. I'm guessing your house is also ready for the holidays." He longed to see the Christmas tree he'd cut for her adorned with lights and ornaments.

"Yep!" She smiled broadly as she lifted up on her toes. "I'm making sure I have the Christmas spirit everywhere I spend my time—here and at home." Her expression fell a little. "If there's a downside to this holiday season, it's that my aunt will be going to California for Christmas. We have family there that she hasn't seen in a long time, and some of them are older, so . . . Anyway, she won't be coming here, but we'll have lots of Christmases to look forward to in the future." She paused. "I think I told you that she raised me, right? But I'll probably spend Christmas day with Jake, Eva, and their family."

Abraham wanted nothing more than to ask Yvonne to his parents' house for Christmas, but his parents were probably already confused or upset about Brianna staying with him. Bringing someone new would confuse them further, and if he broke things off with Brianna right before Christmas, that would be awful. He needed to accept that he and Yvonne could only be friends, at least for now.

"Go easy on the gift giving." Abraham paused as he recalled all the Christmases with his family. He had never missed a one, even after he chose not to be baptized. "Presents are always modest, usually something homemade or simple in nature."

Yvonne sighed. "Well, I love the 'simple in nature' part. Their simpler ways are one of the things that brought me here in the first place. But homemade? Hmm . . . I'm not very crafty."

"I've got a pretty decent shop in my barn with lots of tools and saws. I could help you make something." He thought for a few moments. "Maybe some sort of keepsake box for the *boppli*. Sorry, I mean for the baby." Abraham told himself that friends helped friends. It couldn't just be that he would do anything to be around her.

140

"Wow." A gleam of interest lit her hazel eyes. "That would be a great idea, but . . ." She nodded to his arm.

"I'll just supervise. You'll have to do all the work." He grinned before he winked at her, which seemed to spontaneously come out of nowhere.

"Um . . . Is it going to be okay with Brianna if I come to your house? I mean, you'd only be helping me with a project, but . . . uh, if she's there at the house, I don't want to upset her or anything."

"Yvonne, Brianna left this morning. She was only there to take care of me. We weren't living together then, and we're not planning to." He had told her this in a text, but it felt important to drive the point home. "It wasn't the type of cohabitation Brianna made it out to be."

Abraham surprised himself by sharing so much, something that came easily with Yvonne for some reason.

She pulled her eyes from his. "It's really none of my business. I just don't want to cause any problems with you and Brianna."

"There are already problems." He swallowed hard as he avoided her inquiring eyes. "Sorry. I probably shouldn't have said that."

"No, it's okay. But I'm sorry to hear that. Brianna led me to believe that things were pretty serious with you two." Her eyes were sharp and assessing but with a hint of something else. Was she really sorry to hear that he and Brianna were having troubles?

"And that's the problem. She's taking things way too fast for me." He shifted his weight and took a deep breath, then grinned a little. "I guess I move at a slower pace. You

141

date someone for a while, decide if that person is right for you, fall in love—maybe—then get married and have a family, all in that order. I don't want to live with anyone before I get married."

She smiled. "I think your aspirations are admirable. Not a lot of men feel that way." A faraway look found its way into her eyes, and for a couple of seconds, she seemed somewhere else. "Trevor was like that. He wanted to do everything in that order too."

Abraham thought about how hard it must have been for Yvonne to lose the man she'd planned to marry. He could feel a blush creeping into his cheeks as he looked down at the wooden floor and shrugged. "I guess it's the way I was brought up. I feel it's right in the eyes of God."

"You know, before I met Eva and Jake, I was kind of messed up about God and religion in general, but they had such a strong faith that I wanted to explore what motivated such dedication to God. I wasn't raised as a Christian, so it took a lot for me to convert. But when I did, my life took on a whole new meaning."

"Why is it so easy for me to talk to you?" Abraham folded his arms across his chest and tipped his head to one side.

Her cheeks reddened. "I feel the same way. Even at the wedding when we took that walk. That's what I remember most—that you let me talk about Trevor, how I was really feeling, and I didn't have to pretend that I was okay."

Abraham offered a gentle smile, wondering if they were getting too personal. "By the way, I think it's great that you're keeping the dog and have worked through your fears."

She chuckled. "I'm *working* through my fear. I don't think Blue would hurt me for a minute, but there is one thing I don't know how to handle."

Abraham raised an eyebrow.

Yvonne groaned. "Argh. That dog needs a bath. Bad. He has gained a little weight in the short time he's been hanging around, but his fur is still so matted, and he smells." She crinkled her nose. "But I'm wondering how he'll react if I try to bathe him in the bathtub. And it's a clawfoot tub, so I don't think I can lift him in, and I'm not sure he would willingly get in on his own. But it's too cold to bathe him outside, obviously." She pointed out the window as she let out a little gasp. "Look, it's snowing."

Abraham looked over his shoulder. "Yeah, I guess. Not much. It probably won't stick to the ground."

"It doesn't matter," she said dreamily. "It makes it feel even more like Christmas. It rarely snowed in Texas, and it never snowed on Christmas Day. At least, not in my lifetime where I was living. I hope we have a white Christmas."

Abraham prayed right then and there that Yvonne would get her white Christmas. "I'm guessing you've probably never shoveled snow, then?"

She grinned as she playfully batted her eyes at him. "How hard can it be?"

Abraham burst out laughing. "Guess you'll find out." After he gained some composure, he said, "Do you want me to come help you bathe that dog?" The familiar guilt wrapped around him as he thought about Brianna.

Yvonne brought both hands to her chest. "Would you? That would be great. I'm sure once I see how he reacts, and when he trusts me even more, it shouldn't be a problem. But I'm scared to attempt it by myself."

"No problem. When do you want to do it?" Abraham hoped it would be soon.

"What about Sunday, midmorning? Tomorrow I'm working." She drew in a breath. "Oh, wait. You probably go to church on Sunday, and I don't want to keep you from that. It's on my to-do list to visit some churches in the area, but as of now, I don't have a church family."

Abraham was quiet as he decided if he wanted to share a secret with her, something he hadn't told Brianna or even any of his family. "I, uh . . . won't be going to my church this Sunday. The Amish worship service is being held at my brother's house. I'm not actually attending the service, but I'll be there. My older brother—Leroy—lives with his family in our family home, where I grew up. When any of my brothers are having the service, I go. But I don't go in." He caught her confused expression. "It's dumb. I stay outside with an ear to the wall for most of the service. I'd be welcome in any one of their homes even though I'm not a church member, but I prefer to stay outside and listen. Silly, huh?"

She shook her head. "Not at all. I loved listening to the worship service at Eva and Jake's wedding. I didn't understand most of it, but there was a feeling of fellowship that I'd never felt before." She cocked her head to one side, her mouth parting slightly. "You really miss it, don't you? The worship service?"

Abraham missed more than just the church service, especially now, at a time when he was questioning the choices he'd made in his life. But he wasn't ready to share that with anyone, not even Yvonne. "Yeah, I do. And it's kind of my private little thing. I park down the street after everyone is inside, then make my way up to the house. I leave before the service is over and people start coming out of the house, which is crazy. I mean, they're my family. But it's just something I like to do. If people knew I was there, especially my family, they would try to talk me into getting baptized into the faith."

She stared at him for a long time before a faraway gaze took her somewhere else in her mind. "I'd love to be able to do that—to hear the service but not have anyone know."

"Then come with me." His stomach roiled as soon as he said it. Not because he didn't want her to go, but because it sounded so bold.

"Really?" She spoke barely above a whisper. "But you said it's your private thing. I don't want to intrude on that."

"You'd be going with the same goal as me: to enjoy the service but without anyone knowing. I wouldn't mind at all, and after listening to the worship service, we could go wash that dog of yours." He laughed. "Try to, anyway."

"I think that would be great." She smiled, and Abraham thought his heart might melt.

In the past fifteen minutes, he'd offered to help Yvonne make a homemade gift, wash her dog, and take her to hear the worship service. He was going to have to find a way to break up with Brianna so he could spend more time with Yvonne without feeling guilty or ultimately hurting Brianna any more than he had to. But he was still questioning the timing during the holidays. He would need to think on it.

He finally said, "Then it's a date."

CHAPTER 11

Sunday morning, Yvonne threw on a pair of jeans and a peach-colored sweater and took extra care with her hair and makeup. She was looking forward to spending time with Abraham way more than she should be.

"I'm going to leave you in the house because it's lightly snowing outside. But I'll be home later, with help, to give you a bath." She leaned down to where Blue was lying in front of the fireplace. "And I can't add a log to the fire because I'm leaving for a while." She scratched behind his ears, which always caused him to thump his tail against the fluffy extra-large bed she'd bought for him, even though he didn't have much of a tail. The cover on his bed would need to be washed, too, after he had a bath, assuming she and Abraham could make that happen.

Abraham. She felt like she was doing something wrong by going with him to spy on a worship service. It wasn't

146

the spying that bothered her. It was the fact that he had a girlfriend. But unless she was misreading him, he enjoyed spending time with her too.

Just friends, she reminded herself. He had called it a date, and the comment hadn't gone unnoticed by Yvonne, but lots of people said the phrase without meaning *date* in the romantic sort of way.

By the time she had her gray coat and gloves on, Abraham was pulling into her driveway.

"Be good, Blue." She stared at her furry friend and shook her head, smiling. She had a dog. Who would have ever thought she'd be mommy to a giant fur baby in need of some serious maintenance? In addition to enjoying Blue's company, she was also working to push past her fear of dogs, and for that, she was proud of herself.

She pulled her hood over her head and ventured out into lightly falling snow. "Hi," she said as she climbed into Abraham's truck.

"Well." He put the truck in Reverse, then looked at her and frowned. "This probably wasn't the best-laid plan. You're going to freeze to death standing on Leroy's porch secretly listening to the service."

"I'll be all right." Yvonne had already thought about that but wasn't going to miss out on this adventure. Guiltily, she was more excited about spending time with Abraham than she was about hearing the worship service, although that would be special too.

"How would you feel if we skip our spy mission? I think God would understand considering the weather. We could get some breakfast and then go wash that dog of yours." He glanced her way, then stopped at the end of her road, obviously waiting to hear which way he should turn.

"Would you have gone without me? I don't want you not to go because of me." She slid down the attached hood on her coat.

He shook his head. "No. It's starting to snow harder. I would have canceled, I think."

"Then breakfast sounds great." Now it felt almost like a real date. "Or I'd be happy to go with you to your church."

He looked at his watch. "It's half over with."

She nodded.

Abraham chose a little café outside of town. "Is this okay?" he asked as he parked.

"Yep." She pulled up her hood again before she stepped out of the truck.

After ordering coffee, Yvonne finally warmed up enough to take off her coat. As she draped it over the chair behind her, she said, "It gets really cold here."

Abraham laughed. "It's thirty-eight." He shook his head. "Girl, you are in for a rough winter if you think this is cold. I mean, it's too cold to sit outside and listen to the worship service, but wait until we get real snow and temperatures that are near zero or below."

She shivered. "I can't even imagine. I need to make sure I have plenty of firewood. Eventually, I'll do something about the insulation in that house, but only if I end up buying it down the road. I did get an electric heater for my bedroom."

"I'll make sure you have plenty of firewood." He stared at her from across the table as if he had something more to say, but he just took another drink of his coffee. He had offered to help her make a craft for Jake and Eva's baby and to wash her dog. He'd already cut her a Christmas tree, and now he'd said he would keep her supplied in firewood. *Hmm . . .*

As they studied their menus, she lifted her eyes over the edge of hers to have a long look at him. She wasn't sure she'd ever felt so comfortable around a man, except for Trevor, and it had taken months for her to feel that way with her fiancé. It didn't hurt that Abraham was incredibly good-looking with his dark hair cut neatly and parted on the side. But it was his eyes that mesmerized her—cobalt-blue eyes that seemed to see through her sometimes.

After they had ordered, he asked, "Do you have any blue Dawn dishwashing liquid? It's the best for washing a dog, or so I was told by the town vet."

She chewed on a piece of bacon, shook her head, then said, "I have dishwashing liquid, although I don't remember what kind, but it's not blue."

"I'm sure that will be fine." He chuckled. "Assuming your pal, Blue, wants to cooperate."

"Guess we'll see." Yvonne grinned, but her thoughts drifted to Brianna, and she wondered how she would feel if the shoe was on the other foot—if she was the one dating Abraham and he was having breakfast with Brianna.

Friends. We're just friends. Friends that were making various plans to spend time together.

Brianna paced her kitchen late Sunday morning. She hadn't heard from Abraham but one time since she'd left his house Friday morning. He had called her Saturday midday to say that he had errands to run, that his arm ached, and that he planned to just rest over the weekend. When she offered to go with him to run errands, he stumbled around and said it was boring stuff—a trip to the lumberyard, a visit with an Amish man about possibly buying a chunk of land he had for sale, and a couple of other things. He was right. It did all sound boring to Brianna. But when she asked him about coming to her house or her going there on Saturday night, he had said he just wanted to go to sleep early.

What was he doing today? Did he go to church? Was he visiting his family? Brianna recalled the disapproval that had shown on his parent's faces when she'd answered the door at Abraham's house. Things got worse when they walked into the bedroom. They had to have noticed her things on the bedside table. His father had done the talking and briefly chatted with Abraham, but his mother had mostly just held a firm frown on her face.

She poured another cup of coffee, then paced some more. Something wasn't right. She'd had the feeling for a while, and it wasn't going away. If she pushed Abraham too hard, the consequences might not be in her favor. But . . . she bristled as she thought about Yvonne. No way she was going to let that woman snatch away Abraham, but she needed to play things cool.

After two more cups of coffee and more pacing in the kitchen, playing things cool didn't sound so appealing. She headed to her bedroom to get dressed.

Abraham faced off with Yvonne's pet, who displayed an impressive rack of sharp teeth and blood-red gums as he stood poised to pounce on him at any moment. The animal's eyes blazed amber fire as his nostrils flared.

"Oh, no." Yvonne shut the door and stood beside him. "I've never seen him like this." There was a thread of hysteria in her voice, and Abraham could only assume she was recalling the dog that had attacked her when she was young. "What do we do?"

"Uh . . . don't make any quick movements, for starters." Abraham put his arm in front of Yvonne to get her behind him, but the dog released a low, guttural growl.

"Wait," Yvonne said as she took a few steps away from Abraham. "Blue, come here, boy."

The animal trotted to her and sat in front of her, baring his teeth at Abraham.

"He's protecting you," Abraham said softly. "He's not going to hurt you. Just pet him and let him know you're okay, that I'm not a bad guy."

Yvonne used both hands and stroked the dog's ears. "You're okay, Blue. He's a friend. He won't hurt you."

Blue's long tongue swiped all around his mouth, then he yawned, seemingly pacified. But Abraham wasn't convinced that the dog still wouldn't go after him. "Maybe come and hug me, talk in a sweet voice, and let him know that I won't hurt you."

Yvonne's eyes widened. "Will that work?"

Abraham sighed. "Maybe. Or maybe he won't want me too close to you, and he'll rip me to shreds." He swallowed hard as Yvonne slowly walked toward him.

The dog growled, the fire in his eyes returning.

Yvonne put a hand on Abraham's arm, rubbing it gently. "See, Blue, this man is just fine. He's a friend." Then she wrapped her arms around Abraham's neck but kept her head turned and facing the dog. "It's okay, buddy. Come here and see that he's okay."

Abraham momentarily forgot about his apprehension and focused on the feel of Yvonne next to him, one of her soft hands cupping the back of his neck above his black sweatshirt. He'd peeled his coat off right when they walked inside, and it was flung over his wrist, but he was wishing he had it on. More protection if Blue decided to take a bite out of one of his arms.

He held his breath as the dog walked toward them, then held out the back of his hand as he'd been trained to do, and Blue sniffed his knuckles, then his legs as he circled him. Yvonne still had her arms around him, which made him more nervous than the dog. He feared he might kiss her, and he was pretty sure Blue might not like that. Not to mention Abraham would feel horrible.

Yvonne eased away and squatted down. "You're a good boy." As she scratched him behind his ears, Abraham lowered himself to their level, and Blue allowed him to scratch his head.

"I'd say you've got yourself a pretty good watchdog." Abraham smiled as the dog relaxed on his belly. Blue licked his lips again, but the aggression had subsided. "But as great as that is, you might want to get some training for him, maybe obedience school. There are ways to let a dog know that you're in danger. You don't want him attacking every person that comes near you."

"Wow." She sat down on the wooden floor, her teeth chattering. Blue rolled onto his side and eased his head into her lap. "You're a good boy, Blue, but you sure do stink." She crinkled her nose and shook her head. "I'm feeling doubtful that he's going to let us lift him into the bathtub."

"I guess we'll see." Abraham rubbed his hands together as he noticed a chill. "This house really doesn't have good insulation, like you said. I can feel cold air coming through the walls." He nodded toward the fireplace. "Do you want me to get a fire going?"

She stood. "That would be great. And I'll plug in my tree so you can see it lit up."

Abraham set his coat on her couch, still moving slowly since Blue was keeping an eye on him. "The tree is beautiful," he said when the lights flickered on.

"Thanks. A nice man cut it down for me and delivered it." She grinned as she stood back and admired the tree, then turned to him. "I love it. Thank you again."

"You're very welcome." He joined her by the tree. "You did a great job decorating it."

"I had a good time doing it." She glanced around, smiling. "I really love it here. I love this house." A quick roll of her eyes. "Although I wish it was a little easier to keep warm. And I like my job . . ." She paused and stared right into his eyes. "And the people here."

Something about the way she said it, and the way she

153

held his gaze, told him she enjoyed him being here as much as he liked her company.

Brianna, Brianna, Brianna. He didn't think he could wait until after the holidays to ease out of the relationship. Hurting her caused his chest to ache, but he'd never felt around Brianna the way he felt with Yvonne. There was a level of commonality that he and Brianna didn't share, and he was attracted to Yvonne inside and out. Brianna was kindhearted, but they were very different. Her physical beauty had drawn him in, but he didn't see himself ever feeling about Brianna the way he was starting to feel about Yvonne, a woman he barely knew.

"It's a great place to live," he said before he forced his eyes away and turned toward the dog. "Are we going to try to clean up this guy?"

Yvonne squeezed her eyes closed and flinched. "I don't know." She slowly looked at him. "What do you think?"

"Well, you know the old saying: 'You can lead a horse to water . . .'" He walked to the fireplace, added several logs, and sighed as he stoked the embers until flames caught. "All we can do is try."

"Is it okay if I put on some Christmas music?" Yvonne picked up her phone from the coffee table. "I could be imagining it, but I think Blue likes music."

Her Bluetooth speaker slowly came to life with Andy Williams singing "It's the Most Wonderful Time of the Year." "Is this okay?" She grinned. "I like the oldies."

"Me too." He eyed the tree, gazed at the glowing look on Yvonne's face, felt the warmth of the fire, and wished he could stay here forever. Then he looked at the dog. "Okay, big fellow, let's see if you'll get in the bathtub."

Yvonne called Blue to the small bathroom with its claw-foot tub, antique sink, and commode. The three of them barely fit in there. She got down on her knees and started running water in the tub, keeping her hand under the flow until it was the right temperature. Blue mostly kept his eyes on Abraham.

"If you can lift his front end, I'll get the back, and maybe he'll let us lift him in." Abraham moved around to the back of the dog. "On three," he said.

"What about your arm?"

"I've still got one good one." He chuckled.

"Okay, if you're sure." She turned to the dog. "You've got this, Blue." Yvonne scratched his ears before she put her arms behind his front paws and started to lift the dog. Abraham held his breath as he lifted the dog's back end with his good arm. He was out of the sling, but he still couldn't lift much.

Together, they managed to get him into the tub.

"Good boy, Blue!" Yvonne cupped water in her hands and gently poured it over the dog, and surprisingly, Blue settled into the warmth.

"That's got to feel good." Abraham knelt down beside her. "Where's the dishwashing soap?"

"Oops. Under the sink." She started to get up.

"I'll get it. He'll probably try to follow you."

Abraham returned with a green bottle of dishwashing soap. "Here goes nothing." He drizzled a little on the dog's matted back. Then they both lathered him up. "Wow. He's doing great." Keeping his hands on the dog, he said, "You've sure come a long way with this fellow in a short time."

She laughed. "I still can't believe you had to come over after I honked my horn so many times."

Abraham loved the sound of her laughter, and with the Christmas music playing in the background, he couldn't think of anywhere he'd rather be.

Without warning, Blue stood up and shook, slinging soap and water all over both of them. Yvonne put a hand to her mouth, her eyes wide. Then she burst out laughing. "I'm so sorry." She reached up and wiped soap from his face, then laughed some more.

"You don't look much better," he said, grinning, as he reached for a glob of soapy water stuck to her face. He took his time wiping it way—too much time, his hand lingering, cupping her cheek. They were having a moment, and Abraham wasn't sure if he could stop his lips nearing hers, but she eased away.

Yvonne cleared her throat. "Um, guess we should get this monster rinsed and dried off."

After two more sprayings and more laughter, they finally got the dog on the bath mat and began drying him off.

"Success," she said as she rubbed the top of Blue's head. "Good boy."

Abraham couldn't take his eyes off her. He wasn't ready for this day to end. "There's a lot of daylight left if you want to go to my place and check out the wood I have in the barn. I'm sure we can find something to build a keepsake box for Eva and Jake's baby."

Blue left the bathroom, and they stood up to follow him. The dog took his position in front of the fire, stretching his paws out and putting his head down on the fluffy bed.

"He looks like he's praying." Abraham walked closer to the fire since his clothes were speckled with soap and water. Mostly water.

Yvonne laughed. "That's exactly what I thought the first time I saw him lying down like that." She paused, lowered her head, and sighed. Abraham was pretty sure he was about to get the boot, that she was going to decline the invitation to his house.

"Um . . ." She offered up a half smile. "Do you think we could work on the baby project another day?"

Abraham swallowed back his disappointment. "Sure. Of course. No problem." He shrugged and forced a smile. "Just whenever is a good time for you, let me know."

Before he could turn to get his coat, she touched his good arm, and he couldn't move. Nor did he want to.

"I had originally planned that after we went to worship service and bathed the dog . . . Well, I wanted to watch Christmas movies, kind of a marathon."

"I totally understand." He went and lifted his coat from the couch.

"I have popcorn," she said, grinning. "Any interest in staying?" She pointed to the dog. "Since Blue seems to like you now."

She was inviting him to stay. Abraham couldn't think of anywhere else he wanted to be. "Sure. I'd like that."

She smiled, and once again, he knew he needed to break it off with Brianna. He wanted to spend the holidays with

Yvonne, and even though he'd feel terrible for breaking up with Brianna at this time of year, it wouldn't be fair to lead her on when he knew who the person was that he wanted to spend time with.

CHAPTER 12

Brianna had driven by Abraham's house a dozen times. If he'd gone to church, he should have been home hours ago. Her stomach churned with the realization that he had to be with Yvonne. She'd driven by Leroy's farm and Abraham's other brother's place. His pickup wasn't at either of their homes. Brianna had no idea where Yvonne lived, and as she circled town again, she racked her brain trying to think of a way to find out where the woman's house was.

After another thirty minutes of driving down dirt roads that led to nowhere, she found Jake and Eva's house. She'd never been there, but she remembered Abraham telling her where his friends lived.

She sat in the car long enough that she saw someone peer out the window, and she knew she had to come up with a plan. Luckily the snow had stopped. Brianna hated snow, but at least it wasn't sticking to the ground, just doing a number on her hair. She hadn't taken the time to get a hat of any sort. She'd been too anxious to find Abraham.

After a deep breath, she got out and knocked on the door, and Jake answered right away. "Hi Jake, I know we haven't met, but I'm Brianna, Abraham's girlfriend." As she said the word, she tried to recall if Abraham had ever introduced her that way. Maybe in the beginning when they were first dating.

"Of course." He opened the door and stepped aside. Brianna walked into the warm living room, which smelled of baking bread. It didn't have the musty smell of Abraham's house that never went away despite all the cooking Brianna had done during her stay there. Her scent burners and candles hadn't done much to help either.

"I'm so sorry to barge in on a Sunday, but I'm trying to find Abraham. His phone stopped working, and I'm not sure he has his new phone set up." She forced herself to smile. "He's not very high tech when it comes to those things." She waved a dismissive hand even though she knew Abraham had a functioning phone since his voice mail was set up. He just wasn't answering her calls. "Anyway, I think he might be at Yvonne's. He was helping her get rid of a stray dog that showed up, but I have a leaky faucet that is going to flood my bathroom if I don't get it repaired very soon. So, I really need to find him."

Jake looped his thumbs beneath his suspenders and nodded. "*Ya, ya.* He told me about the dog, something about it needing a home." He picked up a pad of paper and a pencil, then began to draw a map. "I don't know the address, but this is how you get there." He handed her the slip of paper.

"I have her phone number, of course, since she runs the bookstore. Would you rather call her?"

"I met her at the bookstore, and we exchanged numbers, but there isn't an answer," Brianna said, lying again.

"She's in the country. I suspect she doesn't get very *gut* cell service." Jake shook his head. "We don't get great service here, but since we aren't really supposed to have the phone, except for business . . ." Grinning, he shrugged. "Hard to complain about it too much."

She put the map into her purse. "I won't keep you. My bathroom leak is probably becoming more urgent by the moment." She tried to laugh. "Thank you so much."

"You're welcome." Jake walked her to the door and opened it, but before she stepped out into the cool, she turned to him. "My deepest apologies. I should have asked how your wife, Eva, is doing?"

"She's doing fine. She's just bored and ready to have this *boppli*." Jake chuckled. "We are all ready for her to have the baby."

"Please give her my best. And thank you again for taking the time to draw me a map."

Brianna couldn't get the car into Reverse fast enough. If Abraham was at Yvonne's house, there was going to be hell to pay.

By the third movie, the popcorn turned out not to be enough, and Yvonne made them grilled cheese sandwiches and heated a jar of premade tomato soup. It had been a long time since breakfast. Abraham would have starved just to be in her company, though.

"It's not as good as homemade." She placed two bowls on the coffee table, where they had chosen to eat since it was the warmest place in the house. They each had a sandwich on a plate. "But it's my favorite tomato soup that comes in a jar." She sat beside him.

"I'm sure it's great." Abraham lowered his head and smiled on the inside when she did too. He didn't think Brianna prayed before meals—

He made another mental note to stop comparing the women.

When she lifted her head after he did, Abraham stared at her. He couldn't help it. Everything about this day was perfect. And Yvonne wasn't just beautiful on the outside. She was equally as gorgeous on the inside.

When his phone vibrated in his pocket, Abraham shifted his weight on the couch. He was sure it was Brianna again. She'd called four times in the past twenty minutes, and she'd called earlier in the day, but she hadn't left any messages. She would want to know how he'd spent his day. Abraham didn't want to lie to her, but he suspected that if he told the truth, she was going to be upset.

"I can hear your phone buzzing in your pocket." Yvonne dabbed her mouth with a napkin. "You're welcome to answer it. I can even step into the other room."

Abraham shook his head. "No, no. It's fine." He didn't want to take away one moment of time with Yvonne. "Can I just tell you that I had a great time today? I enjoyed breakfast"—he pointed to his supper in front of him—"and this fabulous meal." Laughing, he said, "And I'm super proud we got ol' Blue cleaned up."

Yvonne had wanted to ask him about Brianna all day. She also wondered if that was who kept calling him. They'd done nothing wrong today, but there was a damper on their time together because Yvonne felt guilty and bad for Brianna.

She'd told herself that she was going to distance herself from Abraham, and she'd done just the opposite. But his relationship with Brianna wasn't any of her business. Or was it? Today had felt like a small step past friendship. She wasn't sure she wanted to fuel this fire, so instead of telling him how much she had enjoyed the day, she said, "I need to wash Blue's cover on his bed. I just put a clean dog on a filthy bed, but at least now I know that he isn't opposed to baths."

"I know a good vet if you want to take him to get shots and have him checked out." Abraham laid his napkin across his empty plate. "And he's going to be a good watchdog, too, but I'd still consider some training for him. He might have eaten me alive today if you hadn't shown him that I was an okay guy." He smiled and even winked at her.

Abraham Byler was more than an okay guy, and he was flirting with her, whether he realized it or not. "I probably will look into obedience training." She rolled her eyes. "I'm just floored that I have a dog. I've spent much of my life terrified of them."

"Well, you're out here by yourself, so it's good to have some protection. Controlled protection."

They were quiet for a while, just the sound of the fire crackling and Blue lightly snoring.

"I guess I should go. I've got an early shift." He stood and picked up his plate and bowl.

"I'll take those." Yvonne held out her hands, collected their dishes, then carried them to the kitchen. When she returned, Abraham had on his coat.

"It's snowing again." He smiled.

Yvonne gazed into his eyes, surprised to find herself wishing for a kiss. What was she thinking? He was off-limits. "I'll keep hoping for that white Christmas."

"I hope you get it." He spoke in a husky voice, and Yvonne found herself holding her position, not getting too close to him, even though it seemed a hug might be in order after such a fun day . . . with a friend.

"Just let me know when you want to work on that keepsake box. My schedule changes, but some days I'm home by around three." He slowly made his way toward the door.

"I appreciate the offer." A safe, noncommittal response.

He was clearly waiting for her to join him by the front door. Brushing arms, she eased around him and opened it. The moon cast shadows on the falling snow that glistened like fairy dust. She wished things were different, that Abraham wasn't attached, and that they could have their own fairytale.

"Well, have a good week," she said. "And thank you for helping me with Blue."

"You're welcome." He smiled, then turned to leave.

Yvonne waited to see if he would look over his shoulder. When he did, their eyes locked. She wondered if he felt any level of sadness, the way she did. Or had Yvonne misread every flirtatious gesture all day long, and was he on his way to see Brianna now? Maybe it was just like Brianna had told her at the bookstore—that Abraham was a nice guy . . . to everyone.

She waved as he backed out of her driveway.

Brianna shook with fury as she changed into her night-gown, then climbed into bed, her second glass of merlot on the nightstand. It had taken everything she had not to ram her car into Abraham's truck when she saw it in Yvonne's driveway, then storm the house and yank that woman by the hair. But she would have lost Abraham for sure. Or maybe she already had? Right now, she wondered if Abraham would lie to her about where he'd been all day. If he did, then there was more than just friendship going on between him and Yvonne.

She lifted the glass to her lips, but startled when the phone rang, spilling several drops on her blue-and-white comforter. After a few cuss words, she took a deep breath and answered. "Hey, stranger. I've been trying to get hold of you all day. Are you okay? Is your arm all right?" She couldn't have sounded any more sugary sweet if she tried. "I wasn't sure if you went to church this morning."

"I'm sorry. I'm fine. Yesterday, I slept most of the day. My arm was still sore, but I felt like I was recovering from all those pain pills, although I was groggy. But I feel bet-ter today—still sore but much better." He cleared his throat.

"Anyway, I didn't go to church today. I ended up helping Yvonne, the woman who works for Jake, get her dog cleaned up. She was going to get rid of it, but I guess she got attached and changed her mind. I helped her get it in and out of the bathtub. I could only use one arm, but it worked out okay."

Exactly how long were you there? Did that take all day? You couldn't answer my calls? She took a sip of wine, set the glass down, and took a deep, calming breath. "Aw, that was so nice of you to help her. You've helped her with her dog, and you also gave her a Christmas tree. You're just that kind of guy, very thoughtful." Brianna was trembling. It took all her effort to stay composed. "I have three video calls with clients tomorrow about some tax issues they are having, but let me know when you feel up to getting together. The rest of my week is wide open, except for a massage I have scheduled for Thursday."

"Yeah, that sounds good." He paused, coughed a little. "I'll call you. Have a good evening."

"You, too, babe."

"Bye."

Brianna stared at her phone. Something was definitely not right.

After she hit End, she tossed the phone on her bed and picked up her wine glass. There was a third of it left. She threw it as hard as she could, shattering the glass as red wine splashed against the white walls, then slowly trailed downward like blood, pooling atop her white tile.

She smiled and lay down.

Abraham ended the call and stared at his phone for a few seconds, his jaw hanging open. The conversation had gone way better than he could have imagined. Brianna hadn't interrogated him at all. She'd been kind and left the ball in his court as to when they would see each other. That was good, as it would give him time to analyze his situation. Although he didn't think evaluating scenarios would change his growing feelings for Yvonne, even though she'd seemed a bit distant toward the end of the evening.

He kicked his socked feet up onto the coffee table and leaned his head back. When he closed his eyes, the scene with Maureen and Will played out in his mind, as it always seemed to do these days, no matter how hard he tried to forget it. He could still hear the venomous way Maureen had spoken to him when he'd stopped to see her. He hadn't told anyone yet, but he wasn't sure he could ever draw his gun again, and that wouldn't make him much of a cop.

Once again, he found himself questioning his decisions. When he was younger, he'd thought that becoming a policeman was a way to have one of his people on the side of the law—that he'd needed to be there to provide a moral compass. But instead, he'd discovered everyone on the force was honorable and fair, no different from himself. In a way, it had negated his entire reason for leaving his community to become an officer.

And he missed that life. He missed farming, building things with his hands, attending Amish worship services, and going to cattle auctions—all things he no longer had time to do. He missed his family. They were still there for him, and vice versa, but it wasn't the same. Recently, he had questioned his decision to become a cop more and more. He had witnessed violence before on the job, even been involved in altercations, but shooting his weapon had left him feeling wounded, and not just physically. There was a sense that he'd gone against God, and he wondered how he didn't foresee that coming at some point.

His phone buzzed on the couch beside him, and he hurriedly answered since Jake rarely called him.

"Hey, Jake. Is Eva okay?" *Maybe the baby came early.*

"*Ya, ya.* Everything is fine. I just wanted to make sure your girlfriend found you."

"Who? Brianna?

A long pause. "How many girlfriends do you have? *Ya,* Brianna."

"Actually, I just talked to her. Why?"

"She came by our *haus* looking for you. She said she thought you might be at Yvonne's helping her with a stray dog. She had a leaky faucet, and she was worried about it flooding the *haus*. She asked for Yvonne's address, so I gave it to her." He paused. "I hope that was okay."

Something about the way Jake said, "I hope that was okay" sounded weird. Did he think something was going on with Yvonne? "Sure. Yeah, that's fine. Thanks."

After the call ended, Abraham scratched his head. Why hadn't Brianna mentioned anything about a leaky faucet? Why hadn't she shown up at Yvonne's house? He was tempted to call and ask her about it, but it was time to start slowing things down with her, and calling—for any reason—might give her false hope, even if it was to ask a valid question.

He looked at the time on his cell phone when he heard horse hooves on his driveway, then peered over his shoulder and out the window. It took a few minutes for his visitor to step out of the buggy and into the moonlight.

His chest tightened as he opened the door. It was almost nine o'clock. "Leroy, is something wrong? Is it *Mamm* or *Daed*?"

"*Nee, nee.* Everyone is fine. I know it's late, but I saw your lights still on, and I didn't see another car here, so I'm assuming Brianna isn't here?"

"*Nee*, she's not." Even though his brother had said his parents were fine, Leroy's strained expression, and the fact that he wanted to talk to Abraham alone, hadn't allowed his chest to relax.

"I'm on my way home from a meeting with the bishop." He rolled his eyes. "A meeting that went on much later than it was supposed to. Can I come in?"

"*Ya, bruder,* of course." Abraham was aware again how easily he fell back into the Pennsylvania Dutch dialect when he was around his family. "What's going on that you had to have a meeting with the bishop?" *And why are you here to discuss it with me?*

Leroy followed him to the living room and sat in the recliner. Abraham returned to his spot on the couch and resumed his position with his feet on the coffee table.

His brother grunted. "*Ach,* the matter didn't really warrant a meeting. It was about how several businesses in the area didn't have hitching posts, and a couple of the elders wanted to enforce a rule not to patronize those establishments. It didn't go over well." He waved a hand. "But that's not what I'm here to talk to you about." He lowered his head and folded his hands in his lap before he looked back at Abraham. "*Mei bruder*, you didn't get baptized. You chose to become a lawman. And while none of us were happy about those choices, we've supported you."

Abraham waited, wondering where his brother was going with this conversation.

"But I have to tell you . . ." Leroy shook his head. "I don't know what your situation is with Brianna, especially since she isn't here right now, but *Mamm* and *Daed* said it looked like she was living here when they stopped by."

"She's not," Abraham quickly said as his pulse picked up.

His brother was quiet.

"Leroy, Brianna was only here tending to me after the shooting. Our living situation wasn't what you or *Mamm* and *Daed* think. Nothing happened."

His brother unfolded his hands, took off his black felt hat, and ran a hand through his hair before replacing it. He was still in his black coat. "I know things changed for you a lot when you chose another life, but I'm glad to hear that you aren't living together and that you appear to be making healthy choices. We'd all like to think that even though you left the faith, your morals remained intact when it comes to *Gott*." He held up a palm. "And it's not *mei* business. I know that. But I'm relieved."

All of Abraham's emotions were bubbling to the surface, but he didn't know how to express himself.

"Is she the one? Brianna? Do you think you'll eventually make her your *fraa*?"

"No." Abraham's eyes widened when Leroy's did.

"*Ach*, wow. You didn't even hesitate." He took his hat off again and set it in his lap.

Abraham leaned his head back against the couch and closed his eyes. "She's not the one."

When he lifted his head, Leroy's eyes were wide again. "Really? The woman is absolutely beautiful."

"We both know that there needs to be more than physical beauty for a relationship to work." He sighed. "I'm actually trying to figure out a way to break things off with her, but it seems cruel to do that right before Christmas when she doesn't have any family here." He waited for his brother to absorb what he was saying before he went on. "I-I am having strong feelings for someone else. Yvonne, the woman who took over Jake's bookstore. Nothing has happened with her, either, and it won't until I've ended things with Brianna. But even a relationship with Yvonne might not work out for me."

Abraham realized the next part of this conversation was even more serious than the first. "I'm questioning my choices about *mei* life. About being a cop and about leaving the faith."

His brother looked at him sympathetically. "Is this about Will, about the shooting?"

Abraham nodded. "What if I had killed Will?"

"What if he had killed you or his *fraa*? I know violence isn't our way, but when you became a policeman, you took vows to uphold the law."

"Which law? Our law or the laws of *Gott*?"

Leroy stared at him long and hard. "That's the question we all asked ourselves when you made decisions not to get baptized and to pursue law enforcement. It was such a far cry from the way you were raised that it was hard for us to understand."

"I've held strictly to my beliefs, Leroy, with few exceptions. But this thing with Will has me shaken up. You know how it is—a burglary here and there, domestic issues, car accidents, and such. I can't recall any murders or serious crime. But I should have foreseen something like this coming."

"Have you talked to anyone else about it?"

"*Nee.*"

"Maybe talk to the bishop?" Leroy tipped his head to one side. "You know you can still go to him, and he's a wise man."

"I know." Abraham leaned his head back against the couch cushion again, then finally looked at his brother. "I feel this nudge to return to the faith. Maybe I'm hoping God will cleanse me for what I did."

"That's *gut*," his brother said as he smiled. "You know that would make the family happy."

Abraham sighed. "I would be baptized, and I could never be with Yvonne, then."

"*Nee*, you couldn't." Leroy put his hat on and stood up. "*Bruder*, you have much to think about." He pointed toward the hallway. "I've been on the road a while. I need to use your bathroom."

Abraham nodded, but before his brother was out of sight, he said, "Can you just keep this conversation between you and me?"

"*Ya*, I will." Leroy smiled slightly before he rounded the corner.

When Leroy walked back into the living room, he opened his hand, palm up. "These boots of mine are clunky, and I tripped on your bath mat. When I lifted it to straighten it, I found this." He walked closer to Abraham, holding a small square-ish piece in his hand. "Is it from your phone?"

Abraham's stomach lurched as he swallowed hard. "Uh, maybe. My phone quit working, so I got another one. I guess this could be the SIM card from my old phone." He held open his hand, and his brother dropped the square into his palm. "Thanks."

As he walked Leroy to the door, his brother said something about his job, but Abraham didn't catch it all. He was thinking about how miserable he'd been for four days without a phone. How had his cell-phone SIM card gotten underneath his bath mat? He could hardly get to the bathroom during those days, and he barely even knew what a SIM card was, much less how to remove one. But he was pretty sure that the person who'd been temporarily living with him knew how, and his insides burned with anger. But this wasn't something he wanted to share with his brother, so he just waved and thanked him for coming by.

Leroy said, "*Gut* to see you," the way he always did.

Abraham nodded before he closed the door, then just stared at the small card in his hand. This was the second question he had for Brianna, and the urge to call her was even stronger than when he'd found out that she sought him out at Yvonne's but never showed up or mentioned a leaky faucet. Something was amiss.

But he didn't call her. Maybe he never would.

CHAPTER 13

O n Wednesday afternoon, Yvonne waited for Larry Boone to show up. Everything was ready for the book signing. She'd set up a table, covered it with a white tablecloth she'd found in the back, and set up chairs for the author and customers. She'd also lit two cinnamon-scented candles and placed them on the counter to add to the holiday ambience. It was festive at the bookstore, but Yvonne was having trouble staying in the Christmas spirit. She hadn't heard from Abraham since he left her house Sunday evening, and it bothered her even though it shouldn't.

She was percolating coffee in the back when the bell on the door jingled, so she rushed to the front of the store, rounding the corner just as Jake walked in.

"*Wie bischt?*"

Yvonne smiled. "*Gut.* I think we're all ready."

Jake grinned and pointed a finger at her. "Listen to you. Learning the *Deitsch.*"

"Well, not much, but it's hard not to when I hear it spoken so much." She knew *"Wie bischt"* was a general greeting that was sometimes a question meaning "How are you?" and sometimes just "Hello."

She walked around the counter, popped open the cash-register drawer, and said, "Yesterday, I went to the bank and got some smaller bills. If we have much of a crowd at all, I think it will be Amish women, and they tend to pay with cash."

"That's why I pay you the big bucks. Always thinking ahead." He tapped a finger to the side of his black felt hat. Most of the Amish had switched from straw hats to felt or sweater caps since the temperature had dropped.

She chuckled. "Um . . . Well, I don't know about big bucks, but I like my job. How's Eva?"

"The same. Bored and ready to have the *boppli*. I just stopped by to see if you needed help getting the fire going." He nodded toward the wood-burning stove that sat off to the side. "But I see you've got it under control." He rubbed his hands together, then moved closer to the warmth of the fire.

"Yeah, it's fizzled out on me a few times lately, but today, I seemed to have done okay. Maybe it's the practice I have at home, keeping the fire going in my fireplace."

"I can't stay. Lots to do. But Eva wanted me to let you know that she's called everyone who has a cell phone and told them about the book signing. Hopefully, you'll have a good crowd."

"I hope so. I just made coffee, and I've got a plate of cookies I was getting ready to bring in." Yvonne had confirmed with the author yesterday that he was in town. "Larry Boone is staying at the Peony Inn."

Jake burst out laughing. "Well, I'm sure Lizzie and Esther are entertaining him."

"Oh, I'm sure." The widows were known and loved by everyone in town, even though Lizzie strayed from the Amish ways sometimes and marched to her own drumbeat.

"Best of luck." Jake waved as he took large strides toward the exit.

"It's your store. Hopefully you'll make some money!" she hollered just before he was out the door.

She'd looked up Larry Boone on the internet. On the phone, he had sounded like an older guy, but his picture said otherwise. He looked to be fortyish, and she recognized him when he stepped out of a black Jeep in the parking lot. When he retrieved a large box from his back seat, Yvonne rushed to hold the door open for him.

"Hello, and welcome." Her teeth chattered as the cool breeze wafted into the store. But it wasn't snowing, and as much as she loved flurries, nice weather would bring more people.

"Thanks," he said as he slid by her, placed the box on the table, and extended his hand. "I'm Larry, and it's a pleasure to meet you."

Yvonne smiled. The man's picture online didn't do him justice. He had thick tawny-gold hair parted on the side with a swath that fell casually across his forehead. His dark-brown eyes framed a handsome square face, and he was tall . . . like Abraham.

She willed the image of Abraham from her mind.

"Despite the chill in the air, it's a beautiful day, so hopefully you will draw a crowd." Yvonne clasped her hands in front of her and smiled.

Larry shrugged as he smiled back. "You just never know about these things, but since I was going to be in the area and had plenty of books, I thought it was worth the effort. I appreciate you hosting the event."

"Of course. We're happy to have you." She held up a finger. "I was just going to get a platter of cookies from the back."

"Sure. I'll get set up."

A moment later Yvonne returned and placed the cookies on the counter. "So, what brings you to Montgomery?"

"I have cousins in Bedford. I've done book signings there and in most of the larger cities and towns over the years." He glanced up at her and grinned as he unpacked books. "I thought it would be cool to do something in the heart of Amish country."

"Well, Montgomery isn't huge, but there are a lot of Amish in the area. And they love to read, so I'll be hoping you do well. Can I get you some coffee?"

"That would be great."

When Yvonne came back with a cup in her hand, she sloshed a tiny bit over the side when she saw Brianna talking to Larry, laughing and smiling, dressed in a gorgeous blue-and-white pinstriped pantsuit. Yvonne took notice of her own blue jeans, black boots, and stylish black sweater she'd chosen. In comparison to Brianna, she might as well be wearing overalls or something equally as unnoticeable.

Brianna turned her attention to Yvonne. "I used to be a

huge reader, so when I heard you were having a book signing, I didn't want to miss it." Brianna glanced at Larry and
flashed a bright smile his way. Yvonne wondered if Brianna
knew the author wrote children's books. Abraham must
have told her about the book signing. Eva wouldn't have
called her. Although Yvonne had hung flyers all over, so
maybe Brianna had seen one.

"I'm happy you're here," Yvonne said before she took
a tissue from the counter and wiped the spilled coffee from
the side of the cup and handed it to Larry.

"Oh, wow." Yvonne pointed out the window at a line of
Amish buggies coming up the road. "I think you're going to
have a good day."

Larry pressed his palms together. "Wonderful."

Yvonne greeted each of the Amish women as they came
in the store. Some of them took seats in the folding chairs
she'd set up, and others stood. Brianna took a seat in the
front row.

Lizzie and Esther trailed in behind the other women,
and Lizzie lagged behind until it was just her and Yvonne
standing near the entrance. "That is one of the most handsome *Englisch* men I've ever seen. And he is staying at the
inn, so I've already learned that he isn't married and doesn't
have a girlfriend." She gave a taut nod of her head. "You're
welcome."

Yvonne glanced around to make sure no one had heard
Lizzie. No one seemed to notice them. The Amish women
chatted among themselves, and Larry was still unpacking
books and laying pens and bookmarks on the table. Brianna
was typing something on her phone.

"No matchmaking, Lizzie." She pointed a finger at her. In addition to running the Peony Inn, Lizzie and Esther were known matchmakers. Sometimes it seemed like a full-time job for them. They'd even given a nudge to help get Jake and Eva together, and Yvonne had heard of plenty more antics the sisters had pulled, trying to get couples together.

"I'm just concerned for you," Lizzie said, still whispering. "It's tragic, what happened to your fiancé, but you must find the will to nab a husband." She sighed, shaking her head. "In some circles, you're already considered an old maid." She patted Yvonne on the arm. "And we can't have that happen to a beautiful, available woman like you." She was still wagging her head when she went to sit by her sister.

Yvonne stood speechless for a few seconds as she tried to absorb Lizzie's thoughts on her singlehood. After gathering herself, she was getting ready to introduce Larry to the audience when a car pulled into the parking lot. She swallowed hard. *A police car.* Abraham was the last person she would have expected to see at a book signing for children's books, but he was obviously here to be with his girlfriend.

Abraham stepped out of his car and checked the messages on his cell phone, then glanced around. He was pleased to see so many Amish buggies tethered to the hitching post. He'd seen the flyer about the book signing taped on the window outside Stop 'N Sea, his favorite place to get a fish sandwich. Now he just hoped he didn't get a call since he was on duty.

He had intentionally stayed away from Brianna and Yvonne, hoping to clear his head when it came to both women. In the end, he couldn't get Yvonne off his mind, and this was his excuse to see her.

Brianna had called once daily, and Abraham had answered each time. He didn't ask her about her supposed leaky faucet, and she never mentioned it, nor did he say anything about Leroy finding the SIM card to his old cell phone under the bath mat. Even though he wasn't much of a gadget person, and hadn't learned more than the basic technology he needed for his work, it had only taken a couple of minutes to locate the compartment where the SIM card went in his old phone, and it wasn't there. He'd analyzed why Brianna would have taken it out, and he'd also recalled how isolated he had felt without a phone and only Brianna to talk to and see. That was her plan, he realized—to have him all to herself. Every time he recalled those days she'd stayed at his house, he wished he could go back in time. He should have stayed with Leroy and his family or one of his other siblings, even if it had been crowded.

Each time Brianna had called these last few days, Abraham had come up with an excuse why he couldn't come to her house or why she couldn't come there. Some had been little white lies. For two days, he'd feigned a stomach bug. The other couple of days, he'd worked late intentionally so he wouldn't have to lie to her.

As he walked in the door of the bookstore a few minutes late, the bell on the door jingled. Yvonne paused what appeared to be an introduction to the author. Abraham smiled and mouthed "Sorry," then went to take a seat. Most of the chairs were taken by Amish women. But then his eyes landed on the woman in the blue-and-white pinstriped suit. What was Brianna doing at a book signing for children's books?

She was probably wondering the same thing about him.

He smiled at Brianna, knowing he had no choice but to sit by her. He excused himself as he passed by some of the Amish ladies, then sat in the middle of the front row by the woman who thought she was still his girlfriend—something he needed to take care of soon. He'd been trying to ease into it.

Brianna smiled as she reached for his hand and held it tightly. Yvonne paused again and cleared her throat before she finished her introduction, then took a seat on the stool behind the counter. Her eyes were on his and Brianna's hands, and Abraham longed to snatch his hand back, but this wasn't the time or place to upset Brianna. At this point, he wasn't sure what the woman was capable of. He just wanted out of this relationship, whether there was anything to pursue with Yvonne or not. Abraham wasn't even sure it was a good idea to get involved with Yvonne when he had his own unresolved feelings about the choices he'd made regarding his job and leaving the Amish faith. But he'd felt drawn to be here today. Now, he prayed he would hear the familiar buzz of his radio on his hip and be freed of this uncomfortable situation.

Luckily, the author didn't talk long and started signing books right away. A dozen Amish women moved toward his table. Brianna finally let go of his hand, then leaned close to his ear.

"I'm surprised to see you here." She gave him a thin-lipped smile, and that was never good. He wanted to say, "Ditto."

"I wanted to get some books for my nieces and nephews." It was a quick response, and he would make it true by purchasing some of the man's inventory. "What about you?" He raised an eyebrow. To his knowledge, Brianna didn't have contact with her parents, and she had no siblings.

"Christmas gifts for some of my clients who have children." She was either quick on the uptake, as he was, or she was lying, as he'd been known to do lately—something he didn't feel good about. It only proved they weren't suited for each other, no matter how beautiful she was on the outside.

And Abraham knew better than to even look in Yvonne's direction, but several times, he'd felt her eyes on him and Brianna.

"I guess we better go get in line." Abraham stood and waited for Brianna to do the same, then followed her to where the others were waiting to get signed books.

Yvonne had joined Larry Boone and was writing names on slips of paper, then handing them to him, obviously so he would get the spellings right. And she was collecting money and making change. A couple of women stood by the counter, probably waiting to pay with credit cards. By the time Brianna and Abraham stepped up to the table, there were only a couple of people left behind them.

"Hi, Abraham." Yvonne barely looked at him before she cleared her throat. "And hello again, Brianna."

Larry Boone didn't seem to notice when Brianna reached for Abraham's hand and held it. But the man's eyes veered to Yvonne repeatedly, and for the first time in a long time, a tinge of jealousy seared into Abraham's heart.

"One signed to me, please," Brianna said after Yvonne had confirmed there were two *n*'s in her name. "Then can you just sign your name on three more books, please?"

Larry nodded. When he was done, Abraham fought not to look at Yvonne, said he wanted four books, then wrote down the names for Larry after Yvonne said she needed to go tend to the ladies paying with credit cards.

"Oh, Yvonne . . ." Larry said before she got too far away. "Dinner after you close this evening?"

Abraham's stomach clenched as he fought not to react. Larry Boone was a handsome man, even Abraham could see that, and he and Yvonne probably had a lot in common— love of all things bookish, for starters.

"Um . . ." Yvonne glanced at Abraham and Brianna, then looked back at the handsome author. "Sure. That sounds great."

Abraham had cash on him, but he forced his hand from Brianna's and reached into his back pocket for his wallet. "I have to go pay with a credit card."

"Me too." Brianna was quickly in step with him, and after they waited in the short line, Yvonne handled Brianna's purchase, then his. "Thank you both for coming," she said directly to Brianna, but she never looked at Abraham.

After they left the building, Abraham stopped and looked around. "Where's your car?"

Brianna pointed to her left. "Oh, it's on the side of the building. I was trying to make room for the buggies." She latched on to his hand. His felt clammy against her cold palm. "I know it's only four, but do you want to get an early dinner? We haven't spent any time together lately." She rolled her lip into an exaggerated pout.

Abraham opened his mouth to tell her he was on duty, but he didn't want to wait any longer to get the inevitable talk over with, and a public place might be best to have the hard conversation. "Sure."

Brianna followed Abraham's police car to Stoll's Lakeview Restaurant. He'd let her choose, and even though she wasn't fond of buffets, Abraham was, and she wanted to show him she could put his interests first. She wasn't sure how much she would be able to eat. Her appetite had fled the moment Abraham walked into the bookstore. He wasn't there to buy books for his nieces and nephews any more than she was there to purchase books for her clients. He was there to see Yvonne, which was the only reason Brianna had parked her car out of view and attended the stupid event—to see if he would show up. Abraham was predictable, and as they pulled into the parking lot at the restaurant, her prediction was that he was going to break up with her.

Each time they'd briefly talked on the phone over the past few days, he had been distant and noncommunicative. She could have been talking to a mere acquaintance, not the man she was in love with. This reminded her of her breakup with Mitch. It had started out just like this. Her ex had put distance between them when he started seeing someone else. There was so much lying and betrayal. Brianna would have never pegged Abraham as a cheat. Maybe she was wrong about everything. She would know soon enough.

They walked in together, and Brianna waited until they were seated with their food from the buffet before she said, "My, my. That author is a handsome fellow. I'm sure Yvonne was thrilled that he asked her to dinner." Abraham didn't look up from his plate, but he nodded. "It's so horrible about her fiancé dying. I hope she finds happiness again. I'm sure she and Larry Boone have much in common." She smiled but didn't take her eyes off Abraham, and he reacted just as she could have predicted. His eyes were icy and unresponsive, his head down as if he was concentrating intently on his grilled chicken, like it might grow wings and fly off his plate.

Just do it. Get it over with. She'd had her heart broken before. She'd get over it.

They finished eating in silence, except for an occasional comment about the food or the weather. Finally, he took a deep breath and wiped his mouth with his napkin. For the first time since they had sat down to eat, he looked her straight in the eyes. "Brianna . . ."

"You don't have to say it, Abraham. It's okay. You want us to stop seeing each other." When relief swept over his face and his shoulders relaxed, she wished she'd made him say it. "I'm not stupid."

"Brianna, I know you're not stupid. Not at all." He paused, and she readied herself for the part where he would tell her how wonderful she was but that she wasn't the right person for him. She doubted he would come out and say that he had romantic interests in Yvonne. "I'm just going through some things right now, and it wouldn't be fair to you if we keep seeing each other."

She stiffened. "Might I ask what kind of *things*?" He had just veered from predictable.

Sighing, he leaned back against his chair and rubbed the back of his neck. "The thing with Will and Maureen has me feeling weird. I'm not sure I want to be a cop anymore."

Brianna's jaw dropped. This was the last thing she could have predicted from this predictable man. But what did a change in careers have to do with breaking up?

"And that's not all." He locked eyes with her. *Here it comes.* Now he was going to tell her how wonderful she was. "I'm questioning my decision about straying from my Amish roots."

Her eyes widened as her mouth fell open for a second time. "Huh?"

"I'm considering baptism into the Amish faith."

She searched his face for any hint that this was a joke, but his solemn expression said it wasn't.

"I'm not for sure yet, but I don't see you converting to the Amish way of life if our relationship progressed in a more serious direction."

Brianna had thought it was serious for a while now. She fought a smile, her own relief wrapping around her. There was still a chance for them. She hadn't lost him to another woman.

"Abraham, you could have discussed this with me. We could have talked about it instead of you being so aloof. I don't see why we must stop seeing each other while you contemplate which direction you'd like to take your faith and your life. Now that it's out in the open, things can be different, open for discussion."

He shook his head. "No, Brianna. It's not fair to you, and I need this time to myself. You're a wonderful person, beautiful and kind. You'll find someone more suited to you. I'm sorry. I really am."

There it was, that predictability. Maybe he was thinking about being Amish again, which sounded unthinkable as she gazed at him in his police uniform. But there was more to it. And her gut told her it was Yvonne. Adrenaline shot through her veins and left her skin feeling like it was on fire as she struggled to control the rage inside of her. But if she was going to stay in the game and battle Yvonne, then she would need to play it cool. It would be easy enough to talk him out of his foolish idea to return to the Amish way of life. He'd been away from the life too long to go back to driving a buggy and living without electricity. And he'd been right about her not converting. *No way.*

She blinked back tears that she could call upon when needed, in times of joy or sadness. "I understand. And of course I wish you all the happiness in the world. I'll be praying that you make the best decision for yourself." She didn't know how much praying she would do, but she needed to find out how the deck was stacked. How much of this was truly about religion, and how much involved his feelings for Yvonne? Until she had those answers, she wouldn't know how to play her hand.

Abraham swallowed back a knot in his throat. He couldn't stand to see a woman cry, especially when he was the cause of the tears. "Brianna, please don't cry. I'm so sorry."

She put two fingers to her trembling lips but didn't say anything. Abraham was shocked that she was weeping. He had been more worried about her screaming, toppling tables, or other things that now sounded silly in his mind. She'd told him she loved him, and while it was premature, he should have known that she would be more hurt than mad.

"What can I do?" His own eyes were getting moist.

"Just find what you're looking for, Abraham. I only want you to be happy, and I understand now what a struggle this must have been for you, keeping your feelings inside." She sniffled.

Abraham had kept a lot of his emotions inside. He had told her the truth, just not all of it. He didn't see any reason to hurt Brianna further by telling her how much he cared about Yvonne—another relationship that had nowhere to go if he chose to be baptized.

"Thank you for being so understanding, Brianna. It means a lot to me." Abraham hadn't given her enough credit. She was taking this like a mature woman. "I just want you to be happy too."

Abraham's radio buzzed. *Perfect timing.* He'd said and done what he needed to, and this would make it a clean break without hugs and more tears. "I have to go." He stood and went around to where she was sitting, then kissed her on the forehead as he placed forty dollars on the table to pay for the meal.

"Be safe," she said through her tears as he walked away.

He couldn't turn around or she might see his watery eyes. Hurting another person, no matter the reason, was painful. He said a silent prayer that Brianna would find the person of her dreams and be happy.

CHAPTER 14

Yvonne finished settling the money part of the book signing with Larry, then handed him a check. "You did great. Thirty-seven books in our small town is awesome."

Larry chuckled. "Thirty-seven books are awesome in *any* town, big or small."

Yvonne tried to smile, but her heart was heavy, and she knew she wouldn't be good company for dinner. "Do you mind if we skip that dinner tonight? I'm exhausted, and it occurs to me that I need to let my dog out." She cringed at how silly that sounded, but it was true. She also wasn't up for small talk. Seeing Brianna and Abraham together had hit her harder than she thought.

Larry raised an eyebrow. "Are you sure? I'm leaving tomorrow."

Yvonne nodded. "Yeah, I'm sorry. But I'm so happy your book signing went well."

He smiled. "Me too."

As he lifted what was left of his box of books, she walked him to the door. The last thing Yvonne needed was a handsome guy trying to have a one-night stand with her, something she'd never done and had no plans to do. Larry was definitely good-looking, but since he oozed charm, Yvonne couldn't help but wonder if he had lots of one-nighters with women. It was wrong of her to judge him, but either way, she wasn't up for dinner.

After she called Jake to tell him about the book signing, she started closing up the store. By the time she got home and onto her front porch, she could hear Blue's feet tapping against the wood floors as he made his way to the door. He bolted past her to go do his business but was quickly back on the porch waiting to join her inside. She left a sign on the door of the bookstore and went home each day at lunch to let him out, but her furry roommate was always anxious to go out when she got home. Maybe he needed a doggie door since he had proven himself to be a good boy in the house.

She opened the door to let Blue back in, and he rushed across the threshold along with a burst of cold air. Yvonne leaned down and let him lick her on the face while she scratched his ears. She thought about Trevor. He would have never believed she had a dog. Her aunt had been shocked as well when Yvonne had told her. But in their short time together, Blue had become a fixture in her life.

Yvonne scurried through the house, plugged in her electric heater in the bedroom, then started on a fire. Blue curled up on his bed in front of the fireplace. She was fanning the flames when Blue began to growl, something he rarely did. He'd done so at first with Abraham, and twice during the night recently. But after looking out the window both times, she'd seen deer outside, their shadows visible against the light from the lamp in the yard.

"You're okay, Blue. It's probably deer or some other animal." She added another log to the fire, still shivering.

Her dog, who was filling out nicely and clean now—including his bed cover—began to pace the living room, still growling as he went from window to window, then to the front door before he rushed to the back door in the mud room. It wasn't even all the way dark yet, so Yvonne followed him, peeking out windows and trying to talk to him in a soothing voice. She wasn't afraid of him at all anymore. But she was afraid of what might be outside. In the past, he'd zoned in on one area and barked until Yvonne identified the deer, then managed to get him settled down. This felt different, and she walked on shaky legs to where Blue now stood just inside the front door barking loudly.

She recalled Abraham saying Blue would make a good watchdog, so she opened the door, and Blue almost knocked her down as he swept past her and dove off the porch, sprinting into a run until he was out of sight in the woods that surrounded her yard.

Her heart pounded, and she wished she had kept him inside. What if he tangled with something stronger than he was? She'd been told there were bobcats and cougars in the area, although they were rarely seen. Deer hooves could also do some serious damage. She knew that from living in Texas.

As she stood in the doorway with a racing heart, chattering teeth, and her arms folded around her, she called out to him. "Blue!"

In the distance she could hear him barking. At least he was okay.

She closed the door and waited, returning about fifteen minutes later with a blanket wrapped around her. As she walked onto the porch, she shook all over from the freezing temperature. "Blue!"

She couldn't hear him barking now. Her chest hurt as she repeatedly called his name and wondered when she'd become so attached to her dog. It had snuck up on her. Tears built in the corners of her eyes. "Blue!"

Giving in to emotion, she bent at the waist, thoughts of Trevor swirling around in her mind. Comparing her fiancé's death to the possibility of losing a dog she'd only had a short time was wrong, but she still felt a familiar sense of loss.

She went back inside and bundled up in her coat, gloves, knitted cap, and heavy boots. Then she turned on a flashlight and headed outside again, down her porch steps, and toward the woods. "Blue!"

As she reached the end of her yard, with only thick woods ahead of her, she stopped. It was freezing outside, she couldn't hear Blue barking, and God only knew what was in the woods ahead of her.

Yes, God. She bowed her head and asked Him to keep Blue safe and warm. Then, with tears in her eyes, she shuffled back to her house and waited on the porch another ten minutes. But all she could hear in the distance were coyotes. She wanted to call Abraham, but he was most likely with Brianna.

Abraham's shift hadn't ended until almost eleven, and as he kicked off his shoes by the door, he sighed. Breaking things off with Brianna had whipped him emotionally, and then he'd had several work calls throughout the evening. Luckily, nothing serious.

He longed to call Yvonne, if for no other reason than to hear her voice. But she'd had dinner with the author this evening, and for all Abraham knew, she could still be spending time with him. Maybe it was for the best. Being around Yvonne would make him question the possibility of returning to his Amish ways, especially if there was any chance of being with her as more than a friend.

He'd been a police officer for a long time. After leaving the Amish faith at nineteen and getting his GED and some college courses, he'd been provisionally hired by the police force and gone to the police academy, then started his career in law enforcement. Could he really give up his English life and return to the simpler ways that he so often craved? Was this just a reaction to shooting Will and being shot in the process? Or was there more to it? Had he ever been completely happy outside of the environment he'd been raised in? At nineteen, he'd been young, ambitious, and thought he was defending a cause. But the passivity that had been engrained in him for as long as he could remember still lingered, and shooting a man was weighing on him.

By the time he showered and got in bed, his mind was still on overdrive even though his body was exhausted. But as he closed his eyes to sleep, only one vision filled his senses: *Yvonne*. There was something emotionally safe about her, a feeling he had every time he was around her.

But could he really share with her how he was feeling about the possibility of overhauling his life? He wasn't sure, but he had to see her.

Yvonne wasn't sure how long she'd stayed awake listening for Blue before she'd dozed off, but she bolted upright when she heard her dog barking on the front porch, and she ran for the door.

"Blue!"

The shivering dog jogged into the house and went straight to the fireplace, where Yvonne sat down beside him and wrapped her arms around him, crying. "Where have you been?"

The dog licked her all over her face, and she nuzzled him with her nose. "You scared me." She scratched behind his ears, and she rubbed his back until he warmed up.

Finally, when Blue got comfortable on his bed in front of the fire, she stood up. She was almost to her bedroom when she turned around. "Blue. Come on." She patted her leg, and the dog lifted one ear as he tipped his head to the side. He didn't appear to be nearly as traumatized as Yvonne. He slowly got to his feet and followed her to her bedroom.

"That's my side," she said after he jumped onto the bed and rested his head on her pillow. "Okay, I'll give it up just for tonight." She climbed under the covers on the other side, and when Blue started snoring, she smiled. She felt safe.

Until Blue started barking at four in the morning. He raced from the bed, went window to window, then door to door, pawing to get out. Yvonne was instantly awake, on alert, her heart pounding in her chest again. But she didn't let him out. She had to believe it was a wild animal nearby that had him so upset, but on the off chance it was a person, it was unlikely they would try to break in with a barking dog inside. At least she hoped not.

Eventually, she was able to get him settled down, and they both went back to bed. She noticed Blue wasn't snoring but seemed only half asleep, with his eyes cracked open. Yvonne couldn't close her eyes. And she didn't feel safe anymore.

Abraham kicked back on his couch Saturday morning, glad to have the weekend off but unsure what to do with himself. Brianna had called last night around midnight, and even though he was still awake, he had let the call go to voice mail. She'd left a sweet message saying that she hoped he would have a good day, and she also told him that she would keep him in prayer, knowing he would make the best decisions for himself. And there was something else . . .

He scratched his chin, then reached for his phone and listened to the message again.

"*Hi, babe. I just wanted to say that I hope tomorrow will be a good day for you. I'm keeping you in prayer, and I know you will make the best decisions for your life. Is it okay if I still miss you a little?*"

It seemed odd that she would still call him "babe," but they'd split up only two days prior to her call. He supposed it would take her some time to get used to the fact that they were no longer a couple. Regardless, he wasn't going to call her back. Time took care of these things, and Brianna would feel better as each day passed.

He wondered if he would feel better with the passage of time. He still had flashbacks of the shooting. He couldn't get Yvonne off his mind. And his thoughts were garbled about his faith and where he should be.

The wind kicked up outside, and a heavy snow began to fall. It had snowed more this December than it usually did, but it didn't stick much and melted the following day. However, today, everything was beginning to cover with white, and Abraham decided to throw caution to the wind.

How are you enjoying this snow? He hit Send on the text to Yvonne.

I love it! She wrote back right away, and she included a happy-face emoji.

Abraham smiled. *It's sticking this time. Are you at work?* He doubted Yvonne knew much about driving in the snow when it accumulated.

He waited. Maybe she had a customer, assuming she was at the bookstore like she was most Saturdays. Or maybe her date with the author had gone so well that he'd stuck around. Their last encounter at the bookstore with each other had been awkward for reasons he was unsure of.

His adrenaline spiked when his phone buzzed.

Yes, it is sticking, and yes, I'm at work. Jake called and said I should close the bookstore early since there might be five or six inches of snow on the ground later. Yay!

Abraham tapped a finger to his thumb as he thought of

a response. He had to see her. It might confuse him further. Or maybe he would have clarity and know he wanted to pursue things with Yvonne . . . Then he would have to give up the idea of being baptized back into the Amish community.

The whole thing was giving him a headache. He just wanted to spend time with her. He wondered if she still wanted him to help her build something for Jake and Eva's baby, but he knew it wouldn't be today in this weather, and he didn't want to wait to see her.

Do you want some company after you get off work? I kinda miss that dog, lol.

He was trying to be cute, but when she didn't answer after about ten minutes, he assumed the answer was no. If so, he had nothing to lose by texting her one last time to see if it made a difference.

Brianna and I broke up.

Yvonne chewed on a fingernail as she shifted her weight on the stool behind the counter at the bookstore. From the way Brianna had made sure everyone, especially Yvonne, knew that Abraham was taken, she assumed he'd been the one to call things off. She'd be lying to herself if she wasn't happy to hear the news, but she did feel sorry for Brianna. She was still thinking about it when he texted back.

I'll bring pizza and a bone for Bruiser.

She chuckled. *You know his name is Blue, lol. And, okay, that sounds good.* Her finger hovered over the Send button, and then she added, *I can text you when I get home.*

Perfect. Looking forward to it.

She almost texted *Me too* but decided to leave the conversation where it was. Her mind was spinning. When she'd met Abraham, he'd clearly taken an interest in her, but she'd been with Trevor. After she moved to Montgomery, she'd learned that Abraham had a girlfriend. This was the first time they were both unattached. Were they free to see if their initial attraction had anywhere to go? It seemed so, and a warm glow flowed through her.

Jake called her around noon. "Go home," he said when she answered.

"It's too early to close. Saturday is usually your busiest day." She stared out at her red SUV covered in white, along with the parking lot and as far as she could see. But she didn't think he meant for her to close this early.

"How many people have been in today?"

"None." She sighed.

"*Ya*, exactly. No one is getting out in this. It will probably melt off tomorrow, but the roads will be covered this afternoon and tonight, and you have no idea how to drive in snow. Go home."

She thought about how much more time she'd have to spend with Abraham. "Okay, if you're sure."

"*Ya*, I am."

Yvonne packed up, locked the door, and took careful steps in the snow to her SUV, wondering if she would finally need the four-wheel drive everyone had said she had to have. Luckily, her house wasn't too far from the bookstore, and she took it slow and easy.

Blue was curled into a ball on the front porch when she

pulled into her driveway, now covered in snow. The dog had refused to go inside this morning when she left for the bookstore, as if he was on guard or something. But he happily followed her into the house, which was chilly but much warmer than outside.

She went through the drill, first going to her bedroom to fire up the electric heater, then getting a fire going and plugging in her Christmas tree. Her excitement was building about Abraham coming over, and she remembered she'd said she would text him.

I'm home. Closed early.

She waited only a few seconds.

Ordering the pizza, and I'll be on my way.

After she took a little time to tidy up around the house, she spruced herself up by powdering her shiny nose, adding some lip gloss, and running a brush through her hair. She left on her jeans and red sweater but slipped into a fuzzy pair of slippers—a pair in better shape than the ones she usually wore. These were white with little bunny ears on top.

"Cute shoes," Abraham said with a chuckle when she opened the door. She took the pizza from him, happy to see he had a bone in one hand. Blue hadn't moved from his spot by the fire, but he was growling.

She took in Abraham's tall stance, his confident shoulders and contagious smile.

"Thanks," she said, grinning back at him. Then she looked over his shoulder. "Aw, it stopped snowing."

"Probably a good thing, or I might have gotten stuck here." He slipped out of his black coat, and she nodded to the coat rack by the door.

"There are worse places to get stuck," she said as she carried the pizza to the kitchen and set it on the counter. When she returned, Abraham hadn't moved. But Blue had. He was inching warily toward him with his ears peeled back, his teeth bared.

"Blue. No. He's our friend." She went and scratched behind the dog's ears. "Don't you remember him? He helped me give you a bath." Turning to Abraham, who still hadn't moved, she said, "This might be a good time to offer him that bone in your hand."

"Wow. Is this the same woman who was originally terrified of this animal?" Abraham squatted down to the dog's eye level. "Here, boy."

Blue stopped growling and eventually took the bone and went back to his bed.

"I know. I know. I need to get him to obedience school. But he's had a rough few days." She sighed as she ran a hand through her hair.

He slowly edged over to the couch, and they both sat down, Blue keeping an eye on Abraham. "'Rough'? How so?"

Yvonne filled him in on the past few nights and how she thought she'd lost Blue when he didn't come back from the woods for a long while. "I didn't realize how attached to him I had become until I thought something happened to him."

"It could have been raccoons, deer . . . even coyotes. I'm glad you didn't venture out in the woods to look for him." He smiled as his eyes shifted to her Christmas tree. "It still looks great."

"It sure drinks up a lot of water, but I'm not complaining. I'm so grateful to have such a beautiful tree." She twisted to face him. "Are you hungry? Do you want pizza now?"

He shrugged. "Whenever you're ready."

She brought them each a glass of tea and a plate with two slices, and as they'd done before, they ate at the coffee table. "I admit that I haven't trained Blue to do much, but he knows not to beg for food. We already had that battle." She nodded toward the dog.

"He sure has filled out."

"Yeah." She smiled. "He's a keeper."

Abraham loved the way Yvonne stared dreamily at the dog she'd been so afraid of. He briefly wondered if she could ever look at him like that.

"So . . ." She set down her slice of pizza. "Am I being too nosy if I ask what happened with you and Brianna?"

He wiped his mouth with a napkin she'd set out and shook his head. "No, not at all. I guess it was a lot of things. She was moving too fast for me, and we just weren't as compatible as it appeared in the beginning. I realized she wasn't the one, and I didn't see us moving our relationship to the next level. She did. It seemed better to break things off now instead of prolonging it." He frowned, choosing not to share about the SIM card or Brianna's lie about a leaky faucet. "But I do feel bad that I did it right before the holidays, and she doesn't have any family here."

Yvonne hung her head, then locked eyes with him. "I

feel bad for her, too, but you did the right thing by not leading her on if you knew it wasn't going to work out."

Abraham was tempted to tell Yvonne his decision didn't have anything to do with her, even though it partly did. He owed her the truth, keeping in line with not leading her on, but he wasn't ready to go full throttle with everything just yet. "And there's something else."

She raised an eyebrow as she chewed.

"I-I . . ." Unexpectantly, his voice shook. This was going to be harder than he thought. "I'm kind of thinking that I might want to be baptized into the Amish faith."

Both her eyebrows shot up, then she swallowed. "Wow. That's, uh . . . huge. Right?"

"Super huge." He needed someone to talk to besides Leroy, someone objective. "I haven't talked to anyone about it, except my older brother, Leroy. I mean, I've been away from the community for a long time, but the possibility has consumed my thoughts lately."

"I know you miss being Amish sometimes." She eased out of her fuzzy slippers and tucked a leg underneath her as she faced him on the couch. "I can understand that. The lifestyle has a lot to offer." She paused and took a drink of tea. "A simpler way of life, void of competition or jealousy, and the all-knowing confidence that everyone in your circle is grounded in their faith. It must have been hard to walk away from that in the first place, especially since it was all you knew at the time."

"It wasn't all I knew," he said. "I had a fairly active *rumschpringe*. But at nineteen, I was mostly a kid on a mission. I thought that because of one incident with a friend, the Amish were being treated unfairly and that I could fix that—fix the police force. And I couldn't have been more wrong. They didn't need fixing. I work with a great group of guys who treat everyone fairly, especially the Amish." He set his plate that he had been holding on the coffee table and twisted his hands. "It's complicated, though."

"I want to ask you something, but I don't want to overstep." Yvonne bit her bottom lip, cringing a little.

"Please ask. You won't be overstepping." He was genuinely interested in her input.

"Does this have something to do with the shooting?" She nodded toward his arm.

He wondered if honesty would make him look like a wimp. "*Ya*, I guess it does."

She stared at him for a long time, as if she might be planning her response carefully. "I've known several police officers and sheriff's deputies, and most of them have never had to draw their weapons. But one deputy who I was friends with while I was in college not only shot a man, but he killed him. It was definitely self-defense, but he never got over it, and he quit his job. You were raised in a very passive environment, so I can understand that the whole thing must have been difficult for you."

If she thought he was wimpy, she wasn't letting on. "I appreciate that. And I have time to think about it. I'll be on desk duty for at least another month." He pointed to his shoulder. "My stitches are out, but the doctor said it's going to take a while for my muscle to heal."

"Then give yourself that time to weigh it all out. I totally overhauled my spiritual beliefs in what I consider to be late in life." She smiled warmly at him. "I know I'm only thirty-three, but you know what I mean."

Abraham had never known her exact age. He scratched his cheek. "Well, I'm four years older than you, but I'd be overhauling my life, not necessarily my spiritual beliefs. Do you think it's weird that I've never been married at my age?"

He'd always felt comfortable with Yvonne, but he wished he hadn't let that question fly out of his mouth.

"Not at all." She shook her head. "I think it's smart and endearing. Whoever you end up marrying will most likely be your forever mate because you waited for exactly the right person."

The moment of truth was coming for Abraham, and he owed it to Yvonne to be honest with her. "There is another problem that's tangled up with my decision about whether or not to return to my Amish roots." He paused, gazed into her eyes. "Actually, it's not really a problem but a person who has me confused as to what I want to do."

"Someone in your family?" She tipped her head slightly to one side as her questioning eyes waited for an answer she probably wasn't expecting at all.

"No." He pointed at her. "It's *you*. Since we're being honest, it's no secret that I had an enormous crush—for lack of a better word—on you since I first saw you at the bookstore." He kept his eyes fused with hers, waiting for her to look away, but she didn't. "Then I saw you at the wedding, I wrote you letters . . . but the timing was off." He shrugged. "Now, you're my favorite person to spend time with." He still hadn't lost the connection as her eyes stayed locked with his. "I guess I'm curious how you feel about that."

She stared at him for a long time before she responded. "I feel like anything I say might influence your decision, and I know from experience what a personal thing our faith journey is."

"You're right." He edged closer to her, propped his elbow on the back of the couch, then leaned his head against his hand, his eyes still clinging to hers. "I was planning not to see you again because I knew I had feelings for you. I thought it would be best because I didn't want to lead you on, in case I chose the Amish way of life."

"Exactly," she said softly as she finally pulled her eyes from his and looked down.

He gently lifted her chin until she was looking at him again. "But there's a huge problem with that because I don't want to stay away from you. Not at all. So, what now?" He tucked her hair behind her ear on one side, his face close enough to hers that he could kiss her—something he'd longed to do since the first day he saw her.

"I guess I've been forewarned," she said softly as she gazed into his eyes.

"I want to kiss you." He leaned even closer. "And I'm going to unless you stop me."

She didn't move at first, not even to blink an eye. Then she moved slowly closer to him and her lips feather-touched his . . . and it was a kiss for his tired soul to melt into. There was a dreamy intimacy that he'd never felt before. There was no doubt she aroused him in a physical way, but it was more than that. It was soulful and divine. Just the way he knew it would be.

CHAPTER 15

Brianna sat on her couch and stared at the photograph of her and Abraham, the one she'd gotten framed for each of them. They were perfect for each other. He was kind, good-looking, and had an honorable career. He didn't make as much money as she'd hoped—or at least she didn't think he did—but he was suitable husband material. He had a flaw, though. Abraham Byler was a liar. He had used a spiritual conflict as a reason to break up with her instead of being honest and telling her that he wanted to spend time with Yvonne.

Brianna couldn't understand why or what Abraham saw in her. She was rather plain, but maybe that was attractive to him since he'd grown up around Amish women. Yvonne worked at a bookstore, which surely didn't produce much of an income. Brianna was having trouble understanding Abraham's attraction to the woman. Then again, Yvonne had had her talons ready to latch on to Abraham from the moment she arrived in Montgomery, and there was no telling what the woman had done behind the scenes to lure in Brianna's boyfriend.

Now, here she was on a Tuesday morning, four days before Christmas, alone. All thanks to Yvonne, a woman who portrayed herself to be good and wholesome while secretly plotting to steal another woman's man. Brianna shook all over when she thought about Abraham in Yvonne's arms. Brianna's good man was also gullible and had allowed himself to be drawn in by someone who obviously had no morals or good intentions.

She put the framed photo in her lap, then clenched her fists together until her nails dug into her flesh and drew blood, her palms spotting with crimson. Slowly, she lowered her hands to the picture of her and Abraham and smeared their happy faces red, wondering if he still displayed his framed photo of the two of them.

Abraham and Yvonne shouldn't be allowed to get away with hurting her this way. There had to be something she could do to win back her man. If she failed, then they would both need to be held accountable for the emotional damage they had inflicted on her.

But first she would be nice, the way a woman should be, something that came naturally to Brianna. Yvonne could learn a thing or two about being nice.

When she thought about Abraham spending time with that woman, she could barely breathe.

Yvonne shivered, despite being bundled up in her coat with gloves on and a knitted cap that Abraham insisted she wear out in the barn.

She eyed the project they'd been working on together since Sunday evening. Yvonne had gone to Abraham's house every day after work this week, and they'd spent part of Sunday together, mostly basking in front of the fireplace when they weren't working in the barn. She'd convinced him to take her small artificial Christmas tree for his house.

"Do you think Jake and Eva will like it?" Yvonne ran her hand over the keepsake box that she'd built under Abraham's instruction. It only needed one final coat of stain, but it should be ready by Christmas, which was in three days.

"I think they will love it," he said as he wrapped his arms around her from behind, kissing her on the cheek.

It would have come so naturally to say, "And I love you," but it was way too soon for that, even though her feelings had snuck up on her. But she refused to put Abraham in a situation where he had to choose—either her or the Amish. And she couldn't help but recall that Brianna had made Abraham uncomfortable with her early declaration of love. Yvonne didn't want to pressure him that way either.

Over the past few days, she'd settled into a routine. Even her dog had exhibited a calm demeanor, and although Blue barked occasionally, it wasn't the guttural growl he had exhibited before.

She'd told herself that she shouldn't see Abraham, that she should allow him the freedom to really choose what he believed his destiny was regarding his faith journey. But she hadn't cared about a man this much since Trevor, and she hadn't had the strength to force the issue. Abraham had said basically the same thing. Until the time came that he knew what his future held, she would enjoy the time they were spending together. Even though they could both be hurt in the end. They knew the risks, but the ball was mostly in Abraham's court.

"This has been fun." She turned around to face him, and he wasted no time covering his mouth with hers and holding her close.

"You're so beautiful," he said as he cupped her cheeks with his gloved hands.

Despite the frigid temperatures, Yvonne was warm on the inside. "*Danki*," she said, grinning.

"Learning a little more of the *Deitsch, ya?*" He tucked loose strands of hair under the black knitted cap he'd loaned her, insisting the hood of her coat wasn't warm enough. "*Mei mamm* made this for me." He raised an eyebrow.

"Ha." She chuckled. "You're going to have to give me something harder than that. You said, 'My mom made this for me.'"

"Hmm . . . harder, huh?" He clicked his tongue a couple of times. "Here's one for you: Blue *is ab im kopp.*"

She slapped him playfully on his good arm. "Hey, don't call my dog crazy."

"Very good." He laughed. "And Blue isn't crazy, just incredibly loyal to you." He breathed cold air as he spoke. "*Die Kelt iss farichderlich den winder.*"

"Ugh." She squeezed her eyes closed. "Too hard." Then she gasped. "Wait! Say it again."

Abraham repeated the phrase.

"Um, something about the cold and the winter."

He smiled broadly, kissed her, and said, "Pretty good. It means the cold weather is terrible this winter."

She leaned into the warmth of his coat with her teeth chattering. "And that's for sure. I can't believe it will get colder."

He turned the electric heater off, put an arm around her, and guided her out of the barn. "You haven't seen anything yet, Texas girl."

She laughed, then heard his phone buzzing in his pocket. "Do you need to get that?" she asked as they went up the porch steps to Abraham's house.

He held the door open for her. "No."

After they were inside, she continued. "Don't you even need to see who it is? What if it's an emergency?"

"I know who it is." He scowled as he helped her out of her coat.

It was much warmer in Abraham's house than hers. If she ended up buying her little farmhouse, that was the first thing she would do—add more insulation like Abraham said he did.

"It's Brianna," he admitted. "She's been calling every day."

As curious as she was, she didn't want to pry.

"I haven't called her back," he added before she could say anything. "And her messages are weird, like she thinks we're still together." He took off his coat, then his gloves. "Coffee?"

She considered the offer. "No, I better go. I stopped on

the way here to let Blue out, but I haven't fed him. And I won't do well driving at night if it starts to snow. I should probably make my exit while I can."

Abraham hung his coat and hat on the rack by the door. "Your leaving doesn't have anything to do with what I said about Brianna, does it?" His eyes held a pained expression.

She rubbed his arms, then leaned up and kissed him. "Absolutely not. But maybe you should call her back. She's bound to be hurting." Yvonne could still recall the torment she'd felt when a college boyfriend had broken up with her. It wasn't the type of pain she'd felt when Trevor died, but it was a powerful ailment at the time.

He eased the phone from his pocket. "She left another voice mail message, and she sent a text just now that says '911.'"

Yvonne brought a hand to her mouth. "Oh, no, Abraham. I should definitely go, then. You have to listen to the message." She took her coat from the couch and had one arm slipped in when Abraham reached for her other.

"No, don't go yet." He put the phone on speaker and played Brianna's voice mail.

"Abraham, I'm so sorry to call." Brianna was crying. "I fell and twisted my ankle. I'm pretty sure I need to go to the hospital, but I can barely walk, much less drive. I know we're not together the way we used to be, babe, but you're my only friend. Can you please call me?"

"See what I mean? Why is she still calling me 'babe'?" Abraham's irritation was obvious from the scowl on his face. "Why didn't she just call the actual 911 instead of texting me?"

Yvonne eased out of his grasp and finished putting her coat on. "You need to go help her."

"Why me?" he asked like a pouting little boy. It was kind of cute but also not very sympathetic.

"You heard her. You're her only friend." Despite her encouragement, Yvonne found it suspicious when adult women didn't have any other female friends. But she wouldn't judge. "Besides," she added. "Brianna did take care of you for several days after the accident."

Abraham rolled his eyes. "Yeah, she did. And that's a story for another day." He sighed. "I guess you're right, though."

A story for another day? She had no idea what that meant. Maybe he would elaborate at another time. "You go take care of Brianna. I'd already told you that I need to take care of Blue." She kissed him on the cheek. "No pouting."

"See you tomorrow?"

"Yes."

After he'd kissed her with all the passion she was getting used to, they said their goodbyes.

Abraham knocked three times on Brianna's door, and she yelled for him to come in. He was glad to see that the framed photo of them that had been on her hutch was gone. Hopefully, that was a sign that she was moving on. Although the multiple phone calls, still addressing him as "babe," and now this . . . It didn't feel like she was moving on.

After his eyes adjusted to the bold colors everywhere, he saw her on the couch with a tissue, dabbing at her eyes.

"What happened?" He stood above her, knowing that if he sat beside her, she'd find her way into his arms.

"I was using my little stepladder to get something from the top of the linen closet—more blankets, actually—and I slipped and fell."

Abraham frowned. "Why is it so cold in here?"

"The furnace stopped working." She shrugged, sniffling. "It hasn't been working since last night."

Abraham sighed. Brianna had a fireplace, but it was sparkling clean, and she refused to use it, said it made the house smell like ashes. Abraham loved the aroma of burning wood and the crackling sounds that went along with it.

"Let's take care of your foot first." He lifted up the ice pack she had placed atop her left foot. "It's pretty swollen . . ." He moved it around until she flinched. "Sorry. You've got a nasty sprain, but I don't think it's broken. If you keep ice on it, it will probably be much better in the morning."

"Are you sure?" She batted her eyes at him, but despite her tears, her lips were shiny, and there wasn't a hair out of place on her head. And her red blouse was unbuttoned enough for him to see her cleavage.

"Well, I'm not a hundred percent sure, but I don't think you need to go to the hospital. If it's worse tomorrow, you should be able to drive yourself to the hospital since it's your left foot."

She grunted. "Really, Abraham? Drive myself?" She dabbed at her eyes with the tissue.

He lowered his head, sighed, then looked back at her. "I have to work tomorrow, but if you really don't feel like you can drive yourself, call me."

Her bottom lip trembled as a tear rolled down her cheek. "You never answer when I call."

Still in his coat, Abraham finally sat down on the couch beside her, and as he had expected, her head found its way to his shoulder, and her arm across his waist, offering him a clear view down her shirt. He eased her away. "Do you want me to have a look at your furnace?"

"Only if you have time," she said as she looked away from him.

Abraham sighed again. "I have time."

He went down to the basement, glad to see that he just needed to flip a switch, and the furnace powered right up.

"The breaker must have tripped," he said when he was back in the living room. "So, I'm going to go." He pointed to her foot. "Keep ice on it—twenty minutes on, twenty minutes off."

"Maybe you could stay awhile?" She blinked back more tears.

"I can't, Brianna." He turned to go.

"Does this have anything to do with *Yvonne*?" She spat the words at him, and he spun around, not completely sure they had come from the same soft-spoken woman he knew. She sounded like another person, her voice louder but controlled.

"What?"

"Don't lie to me, Abraham. We've only been split up a week, as of today. I know you're seeing Yvonne. Someone saw you together and told me." She'd stopped crying, and some other, much less friendly, emotion had taken hold of her.

Abraham scratched his cheek as he took a big breath and tried to recall if he and Yvonne had been anywhere other than one of their houses, and he concluded they had not. No one could have seen them together. Brianna had to have driven by his house and seen Yvonne's car there. He could deny seeing Yvonne, but he didn't want any more lies. Brianna would know he wasn't telling the truth anyway. Maybe being honest with Brianna would help her to put their relationship behind her. It would sting, but ultimately it might help her move on.

"Yes, I have been spending time with Yvonne." He held up a hand when she started to say something. "And I'm sorry if that hurts you. I really am. But, Brianna, you and I are over, and you need to move on."

"A week is supposed to be long enough for me to move on?" Still no tears as she spoke in this unfamiliar voice with a blank expression on her face.

Abraham's stomach twisted into knots, and he just wanted to leave, but he believed himself not to be a heartless man. He sat in a chair to the left of the couch, rested his elbows on his knees, and held his head in his hands for a few seconds before he met her icy expression.

"Brianna, I can't control the way I feel."

She grinned. "So . . . everything you told me about possibly wanting to join the Amish again was a lie?"

He straightened. "No. I wasn't lying. That is still a possibility."

"And I suppose Yvonne will become your little Amish bride?" She tossed her head back and laughed before she stared at him. "Is that your fantasy, Abraham? Do you want some plain woman without any frills? Someone you can dress up in one of those baggy dresses?"

Without a word, he stood up and hurried to the door.

"Go ahead! Run, Abraham. That's what you do. You make people believe you love them, and then you run away!"

Abraham closed the door, resisting the urge to slam it, and went to his truck. As he pulled out of her driveway, he felt like all the blood in his body was rushing to his head, leaving him with a pounding migraine. He drove on, wondering if he could have done things differently with Brianna. He had never told her that he loved her, but he probably should have pulled out of the relationship earlier, when he realized her feelings ran deeper than his.

Brianna called his phone all the way to his house. When he stopped in his driveway, he listened to all four of her voice mails, each one a little more vicious than the last, hurling cuss words at him, including some that he'd only heard on television. After the last message, he blocked her number.

Yvonne wondered how it was going with Abraham as she and Blue enjoyed the warmth of her bedroom. Her electric heater had saved the day again. Which reminded her . . . She checked the weather on her phone and frowned. Only a 15 percent chance of any snow on Christmas Day. Eva had once told her that their weather changed as fast as the direction of the wind, which reminded her of Texas weather. She would hold out hope that she'd still have a white Christmas.

She dozed off to sleep with visions of her time with Abraham. He hadn't called her when he returned from Brianna's, but he knew she was usually asleep by ten. If Abraham had taken Brianna to the hospital, that was often a time-consuming process. They could still be there, but Yvonne didn't feel a tinge of jealousy. She was secure in her new relationship with Abraham. Her feelings for him were strong, considering they had been seeing each other such a short time, but it was as if they had been building up to this for over a year. She reminded herself again about the risk to both their hearts. If he felt called to go back to living as an Amish man, she would not try to block his decision. If anyone knew about spiritual callings, it was Yvonne. It was a personal choice between an individual and God.

She recalled something Abraham had said earlier about Brianna staying with him—how it was a story for another day. Maybe she would ask him about it. Or maybe not. He'd made the statement in a way that insinuated the "story" wasn't a happy one.

It was around two in the morning when Blue started to bark, taking his usual trek through the house from window to window, then door to door. Yvonne had to believe that he sensed animals outside, and she wasn't sure what to do about that, but she wasn't going to let him out and risk him taking off into the woods again. She had let him out a little before ten, so the cause of his upset didn't have anything to do with needing a potty break. Still, it caused her pulse to spike when he displayed this behavior, especially when it was accompanied by his throaty growl. It had happened the night before last too.

Eventually, Blue came back to bed, but it took a while before he was snoring again. Yvonne had trouble falling back asleep, too, but she was locked in tight with her own personal guard dog that wasn't going to let anyone in. Hopefully, the deer or other animals would tire of her place and move on.

The next morning, she woke up late. Again. But she was happy to see that it had snowed overnight. As the sun made its ascent over the horizon, her yard glistened white. She pulled on her robe and followed Blue to the door. Yawning, she pulled it open. Even as the dog darted down the steps, it was impossible not to notice the footsteps that came from the woods, went through her yard, and ended at her front door.

Her throat seized in her chest as she put a hand over her heart, hoping to calm her pulse. Sometime during the night, possibly when Blue was pacing, she'd had a visitor, and it wasn't an animal.

CHAPTER 16

Yvonne waited until she was at the bookstore before she called Abraham. She asked if Brianna was okay, and she listened as he told her every detail of their encounter.

"Wow," was all she knew to say. Brianna was a beautiful woman, but after listening to Abraham relay their conversation, it was hard to reconcile her outer beauty with what was inside.

"Let me just say that it was awful. I blocked her number."

Yvonne cringed. "That's a bit extreme, isn't it?"

"Maybe. But I don't want anything to do with her—or this version of her. And I think she will continue to pull the kind of stuff she did last night."

Yvonne was quiet. Despite the tone of Abraham's conversation with Brianna, Yvonne still felt sorry for her. But she had something else on her mind. "I have some news too." She took a deep breath. "Someone was at my house during the night. I'm not sure what time, but when I let Blue out this morning, I saw footsteps that led from the woods all the way up my porch steps and to my front door."

"What?" The alarm in his voice was evident.

"Yeah, I know. It creeped me out. All this time, I assumed Blue was getting worked up about other animals outside." She sat down on the stool behind the counter and stowed her purse out of sight. "But these were definitely human prints in the snow."

Abraham was quiet.

"Are you still there?" she finally asked.

"Yeah. I don't like this, Yvonne. You're out there all by yourself with no alarm system or any way to protect yourself." He paused. "Unless you have a gun?"

"No. I don't like guns. I wouldn't even know how to use one. Maybe it was just a random thing and won't happen again."

"Maybe. But I'm going to go out to your place and have a look around. I can go around lunchtime if you want me to let Blue out. It would save you a trip."

"You don't have a key, and even though Blue knows you, I'm not sure if he would give you any trouble without me there. I could just meet you there around noon. I really appreciate you offering to do this." She let out a nervous laugh. "Even though you might be tired of helping damsels in distress."

"Don't even compare this and what Brianna pulled last night."

"Well, I'm grateful, and I'll see you at noon."

Abraham hit End on his phone, then tapped a pencil against his desk. The day before yesterday when he'd gotten home from work, he'd had the strangest feeling that someone had been in his house. Nothing had been out of place—he didn't think—but something wasn't right. He'd blown it off when Yvonne showed up to work on the keepsake box, but now he was revisiting how he had felt at the time.

He had checked out all the rooms, and everything was just like he'd left it that morning. *But something was different.* As he mentally retraced his steps, he still couldn't think of anything.

He picked up the top file on his desk and tried to focus on the pending case in front of him, but he couldn't get rid of the niggling feeling that someone had been in his house. And now footsteps at Yvonne's house.

"Hey, Bruce, I need to take off for a while. Can you hold the fort for a couple of hours, maybe a little longer?"

"Sure." Bruce looked up from his own stack of files.

Abraham took his gun from his desk drawer and holstered it to his belt. He hadn't been wearing it since he'd been at a desk all day at work. The feel of it on his hip took him back to the night he and Will had shot each other—which reminded him that he had a deposition coming up for that case. Not something he was looking forward to.

He put on his coat and stepped out into the sunshine that was already melting the snow from the night before. There likely wouldn't be any tracks at all if he waited until noon to go to Yvonne's house. He'd go there first, check it out, then go to his house to have a look around, and meet Yvonne back at her house at noon.

Yvonne smiled when she saw Lizzie and Esther tethering their horse in the parking lot. The sisters were eccentric, especially Lizzie, but Yvonne could use a nice distraction right now.

"*Wie bischt*?" Esther said as they came into the bookstore. "I'm glad the weather is clearing up and the sun is melting the snow."

"Ugh," Lizzie said, scowling. "All that slush outside is worse."

Yvonne realized Abraham wouldn't be able to see any footprints in the snow at her house by noon. But she had seen them and was sure they were made by a person, not an animal.

"I love the snow since we never had much in Texas," she said, smiling. "But I agree that it's not so pretty when it turns to dirty slush."

Lizzie took off her coat, hung it on the rack by the door, then marched to the counter, and set her purse down. "So, I hear you are seeing Abraham Byler?"

Yvonne's eyes widened as she wondered how word had gotten out in such a short time, especially since she and Abraham had only spent time together at their homes.

"Don't look so shocked." Lizzie said as she grinned. "That's the way it is around here. People talk. Word gets out. Your car has been spotted at his house more than once." She leaned over the counter, motioning for Yvonne to come closer. "I also heard that Abraham might be thinking about rejoining the Amish," she whispered, even though Esther was the only other person in the store.

It was one thing for people to gossip about her and Abraham but entirely another when it came to Abraham's faith. She was pretty sure he hadn't intended for that to be circulating on the gossip loop. "Why do you say that?"

"I think it was Leroy's wife who told her sister-in-law, then she told our quilting group yesterday." Lizzie raised an eyebrow. "It's all a secret, though, about his possible baptism sometime in the future." She tapped a tiny finger to her chin, then sighed. "Now, we have a conundrum, don't we? I'm guessing you know about all this."

Yvonne opened her mouth to try to come up with something to say, but Esther arrived at her sister's side.

"Leave the poor girl alone, Lizzie." Lizzie's sister placed a book about gardening on the counter but then smiled at Yvonne as if she was also waiting for more details.

"A conundrum?" Yvonne said.

"Of course." Lizzie narrowed her eyebrows at Yvonne. "If Abraham chooses our way of life, then what happens to his romance with you?"

"I'm not sure you'd call it a romance. We haven't been seeing each other for long at all." Yvonne was aware of the point Lizzie was making. "So, it's probably a bit premature to speculate about things."

"What happened with that fancy lady he was dating? Brianna? He must have kicked her to the curb and taken up with you pretty quick." Lizzie shifted her dentures around in her mouth. "I didn't much care for Brianna. Abraham may have left the Amish, but he's still a moral man living a fairly simple life, if you don't include recent events that involved guns and shootings. Anyway, he didn't seem to mesh with that woman." She pointed at Yvonne. "You're a much better fit." Sighing, she shook her head. "But your situation is complicated."

"Lizzie, stop." Esther tapped her hand on the gardening book, pulling Yvonne's attention. "I'll take this, then get Lizzie out of here so she will stop grilling you."

Yvonne knew she was in a situation that could cause a lot of heartache down the line but cared enough about Abraham that the risk felt worth it. She just hadn't thought much about how it might affect the rest of the Amish community.

After Yvonne had given Esther her change for the book, Lizzie smiled broadly at Yvonne. "I'm available any time you need to talk. I'm a bit of an expert when it comes to matters of the heart." She pressed her palms together. "In the meantime, I'll be praying for you." She grinned and allowed her sister to escort her out, winking just before they left, which caused Yvonne to wonder exactly what Lizzie would be praying for.

Abraham arrived at Yvonne's house, glad he'd come earlier than planned. The footprints in the snow were fading fast, but it was easy enough to see they were human. He squatted down in the melting snow near the woods, where the imprints lay in the shadows of the trees and hadn't lost shape yet. The prints had the markings of running shoes, and his chest tightened as he speculated. He couldn't be sure, but the footprints were small, and at first glance, Abraham thought they might have been left by a woman. He snapped a few pictures with his phone to blow up later.

Blue was going crazy inside Yvonne's house, but Abraham was going to stick to the plan and meet her back here at noon.

He exceeded the speed limit all the way to his house, and a few minutes later, he was inside his home walking room to room. He checked every window in his house and was a little surprised to find the window in the bathroom unlocked. It was a small window above the bathtub, but it would provide access to the house if a petite person wanted to get in. No one had a key to his house, so if anyone had been inside, they would have had to come in through that window.

Abraham stepped into the tub and locked the window. He didn't have much worth stealing. Why would someone come into the house just to look around? His stomach got queasy when he thought of the lengths Brianna had gone to the night before to get him to come to her house. She was small enough that, with effort, she could fit through his bathroom window. But why? And why had she removed his SIM card and hid it underneath his bath mat?

To have me all to herself while she was here. The sick feeling continued to build as he worried Brianna might try to seek some type of revenge for him breaking up with her. That seemed extreme, but he picked up his iPad from the coffee table and powered it up. Then he went to a site he frequently used to run background checks.

How much did he really know about Brianna? She was thirty-four years old. She'd had a bad breakup with a boyfriend who cheated on her. She didn't get along with her family, nor did she have any relatives she stayed in contact with. Brianna had spent Thanksgiving with friends, but she'd never mentioned any of those people following the holiday, only saying she'd had a nice time but would have rather been with him. That was about all he knew about her.

Until now. Her picture popped up when he typed in her information to see if she had a record. And she did. Abraham took a deep breath as his heart pounded, but relief washed over him when he saw that she only had a couple of speeding tickets. It was a short-lived reprieve, though, as he kept scrolling her file, his breath becoming labored when he read that a man named Mitch Hadley had filed a restraining order against Brianna. Abraham thought back to when he and Brianna had first dated, and he recalled her mentioning her ex, Mitch.

What had Brianna done that warranted a restraining order?

Brianna had been up half the night after repeatedly calling Abraham's phone. She suspected he'd blocked her number since she'd received repeated messages telling her, "This caller isn't available." It sounded like the same message she'd received when she learned Mitch had blocked her calls. But on the off chance that Abraham was just out of range—along

227

with an adrenaline rush she couldn't control—she hadn't been able to stop herself.

How dare Abraham humiliate her this way? It was clear that he must have been seeing Yvonne even before he broke up with her, and his explanation about possibly becoming Amish was merely a way to try to spare her feelings, at least in the beginning. Last night, he'd come clean. Abraham Byler wasn't just responsible for her broken heart but also for the enormous dark circles she had under her eyes today.

She rubbed more cover-up onto her finger and applied it beneath her swollen eyelids. Then she picked out a tight pair of blue jeans that hugged her hips in just the right way. After she'd chosen a dark-blue sweater—also snug enough to show off her assets—she put in earrings and slipped into a pair of black boots. The stiletto heels weren't a practical option, but since she'd just faked her fall the night before, her feet slid easily into the shoes. She'd only had to kick her wall a few times right before Abraham arrived to cause it to swell. It hadn't been pleasant, but all the puffiness had been gone by this morning.

Dressed in her power clothes, she was going to pay Abraham a visit at his office, where she would humiliate him the way he had done to her. Except she would do it publicly.

After carefully trudging through melted snow, she made it to her car, trembling with rage by the time she started the engine.

How could he do this to me?

Yvonne hung the sign on the door that read she would return at 2:00 p.m. Tomorrow was Christmas Eve, and there had been a rush of shoppers early but no one in the past hour. Yvonne was sure Jake wouldn't care if she took an extra-long lunch, but she hoped she didn't miss any last-minute patrons. A chance she would have to take.

When she pulled up at her house, Abraham's patrol car was in the driveway. He had been sitting in a chair on her porch but rose when she pulled in. Yvonne could hear Blue barking before she even got out of the car.

"I was tempted to let him out, so I checked the back door to see if it was locked. It was, and that's good," Abraham said when he met her in the yard with a kiss. "But I also thought about what you said, and yeah . . . I wasn't completely convinced he wouldn't maul me before you got here."

Yvonne appreciated him, the kiss, and her loving watch-dog, but as she stared at the mush beneath their feet, her stomach sank. "All the footprints are gone."

"Don't worry. I came here earlier today. I started to worry that the prints would be gone by noon." He pointed to the edge of her yard where the trees hung over the property line. "It was still shady over there, and the sun hadn't melted the imprints. I got plenty of pictures, and you were right. These are definitely footprints from a person, not an animal." He nodded toward the door. "Do you need to let Blue out? He's going nuts, but I'm sure it's mostly because he senses I'm out here."

"Yeah. I'll let him out." Discouraged, she hung her head as she walked to the door, Abraham following her.

Even though she was out in the country by herself, she'd thought she would be safe here. Montgomery was a small town with a close-knit community. She'd never been scared. Until now.

Blue met Yvonne just inside the house while Abraham was wise enough to stay on the porch holding a small bone he had pulled from his pocket. After growling, her dog moved slowly to Abraham, sniffed his legs, then took the bone before hurrying off to do his business.

"Hey." Abraham lifted her chin. "There's something else I need to tell you too." Yvonne could tell by the forlorn expression on his face that this wasn't going to be good news. "I think these prints were made by a woman."

Yvonne swallowed hard. There was only one woman who might despise her enough to stalk her.

"And I also think someone was in my house. I don't have anything concrete to base that on. It was just a hunch, a weird feeling I had the other day. After I came here to take pictures of the footprints, I went to my house and checked every window. No one has a key to my house. But the window over the bathtub was unlocked."

Yvonne pressed her lips together, her heart racing. She hated to ask, but she had to know. "Could Brianna fit through that window?"

He nodded. "Yeah. And I decided to run a background check on her. Her last boyfriend had to take out a restraining order against her."

A knot was building in her throat. "Um . . . I just can't imagine her coming to my house or breaking into yours. Can you?"

He shrugged. "It was the first thought that came to your mind, wasn't it?"

She nodded. "Sadly, yes." Squeezing her eyes closed before she locked eyes with him, she said, "Maybe you shouldn't have blocked her number. Maybe that pushed her over the edge?"

"It doesn't matter. I won't have her scaring you. If she came here last night, it would have been late." He lifted both eyebrows. "Doesn't sound like a sprained foot to me. It was a little swollen, but she definitely exaggerated her injury." He sighed. "There are some other things about Brianna that came to light too. Things that make me think she's a bit off-balance."

Yvonne wondered if this was the story for another day he had mentioned. She was unsure how much she wanted to hear.

"She actually took the SIM card out of my phone during the time she was staying with me. It was like . . . she wanted me all to herself, completely cut off from the outside world."

"Wow . . . That's pretty extreme." Yvonne recognized that she had led a sheltered life. She'd never been involved with the law, gotten into any trouble, and certainly never been stalked or had a break-in. Trevor's death had been by far the most traumatic thing that had ever happened to her. She didn't remember much about her parents' accident and subsequent deaths. But the scenario Abraham was implying caused her stomach to swirl with unwelcome anxiety. "What now?" she finally asked.

"I'll talk to her. I'm sure I can be convincing enough to make her back off. She's just responding to the initial hurt of the breakup. Ultimately, I don't see her as a dangerous person."

"I hope not," Yvonne said softly as she sat in one of the chairs on her porch, Blue rushing to stand in front her. "She's definitely in love with you, and yes, a breakup is painful, but this is all very unsettling." She glanced at Abraham when he sat down in the other chair.

"She won't have trouble finding someone else, but holding on to a man will be her challenge. Brianna is obviously super possessive and overbearing. I think that probably scares a lot of men off. It did me, even though there were underlying issues that made me want to be a free man." He smiled at her, but Yvonne was still reeling from the possibility that Brianna had been at her house sometime during the night.

Her thoughts skipped back to earlier. "Lizzie and Esther were in the bookstore this morning."

Abraham chuckled, which was nice to hear considering the news he'd shared. "I'm sure they provided some much-needed entertainment, especially Lizzie."

"I don't know about entertainment, but she was full of news. Apparently, word has gotten out during the week that we are seeing each other. Lizzie said my car had been spotted at your house."

He sighed. "Probably so, but there's no telling. My folks know that I'm not seeing Brianna. I didn't mention that we were seeing each other, but they do know that I was helping you with a gift for Jake and Eva's baby. Maybe Eva said something about us?"

"Maybe." Yvonne rubbed her forehead. "Lizzie also said

that she'd heard that you might be going back to the Amish and what a conundrum that caused for you and me." She grinned. "And, yes, that's the word Lizzie used—*conundrum*."

Abraham was quiet. "I probably shouldn't have said anything to Leroy. *Mei bruder* probably shared with his *fraa*, and from there . . ." He sighed. "Either way, I've put you in a bad spot. Maybe I shouldn't have told you that I was considering it, but I wanted to be totally honest with you."

She shook her head, noticing again his use of his native dialect. "I'm giving this to God, Abraham. Something I learned to do after I went through Trevor's death and my own faith journey."

Abraham put his elbows on his knees and rested his head in his hands. He didn't say anything. His thoughts about where to take his life had to be weighing heavily on him.

He stood up when his phone rang in his pocket, took the call, then actually stomped a foot against her wooden porch as he ended the conversation. "I can't believe this. I gotta go." He started down her porch steps, then turned around, walked briskly back, and kissed her. "That was Bruce. Brianna just pulled into the parking lot at the station." He shook his head as he took the porch steps two at a time on the way back to his patrol car. "Bruce doesn't really know anything, just that we broke up. But I don't trust that woman."

Yvonne stood up and watched him leave.

Neither do I.

CHAPTER 17

Brianna took several deep breaths in her car after she arrived at the police station. She didn't know what Abraham might have told the other officers about their split, but somehow she needed to keep her dignity intact. She pulled down her visor, touched up her lipstick, then stepped out of the car. With careful steps, she walked to the door.

She'd only been inside the station one other time. It was a small space that usually housed four officers. Today, the new guy, whom she'd met once and had suggested Abraham set up with Yvonne, was the only one present. As much as she wanted to rip Abraham's head from his shoulders, perhaps another opportunity had presented itself.

"Hi, is it Officer Morrow?" she asked politely as the door closed behind her.

"Yeah. Bruce Morrow. We met once before. Brianna, right?" He sat taller, and Brianna realized she'd been so taken with Abraham at the time that she hadn't noticed what a handsome man Officer Morrow was. He was neatly groomed, like Abraham, with a short haircut parted to one side. But unlike Abraham, Bruce had light hair, a leftover summer tan, and a smile that almost caused her to forget why she'd made this trip.

"Yes, I'm Brianna Stone." She looked down at her black boots, took a breath, then blinked her eyes at Officer Morrow, feigning tears. "You met me as Abraham's girl-friend, but we've since broken up."

He slowly stood. Brianna liked that he was tall like Abraham. He motioned for her to sit at the empty chair across from his desk.

"Thank you." She sat, then crossed one leg over the other. "I came to speak with Abraham, but I see that he must not be here." *Unless he's in the bathroom.*

"No. He had to step out." He paused, leaned back in his chair. "Uh, are you here on personal business with Abraham, or is there anything I can help you with?"

Brianna studied him for a few seconds. Officer Morrow found her attractive. She could see it in the dreamy, very un-cop sort of way that he was looking at her. She waved a dismissive hand. "Oh, I guess it was personal but also not important." *And growing less important by the moment.* "So, tell me . . . I know you haven't been here long. How are you enjoying living in Montgomery? And the job?"

"I like it." He grinned in a very boyish way that sent Brianna's senses racing. "But there's not a lot to do on my off-hours. I came here from Indianapolis, and I thought I'd love small-town living, and for the most part I do. But . . . not a lot of social opportunities."

Brianna laughed. "I totally understand. I was in a similar situation before I met Abraham." She needed to be careful since she wasn't sure exactly what Abraham might have told Bruce. "Abraham had the courage to do what I didn't, by breaking things off. It was such a relief, really. We just weren't right for each other." She paused, having captured Bruce's mesmerizing green eyes. "I think maybe it's because he used to be Amish, and I'm a city girl. He just sees things differently than I do. But even though I'm from the city, I craved something a little slower." In truth, she'd left when things became so explosive between her and Mitch. She'd literally closed her eyes, put a pin on a map, and Montgomery was where the pin had landed. She rolled her eyes. "But you are so right about there not being a lot of social opportunities, especially for single people." She suspected Bruce was around her age, early to midthirties.

He flashed that boyish grin at her again. "Well, I'm glad to hear that your breakup with Abraham was mutual. When I heard, my first thought was how much I'd like to take you out, but I figured it was too soon."

Brianna smiled, batted her eyes at him. "Not at all. As a matter of fact, if you asked me out right now, I'd accept the invitation."

His eyebrows lifted. "Really?" He rubbed his chin. "Tomorrow is Christmas Eve, and my mom will lose it if I don't go home to Indianapolis, spend the night, and have Christmas with the family." He stared at her. "This might be a longshot, but since you and Abraham broke up, I'm going to go for it. Do you have any plans for New Year's Eve?"

Brianna folded her hands in her lap, atop her Louis Vuitton purse. "No, I don't have any plans to ring in the new year." This visit was shaping up better than she could have hoped for, even though she still wanted to punch Abraham square in the mouth.

"I need a little time to figure out a nice plan for that night, but if you'd be willing to reserve that time slot for me, I promise to try to wow you." He couldn't seem to wipe the smile off his face.

Brianna nodded. "Then it's a date." The next two days would be horrible, alone on Christmas, but she'd have New Year's Eve to look forward to.

How life can turn on a dime.

They'd settled into small talk when Abraham came rushing through the door, his face red and eyes ablaze with what appeared to be rage. She needed to temper his mood right away before Abraham embarrassed her in front of Bruce.

"Hello." She stood, walked right toward him, and reached into her purse. "You left a few small things at my house that I wanted to return."

His face was still red, but his eyes softened, if only a little. She handed him a small brown bag she had stuffed into her purse. It had been her excuse to see him, but now it was more of a way to say farewell. "It's just a pair of cuff links from when we went to that really nice restaurant in Bloomington." She lowered her voice. "And you left a toothbrush and some other odds and ends." He'd never stayed overnight, but he had left a few things there.

He set the bag on his desk. "Thanks. Now, can I talk to you outside for a minute?"

"Sure, of course," she said in her sweetest voice. "Just give me a minute." Brianna walked to where Bruce was sitting, leaned down, and wrote her phone number on a blank piece of paper on his desk. "Here's my number. I'll be looking forward to New Year's Eve."

Bruce glanced at Abraham and quickly back at her. "Yeah, great. Me too."

Brianna smiled, then marched past Abraham and out the door. He was quickly on her heels.

After they were outside the building, Abraham folded his arms across his chest, then nodded to Brianna's boots. "I see your foot is better."

She chuckled, which cause a shiver of irritation to travel up his spine. "Oh, yes." She waved a hand. "I did what you said, twenty minutes on with the ice and twenty minutes off. The swelling was gone by this morning." She shifted her weight as she grimaced. "I also want to apologize about my behavior last night. Obviously, I was hurt when I found out that you were seeing Yvonne so suddenly after we broke up. But you're right. We aren't suited for each other, and it was for the best."

Abraham wanted to laugh, but if it took a Bruce to get Brianna off his back, then he was willing to stifle his amusement. He wished it wasn't his coworker, but maybe they'd be perfect for each other. Either way, he had to confront her about the footprints at Yvonne's house. He couldn't prove that anyone had stepped foot in his home since nothing was out of place, despite his gut feeling someone had been in the house.

"Well, I'm glad to hear that you realize we weren't the best match." He couldn't help himself. "And you decided this in less than twenty-four hours?"

She shrugged. "Yes, I guess you could say I did. I thought about all the things I didn't like about our relationship, and that took the sting out of the breakup." She flashed him a snarky smile.

"Well, that's great to hear, but I need to ask you something." Abraham was sure she would deny being at Yvonne's house, but he wanted her to know that he was aware of her antics. "I know you were at Yvonne's house sometime during the night. I'm not sure what for, but it's dangerous to go over there unannounced because she has an aggressive dog. I mean, not really hostile to everyone, but he is not friendly to people he doesn't know."

She squinted her eyes at him, frowning. "Why in the world would I go to Yvonne's house in the middle of the night when it's snowing?" She mirrored his stance and folded her arms across her chest.

"I have no idea. I was hoping you could tell me. It scared Yvonne when she got up and saw footprints across her yard and up to the front door."

She grunted. It wasn't very ladylike and reminded him of her behavior the night before. "Well, isn't that sweet how protective you are of your new girlfriend. But I assure you that I was not at her house last night." She eyed him up and down as if she were totally disgusted with him. "Go live your life with someone more suited to you." She heaved her oversize purse up on her shoulder. "I have to find something to wear for my date—someone I'm quite sure *I'm* more suited for."

She spun around on her spike heels and went to her car.

Abraham walked back into the station, eyed the small paper bag on his desk, then shook his head before he looked at Bruce. "I sure hope you know what you're doing." He hadn't told Bruce anything, except that he and Brianna had broken up. A better person would have warned him off, but Abraham suspected Brianna would show her true self to his fellow officer soon enough.

"What do you mean? The woman is gorgeous. I'm not sure why you let her get away." Bruce paused, frowning. "Hey, man . . . If you don't want me going out with her, or you still have feelings for her, just say the word, and I'll cancel for New Year's Eve. We just both kind of found ourselves without anything to do."

Abraham was a little surprised that Bruce didn't already have New Year's Eve plans lined up. From the little he knew about his new coworker, the guy played the field. He often went to Indianapolis, where his parents lived, on his days and nights off. More than once, he'd talked about different women he'd gone out with.

"She's just . . . a handful." Abraham sat down at his desk.

Bruce grinned. "A beautiful handful that I'll happily take off your hands if you're sure you don't have a problem with it."

Again, Abraham considered telling Bruce a little bit

more about Brianna. He decided against it. Just because a person was wrong for him—or Mitch, apparently—didn't mean she couldn't be perfect for Bruce. Why taint the relationship before it started? In truth, he was just happy to have Brianna out of his life. He'd have to bump into her if Bruce continued to see her—which Abraham doubted—but she would be Bruce's problem now. And he wouldn't have to worry about her stalking him or Yvonne. At least, he hoped not.

After Yvonne got back to the bookstore, she had a string of customers in search of last-minute Christmas gifts. It wasn't snowing, so shoppers had stepped out. She hoped she hadn't missed too many customers while she was gone. Only one woman had expressed irritation that she'd come by earlier only to find the store closed. Yvonne apologized, and after offering the woman 10 percent off her purchase, all seemed fine.

After everyone had cleared out, she stared out the window at the slushy white mess on the ground. If the forecast was correct, it wasn't looking good for her white Christmas.

Tomorrow she would spend Christmas Eve wrapping presents to take to Jake and Eva's house on Christmas Day, and even though Eva said her mother and mother-in-law had the meal covered, she wanted to cook something to bring. She wouldn't be seeing Abraham until after she returned from Jake and Eva's on Christmas Day. They planned to spend that evening together.

Everything about Abraham felt so right, but it was indeed complex, even outside of the faith issue. It had gotten more complicated if Brianna was secretly going to hers and Abraham's houses. She was deep in thought about it when Abraham called.

"You're kidding?" she said after Abraham detailed his time with Brianna at the station.

"Yeah, it was weird. It was like she was totally fine with our breakup and ready to move on with Bruce. Overnight, she was all better."

Yvonne wanted to believe Brianna had been truthful, but she had her doubts. "Do you believe her?"

Abraham sighed. "In the spirit of the season, I'm going to choose to believe her. Mostly, I just want to enjoy my time with you."

"Me too."

After they hung up, Yvonne continued to go over Abraham's conversation with Brianna. Maybe the woman was just incredibly fickle and had quickly latched on to someone else. Or maybe she was trying to make Abraham jealous?

Either way, Yvonne was going to embrace the Christmas spirit, too, and force any worries about Brianna to the back of her mind.

It was right after she made that decision that Brianna walked into the bookstore.

CHAPTER 18

Brianna had lost Abraham, but fate had rained down on her and given her a new suitor. She didn't want a bad reputation here in Montgomery to blow this new opportunity. Nor did she want to have to relocate. She couldn't have Abraham and Yvonne running around telling people she was a stalker. This part of Indiana might not offer a lot of social options, but there was a quaintness she had enjoyed when she and Abraham were dating.

Referring to their relationship in past tense still felt odd.

The color in Yvonne's face drained with each step Brianna took toward her.

"What can I do for you, Brianna?" Yvonne sat on a stool behind the counter, her hands palms down on the countertop, her lips pressed together.

Brianna sighed. "Don't look so terrified." When she reached the counter, she heaved her purse up on her shoulder. "Abraham told me that you both think I was at your house, at night, when it was snowing." She shrugged, scowling. "I don't understand why you would think that. Do you think I went there to somehow harm you, to pay you back for snatching Abraham away from me?"

She reminded herself of the reason she was there. To make peace, not cause more trouble for herself. She recalled what she had told Bruce. "Abraham just did what I didn't have the strength to do. We weren't right for each other. But anytime there is a breakup, it's still painful." She lowered her head, blinked her eyes for effect, then looked back at Yvonne. "I'm afraid I acted badly last night, and I feel terrible about it. I've apologized to Abraham, and the reason I'm here is just to let you know there are no hard feelings. We live in a small town." She shrugged. "So, I hope we can be friends. I'm actually going out with Abraham's co-worker Bruce for New Year's." She chuckled. "I don't see any double dating in our future, but our boys work together, so I'm sure we'll bump into each other."

Our boys? Yvonne was seldom speechless, but Brianna seemed six kinds of crazy. She hadn't even gone out with Bruce, but he was already her "boy"? Yvonne didn't believe for one moment that Brianna hadn't been to her house, whatever the woman's reason was. But if her ex had to have a restraining order, and she'd taken Abraham's SIM card from his phone and exhibited such bizarre behavior, there must be at least a small level of danger mixed in with the madness. After Yvonne's thoughts went full circle, she thought it best to just play nice with Brianna and hope that she and Bruce would live happily ever after and not bother her and Abraham. Although she disliked the fact that Bruce worked with Abraham.

"I appreciate you coming by, Brianna." She couldn't tell the woman she wanted to be friends. That would be a far worse lie than she'd just told. "No hard feelings on my end."

Brianna smiled, looking gorgeous, but now that Yvonne had seen what was on the inside, her striking appearance had lost some of its luster.

"Wonderful." Brianna clasped her hands together, still smiling. "Now that we have that settled, I hope that you and Abraham have a very merry Christmas." She chuckled. "And, of course, a happy new year. I think mine will be starting off with a bang." After a quick dismissive wave, she pivoted, then sashayed her way to the door, glancing over her shoulder before she left. "Bye, now."

A cold chill ran the length of Yvonne's spine, and it wasn't just from the burst of air that had swooshed inside when Brianna swung the door wide. She couldn't help but wonder if she would be looking over her shoulder all the time.

Abraham had an uneasy feeling after Yvonne told him about Brianna's visit to the bookstore, but they had both agreed to give her the benefit of the doubt.

It was Christmas Eve, and Abraham had missed not seeing Yvonne the night before. He wouldn't see her again until tomorrow at her house, either, after his family's holiday celebration. He had considered inviting her for Christmas with his family, but they'd technically been seeing each other barely over a week. His family wouldn't understand him seeing someone else so quickly. Even more so, a woman he felt comfortable enough to introduce to his family in such a short time.

Strangely enough, he would have been okay introducing Yvonne to those he loved under different circumstances and when the time was right. As of now, though, he didn't know if there would be a good time. What if he brought her around his family, then ended up choosing to be baptized into the faith? That would mean that he and Yvonne could only be friends and that not only he but his family would have to adjust to how she fit into their lives—or not.

The thought caused his chest to burn. He didn't think he could live without Yvonne, which was ironic since he'd thought Brianna was moving much too quickly after they'd been dating for only three months. But Yvonne had always been in the shadows of his heart, ever since the day he'd met her over a year ago. Equally confusing, he felt called to return to his Amish roots. There was no good end to his situation. A conundrum, as Lizzie had told Yvonne.

He recalled what Yvonne said, that she was leaving it to God. Abraham needed to do that as well. For now, he would enjoy the holiday with her. He was thankful his chief and another coworker had offered to cover the department during the Christmas break. He had several days of uninterrupted time with Yvonne and family to look forward to.

Yvonne made a ham-and-cheese sandwich for dinner Christmas Eve and gifted Blue with one also. They'd enjoyed the warmth of the crackling fire, the ambiance of her beautiful Christmas tree, and watched Hallmark movies after Yvonne finished wrapping gifts. She'd also made a blueberry cobbler to take to Eva and Jake's for Christmas day. It wouldn't hold up to the lavish desserts the Amish women made, but she didn't want to show up empty-handed.

It was still early, not quite eight o'clock yet, but the temperatures were dropping, and her living room was getting chilly even with a fire going.

"Blue, let's go to bed." She poked at the fire until the orange embers glowed with barely a flame left, then Blue followed her into her bedroom, prewarmed by her electric heater.

After Blue took his lounging position atop the covers, Yvonne snuggled into her blankets and comforter, then checked the weather on her phone. An 18 percent chance of snow for the following day didn't sound hopeful.

An hour later, she was a third of the way through a Christmas book she'd chosen just for tonight, when Abraham called.

"Merry Christmas Eve," she said when she answered.

"And the same to you. I'm guessing you're all snuggled in with Blue and with your electric heater running in your bedroom." He chuckled.

"You know me so well." Yvonne yawned. He really didn't

know her that well at all, and vice versa. She didn't know his favorite color, the best day he'd ever had, or his favorite food . . . but in a weird, unexplainable way, she felt like she'd known him forever. Even though he was incredibly easy to talk to, her stomach still fluttered at the sound of his voice.

"Well, I'm hoping to get to know you even better."

Maybe he'd had the same thoughts Yvonne had.

"Have you looked outside?" He spoke through a yawn.

"No. Why?" She placed her bookmark between the pages to hold her place, then sat up.

"I'll give you a hint. Something white is falling from the sky."

"No! Really?" She threw back the covers and rushed to the window. Blue startled for a moment but was soon snoring again. She peeled back the curtain and blinked her eyes into focus at the dusting of white glistening in the moonlight. "Aw. It's snowing."

"It probably won't last, but I wanted you to see it. It's not supposed to accumulate." He laughed. "It wasn't even supposed to snow."

She kept her face close to the window and smiled. "But it is."

He yawned again. "Sorry. I helped Leroy work outside most of the day—and by the way, he apologized for letting the word get out that I was thinking of being baptized. Then *mei mudder* had me setting up a table in the living room for the *kinner* to eat, and other odd jobs, getting ready for tomorrow."

Yvonne wondered again if he heard the Pennsylvania *Deitsch* in his conversation. She wasn't sure if it was her imagination or if he was using the dialect more and more. She placed a palm on the window and leaned even closer. "Shoot. The snow is stopping."

"I was afraid of that. I'm glad I called. And I also wanted you to know that I'm looking forward to seeing you tomorrow night."

She eased away from the window, watched as the snow stopped, then walked back to bed. "I'm looking forward to tomorrow night also." Pulling the covers back, she resumed her position beneath the warm comforter.

He was quiet for a while before he said, "You do know that I would *lieb* for you to meet *mei* family. I just . . ."

She picked up on more of his native dialect. "No explanation necessary. It's much too soon after you and Brianna split up." A part of Yvonne wondered if there would ever be a formal introduction. Abraham might decide that he wanted the Amish way of life long before they met a suitable time frame. She could understand that. Even more so, the spiritual journey and tug-of-war that accompanied those type of faith overhauls.

"What are you doing?" he asked out of nowhere.

"I was reading a book before you called. Blue is snoring." She reached over and scratched behind the dog's ears. He stretched and moaned.

"I'll let you get back to reading, and I'll see you later tomorrow afternoon." She heard regret in his voice. Yvonne felt it, too, wishing they could spend all of Christmas Day together. But she'd told Eva and Jake right after she had arrived in Montgomery that she would spend Christmas with them. And Abraham needed to spend it with his family.

After they'd ended the call, she wondered if he had gotten her a present. It didn't matter either way, but she didn't want him to feel weird that she had gotten something for him.

She tried to focus on her book, but her eyes were heavy, and Blue's snoring was lulling her to sleep . . .

It was around three in the morning when Blue started to bark, jumping right into his routine—pacing from window to window, then to the front door and the one in the back of the house. Yvonne's heart pounded in her chest as she pulled the covers up to her chin. It was one thing when she'd thought animals were outside. Now she knew differently. And when Blue stood at the front door growling and barking as if his life depended on it, Yvonne's bottom lip quivered, her heart still pounding in her chest. She hated guns, but she had no way to defend herself from an intruder. Only her dog.

Why is Brianna doing this? Maybe she was trying to scare Yvonne out of her house, even out of town. It didn't make sense. A part of her wanted to yank open the front door and yell, "Brianna, just come out and show yourself!"

Blue eventually stopped barking and growling, but he didn't come back to bed, nor did he go to his bed by the smoldering fire. He lay just inside the front door in his prayer position, like he'd done when she had first let him in the house.

Yvonne couldn't move, and her heart raced too much for her to go back asleep. She waited until daylight before, yawning and exhausted, she shuffled to the door. Blue was standing, wagging his tail and ready to go out.

As she put her hand on the doorknob, she feared what she might see. There wouldn't be snow on the ground, so she wouldn't see any footsteps. Would she see other evidence that someone had been at her house?

She slowly unlocked the door and pulled it open. Blue rushed out, bolted down the steps, and went to the far end of the yard near the woods. Yvonne stood shivering just inside the door, peering outside as the sun continued to rise. She'd considered calling Abraham at three when Blue started barking, and she thought about it again now. But he would rush over to her house and mess up his Christmas.

She hadn't been hurt. It could have been animals this time. But deep in her gut, she was sure Brianna had been outside her house again.

Brianna woke up Christmas morning face down on her bed, wearing the same blue jeans and black sweater that she'd had on all day long Christmas Eve. Her head spun, and she had the urge to vomit, but it was her throbbing ankle that held most of her attention. She forced herself to roll over, put a hand over her eyes, and groaned. When she finally sat up, she peeled off her sock and lifted her foot, which looked like it belonged to an elephant.

She swung her legs over the side of the bed, but when she tried to put pressure on her right foot, unbearable pain shot up her leg and caused her to cry out. This was a real injury, and it wasn't her left foot. She couldn't even drive herself to an urgent-care facility or hospital. And she couldn't call

Abraham. She needed everyone to believe that she was truly over him, which might become a reality if Bruce could hold her interest. He was handsome enough to have the potential to do so, and she loved a man in uniform. Regardless, she couldn't ask him for help either. She didn't have his number and wouldn't have called him on Christmas Day anyway. She wasn't going to start off this relationship by being needy, even though she certainly needed some help.

When her head started spinning, she lay back down and put an arm across her forehead, closing her eyes as she recalled the events of the night before. She'd poured her first glass of wine around four o'clock, feeling sorry for herself that she was alone on Christmas Eve. By eight she'd had no business driving, but she recalled taking her car on the back roads, mostly looking for a store that was open to buy more wine.

After her unsuccessful outing, she'd come home and found a bottle of vodka. Her head was still spinning, and things were still fuzzy, but she remembered tripping on the rug in the entryway and going down on the white tile floor, her foot twisting as she went down.

She wiggled around in bed but didn't feel sore anywhere else. Eventually, she eased out of her clothes and took inspection, and beyond her swollen foot, she appeared to be unscathed—except for her dignity. Thank goodness no one had seen her drunken display. She enjoyed wine in the evenings, but she'd crossed her consumption threshold much too early into the evening and should have never ventured out.

She covered her face with her hands and sobbed. It was Christmas Day, and she didn't have one single person she could call. Her foot was throbbing. Her head was pounding. Her stomach swooshed and gurgled so badly she hoped she didn't throw up in her bed.

There wouldn't be any turkey and dressing or ham, no gift exchanges . . . nothing.

How did I get here, so alone and unwanted?

Yvonne was the queen of ugly Christmas sweaters, but she chose a dark-blue blouse to wear with her jeans and boots with no heels. Everyone at Eva and Jake's house would be dressed in their usual attire, and Yvonne would stick out wearing a bright red-and-green sweater. Today, she just wanted to blend and observe. She'd never celebrated the holidays in an Amish home, and even though she was looking forward to being with Eva and Jake, she was also eager to take in the traditions of the day. But first things first.

"Come here, Blue." She squatted down and patted her knee. The dog cozied up to her, then licked her face. Yvonne had chosen to forego makeup today, too, since no one else would be wearing any. She handed Blue a shoebox she'd wrapped in silver paper and placed a gold bow on top. "This is for you."

Her furry roommate tipped his head to one side.

Yvonne yawned, something she'd probably be doing all day. She shook her head, feeling silly that she'd wrapped Blue's gift. "Let me help you," she said as she peeled back the paper and lifted the lid on the box.

Blue's stump of a tail started to pound against the wood

floor, and his ears were at full attention as his tongue hung out the side of his mouth. She'd filled the box with pig ears—his favorite—along with a variety of dog snacks and two toys that squealed when they were squeezed.

He went for one of the pig's ears.

"You have a good day, my friend." She rubbed his ears before she slipped on her coat and grabbed her purse from the coffee table. Then she lifted the bag of wrapped gifts by the door and hesitated. Everything had appeared as it should be when she'd let Blue out early in the morning and then again about thirty minutes ago. But her pulse picked up anyway. She hoped it wouldn't always be like this.

With hesitant steps, she trekked across her dirt driveway to her SUV. There wasn't any snow on the ground, and the sun was out. After she stowed her purse and the gifts, she looked around, unsure what she expected to see, but still nothing looked out of order. But Brianna would be more careful now, too, she realized.

She went back for the cobbler, gave Blue more snuggles before she picked up the pie dish she'd baked it in, then put her key in the antique lock. That was when she noticed that something wasn't right. There was clear evidence that someone had tried to pry the door open using a knife or some other flat item. Even though the person's attempt to get in had been unsuccessful, her first instinct was to go back into the house, put the chain on the door, and stay there all day. But she forced herself to run to her red SUV and prayed Blue would be okay while she was gone.

She shook all the way to Eva and Jake's house.

CHAPTER 19

Yvonne's eyebrows rose in surprise when Eva answered the door. "Aren't you supposed to be in bed?"

Eva took the cobbler from her. "I've been given a day off. The doctor said that I'm in my last month. Even if the *boppli* comes early, he or she is out of the woods. I'm still supposed to stay off my feet as much as possible, but it's Christmas." She nodded to the cobbler. "You didn't have to do this, but it smells delicious."

Yvonne pointed over her shoulder. "I need to get the gifts I brought." She was eager to give Eva and Jake the keepsake box for the baby. It warmed her heart every time she thought about how she'd made it herself. Under Abraham's guidance and using his tools, of course. But it was the first time she'd built something she was proud of.

There were around a dozen people bustling about when she returned to the house with the bag of gifts. Jake was an only child, but his father was in a wheelchair tucked out of the way in the living room while his mother worked in the kitchen. And Eva's parents were there, along with her three brothers and their girlfriends.

"Merry Christmas," Eva's mother said when she saw her, embracing her in a warm hug. Yvonne had an unspoken bond with Mary Graber. After Trevor had died, Eva's mother was the only one, outside of her aunt, who'd seemed to really understand her loss.

"How can I help?" Yvonne glanced around the kitchen. Even Eva's brothers' girlfriends were busy preparing pickle trays, buttering bread that smelled fresh from the oven, and chatting amongst themselves. It was festive, and it was exactly what Yvonne needed.

She recalled her Christmases growing up with her aunt and uncle, then just her aunt after her uncle passed. There were gifts and a traditional meal, but Yvonne always thought it to be a bit hypocritical since she was raised to believe there was no heaven. It was nice to be here with Eva and Jake's family, celebrating the true reason for the season, knowing everyone in the house believed they would see one another again after they passed. This was her first real Christmas, she realized.

After she was told by several different women that they had everything under control, she went to the living room and said hello to Jake's father, then to Eva's dad, and she introduced herself to those she didn't know. Eva's brothers, whom she'd met before, tended to stare at her, but she noticed that their ogling was tempered with their girlfriends nearby.

There wasn't a Christmas tree, but it didn't take away

from the festive feel of things. There were poinsettias on either side of the fireplace and holly atop the mantel. Gifts were stacked in various places throughout the living room, all beautifully wrapped. Two things were missing: There wasn't any music in the background. And there weren't any children present. Eva and Jake's baby would be the first on both sides of the family.

With preparations finished, devotions were held, prayers were silently said before the meal, and after everyone was stuffed with turkey, dressing, and every side dish imaginable, it was time to open presents. As Abraham had told her, the gifts were simple, and almost all of them were homemade. Eva's mother had knitted a beautiful winter cap for Yvonne, and they all laughed and joked that Yvonne was going to freeze when winter truly arrived. Jake's mother gave her a box filled with canned items—strawberry jam, pickled okra, and a host of other wonderful foods she would enjoy for a long time to come.

Eva and Jake brought her a large box and set it at her feet where she was sitting in one of the rocking chairs. "Jake made it, but it's from both of us," Eva said as her eyes twinkled.

Yvonne delicately picked at the wrapping paper, wanting to savor this special moment. She was eager for Eva and Jake to open her gift to them too. And she'd be with Abraham later. This was the best Christmas she'd ever had, and it wasn't even over yet.

"Rip it open!" David, Eva's youngest brother, yelled, and everyone laughed.

Yvonne wiggled a finger beneath the shiny red-and-green

wrapping paper, then peeled it back to reveal a box with no hint as to what was inside. Jake handed her a pocketknife, as if he knew she would need it.

After a few cuts through the packing tape, she had the box open, peered inside, then gasped when she realized what it was. "Oh, wow," she said softly before she lifted the large item from the box. "This is amazing, and so beautiful."

"Do you know what it is?" Eva's youngest brother chuckled.

"Hush, David." Eva cut her eyes at him, then looked lovingly back at Yvonne. "Do you like it?"

"I love it." She looked up at Jake, who was standing proudly nearby, grinning from ear to ear. As she recalled how she'd met Jake, when she'd been determined to charm him out of a book she needed for a client, she realized how far they'd come.

"Abraham mentioned that you only had an old log holder by the fireplace and that it had a broken leg. He said the logs all sat lopsided and that it was way too small." Jake's face glowed, mirroring Yvonne's heart.

She ran her hand gingerly over the brass caps that topped each carefully welded piece of the firewood holder in front of her, a shiny black that would surely outlive Yvonne. The holder wasn't just big and beautiful, but Jake had crafted it just for her. "Thank you so much, both of you. This is perfect."

The keepsake box she'd been so proud of seemed small and insignificant in comparison, and she felt herself blushing as she reached for the box and handed it to Eva.

"It isn't much. But I made it." She lowered her eyes,

took a deep breath, then watched as Eva ripped into the silver wrapping paper and easily opened the box containing the gift.

Eva gasped as she looked inside, and Jake leaned down to have a better look. Eva's jaw dropped before she locked eyes with Yvonne. Then she pulled out the keepsake box with tears in her eyes. "Jake, look." She handed the box to her husband. "'Baby Lantz' is carved into the wood."

"It's beautiful, Yvonne," Jake said with such sincerity that Yvonne swallowed the lump forming in the back of her throat.

"Abraham was a good teacher. He helped me pick out the stain and showed me how to use his tools." At this point, according to Lizzie, everyone knew she was spending time with Abraham.

Eva wiggled out of the recliner she was sitting in, assisted by her husband. She threw her arms around Yvonne and whispered, "It's the best present of the day."

Yvonne subtly wiped a tear from her eye, then faced her friend. "*Danki* for having me." She glanced at Jake, blinking back more tears. "Both of you."

Eva and Jake smiled at her use of the Pennsylvania Dutch dialect.

Everyone got back to opening presents. They tended to open one at a time so that everyone could see each gift. The presents ranged from knitted items, such as caps, gloves, and potholders with slots for potpourri inserts, to wooden items made with a lathe and other tools that all the men seemed to own, many of them battery powered. There were handcrafted toolboxes, small pieces of furniture, and even a beautifully carved potato bin. All the gifts were practical, handmade, and better than most anything you could purchase at a store.

Yvonne was radiant on the inside. This was what Christmas was supposed to be. Gifts created out of love. Meals shared with family. And an all-knowing sense that where more than one gathered in His name, He was there. Yvonne could feel God's love and presence, and that was what truly made the day the best she'd ever had.

Later, Eva waddled onto the porch where Yvonne sat, alone, in one of the rocking chairs, reflecting on the day. "I look like a penguin," Eva said as she slouched into a chair. "But I'm enjoying being up and about."

"It won't be long now until you have the baby and you'll be craving some down time." Yvonne smiled at her friend.

"I'm sure you're right." Eva grinned. "We haven't had time to talk. Tell me about you and Abraham."

"It's still very new," she said quickly, but then recalled what Lizzie had said, how she and others knew about Abraham possibly wanting to rejoin the church. "And it's complicated."

"It doesn't have to be." Eva gave her a sympathetic smile. "I wish I could say that our little town was free of gossip, but sometimes I think it's worse here." She tapped a finger to her chin. "But let me make sure I have the facts. Abraham broke up with Brianna. You and he started seeing each other shortly thereafter. And he is considering being baptized back into our faith."

"Yep. That's pretty much it." Yvonne couldn't see any reason to drag Eva into the Brianna drama. "So, you can see the risks." She pressed her hand against her chest. "To my heart. But for now, we're both trusting God to lead the way."

Eva pulled her black sweater snug even though it didn't reach all the way around her large belly. Yvonne had her coat on, but with the sun beating down on the porch, it felt warmer than it was. "After our wedding, when you had left, Abraham told Jake that he had never believed in love at first sight until he saw you at the bookstore prior to that."

Yvonne jerked her head to face her friend. "You never told me that."

Eva shrugged. "I don't think it would have mattered at the time. But you've obviously discovered what a *gut* man he is," she said.

Yvonne sighed. "Yep. A good man that I might lose when and if he chooses baptism. But I know he will be honest with me, and I want what is best for him. He deserves that. And you of all people know how challenging my own spiritual journey was. You and Jake helped me to sort things out."

Eva smiled. "That wasn't us. That was *Gott*." She chuckled. "And a book called *Walk With Me*. And He will be there for you and Abraham too. Just trust in Him."

Yvonne covered her face with her hands.

"*Ach*, what's wrong?" Eva's voice rang with alarm.

After uncovering her face and swiping at a few tears, Yvonne said, "Nothing. These are happy tears. This is the best Christmas I've ever had. I feel the Holy Spirit in my heart in a way that I never have."

Eva smiled again. "Isn't it wonderful?"

Yvonne nodded. Prior to Eva and Jake getting married,

Yvonne had been more of an older sister to Eva. Now the tables had turned. Eva was going to be a mother, and she'd helped Yvonne more than once with her spirituality. There was a sisterly bond, but without one woman having more wisdom than the other. Yvonne thought they complemented each other with their varied outlooks on things, often worthy of friendly debates. Eva was wiser than her twenty years. Yvonne wondered if that was because of how she had been raised. The Amish were introduced to hard work at an early age, but morals were also instilled in them as young children. As teenagers, they had an opportunity to experience the outside world, but almost all of them chose to be baptized into the faith. She could see where it must have been traumatic for Abraham's family when he chose otherwise.

"And you still have the evening to spend with Abraham." Eva twitched, then reached for Yvonne's hand and placed it on her enlarged stomach. "She's kicking."

Yvonne closed her eyes and felt the life moving inside of Eva, and they were both quiet for a while.

Finally, Yvonne eased her hand away. "I'm still quite sure it's a girl," she said as she envisioned a little Eva running around with her friend's dimples and Jake's sapphire-blue eyes.

"I must admit I'm sure it is too." Eva rubbed her stomach. "Tomorrow is Second Christmas for us," she continued as she tucked loose strands of hair beneath her prayer covering. "This might be a long shot, and don't feel like you have to say yes, but would you like to attend our worship service? It's being held at an Amish farm not far from here, at the King place. I know you won't understand a lot of what is going on, but you said you enjoyed the feeling of fellow-ship when you attended our wedding. I spoke with a couple of the elders, one of them being *mei daed,* and they said it would be fine for you to attend."

Yvonne had been told that it was unusual for an outsider to be invited to an Amish worship service, outside of a wed-ding. "I'd like that very much."

"And there's another big meal after the service. Then some of the ladies will deliver meals to the shut-ins in our area." She paused. "Maybe Abraham would like to come too?"

Yvonne couldn't think of anything better than to share that with Abraham. "I'll certainly ask him."

"As for me, I promised to go back to bed when everyone leaves today, but I was told I can leave *mei* prison bedroom and attend worship service tomorrow. I've missed it so much since I've been put on bed rest."

Yvonne heard the longing in her voice. "I know all this bed rest has been awful. We all just want a healthy baby and a healthy you." Yvonne put her hand on Eva's tummy again.

"*Ya,* me too," Eva said. "I had planned to have a mid-wife deliver the *boppli* at home, but since I've had some is-sues, everyone feels like I should deliver at the hospital."

"Probably best. You're going to be a wonderful *mamm.*"

Eva chuckled and pointed a finger at Yvonne. "I think you know more of the *Deitsch* than you let on."

Yvonne grinned. "I'm a quick study."

After Yvonne offered Eva a hand and got her friend to her feet, they both went inside. Yvonne basked in the glory of the day, knowing it wasn't over yet.

Brianna was surprised at how much the swelling in her foot had gone down by late afternoon. Abraham had been right. Twenty minutes of ice, twenty minutes off. She was confident it was just a sprain and not broken. And she was sure she deserved it after faking an injury and for the way she had previously spoken to Abraham. But she didn't want to be limping on her first date with Bruce on New Year's Eve. She'd do the ice regimen daily and hope her foot fit back in her favorite boots by then.

Her headache had subsided, but not enough to partake in a glass of wine or any eggnog. She'd cried on and off all day. Even though she hadn't spent Christmas with her parents in years, she'd always had someone to be with, whether it was a boyfriend or, at the least, people who pretended they were her friends. But this year, even at Thanksgiving, those she had visited felt more like acquaintances than real friends.

With her foot propped up on a pillow on the coffee table, balancing a bag of ice, she thought back to the reason she'd stopped communicating with her parents. She was their only child. After analyzing her childhood, then her teenage years and early adulthood, she knew why. She'd been rebellious, rude, demanding, and an overall brat. The last thing her mother had said to her was, "Do not come back to this house or call us until you have straightened yourself out."

Brianna recalled the rage she'd felt, the determination to

hurt them the best way she could—to never see them again or even talk to them. She was sure her mother had spoken to her out of anger and disappointment and had never intended for their only child not to communicate for years. But Brianna had chosen to punish them to the fullest degree. She'd changed her phone number and hadn't left forwarding addresses every time she'd moved. Her parents couldn't get hold of her even if they had wanted to.

A sick thought caused her to feel like she might hurl the chicken soup she'd forced down earlier. Were her parents even still alive? It seemed likely they would be since they were only in their late fifties.

She leaned her head back against the couch cushion. When had she become so bitter? She could blame Mitch, Abraham, and others . . . but if she was honest with herself, she was the problem. She was unlovable, despite her outward beauty that she'd always counted on to get her through life, to land her a good man, and to enjoy the life she thought she deserved. Maybe you had to give love with genuine intent before you got it back.

Brianna glanced around her modern house set amid an Amish farming community and wondered what she was doing here. She hadn't put up any Christmas decorations. What was the point? No one to share the holidays with. She had no friends to speak of.

She picked up her cell phone. No missed calls. Not one person had called to wish her Merry Christmas. Sniffling, she hit Call on her parents' phone number, which she'd almost deleted more than once over the years.

Her heart pounded in her chest when her mother

answered, and she suddenly had no voice, only a pain that consumed her far more than her foot or her headache.

"Hello?" her mother said for the second time.

"Hi, Mom." Brianna couldn't control the shakiness in her voice. "Merry Christmas." She put a hand to her mouth to control the sobs threatening to spill.

"Brianna?" Her mother's voice was equally as shaky. "Is that really you?"

At first, she only nodded, but finally said, "It's me."

"Are you okay?" her mother asked, sounding tentative, but like she might be crying.

Brianna was consumed with self-hatred as she thought about how much her absence must have tormented her parents. "I'm all right, Mom." It was a blatant lie. She didn't feel okay at all. "I-I just wanted to say I'm sorry and to wish you a merry Christmas."

"Oh, baby . . ." Her mother openly wept, then mumbled something about getting her father. And the sound of his voice made Brianna cry harder than she had in a long time.

After everything she had put her parents through, they both gushed and cried about how happy they were to hear from her. When emotions had simmered, she gave them her address, promised to visit soon, and apologized again for her absence in their lives. She'd never heard her father cry. Until now.

"Merry Christmas to you too. And I love you too." Brianna ended the call, then cried so hard her chest muscles spasmed.

Maybe she'd selfishly needed to hear someone say they

loved her. Had she only called them because she was alone and friendless on Christmas Day?

She was still speculating and crying when her phone rang beside her on the couch. It was a number she didn't recognize, and she was about to hit Ignore when her curiosity got the best of her and she answered.

"Brianna?"

She wanted to believe she recognized the voice, but she wasn't sure. "Yes."

"Hey, it's Bruce. Did I catch you at a bad time?"

She sat taller. "No. Not at all."

"Are you crying?" he asked.

"No. Just allergies." Another lie. She briefly thought about all the fibs she'd told and how each one seemed to leave her feeling bad afterward, even if the lie seemed necessary at the time. And she was still doing it, like a bad habit she couldn't kick. But this was the first time she wanted to try.

"Well, I called to wish you Merry Christmas."

She smiled for the first time in the past two days. "And Merry Christmas to you. Are you enjoying your time with your family?"

"You know how it is with family." He laughed. Brianna didn't know how it was with family, so she didn't say anything. "It's been a great day, and I had originally planned to spend the night, but . . . I was just wondering what you were doing tonight. If you didn't have any plans, I thought I might leave Indianapolis and head back that way."

Brianna blinked her eyes a few times as she eyed her swollen foot propped up and covered with an ice pack. She decided to throw caution to the wind. "I'm not doing anything. I tripped on my entryway rug last night and sprained my ankle. So it's been a slow day for me. I'd love some company." She cringed, knowing what she must look like.

"Wow. I'm so sorry to hear that. Can I bring you anything? We have tons of food left, and I'm sure my mom has a cooler around here. I wasn't sure if you were doing anything. I mean, you and Abraham just broke up, so I . . ."

"I would love some turkey and dressing, and that is so kind of you to offer."

"Fantastic! Let me pack up and get out of here." He paused. "I am really looking forward to seeing you. I'm glad I don't have to wait until New Year's Eve."

She gave him her address, and as soon as they hung up, she did something she rarely did. She squeezed her eyes closed and looked up. *God, please don't let me mess this up.* Maybe it wasn't too late to make some changes in her life.

Cringing, she recalled some of the things she'd done recently. When she figuratively stepped back and tried to look inside herself, what did she see? Even with a guarded and objective view, it was hard to peel back the bitterness, anger, and hurt to find the real Brianna. Worse, she couldn't remember a time when she hadn't felt this way. Was that what others saw in her?

Whoever the real Brianna was, she wanted to be that person again. A better person, she hoped.

She was wise enough to know that changes like she was considering might require some type of therapy. Maybe she would look into that. For now, she resolved she was going to be herself. If Bruce didn't like the real Brianna, then he wasn't meant for her. She was tired of forcing relationships. And there was a freedom that came with that admission.

CHAPTER 20

Abraham finished installing a new lock on Yvonne's front door. He'd had to ask a friend to open the hardware store on Christmas Day, which he hated to do, but he didn't want to wait. "There," he said when he was done and handed Yvonne the key. "We probably need to put a new lock on the back door too."

"Thank you. I'm so sorry you had to do this on Christmas Day." She hugged him, then kissed him, and he engaged in the affection until Blue started to growl.

"Blue, remember, he's a friend." Yvonne dropped her arms to her sides as she eyed her dog before turning back to Abraham. "He's slowly getting used to you."

"I can't believe Brianna is trying to break into your house in the middle of the night." Abraham walked to the fireplace to stoke the fire, shaking his head. "What's the point in it? She might be a bit nuts, but I don't think she's violent." He poked at the fire. "I just don't get it."

"Maybe it isn't her."

Abraham turned around and grinned. "Do you have other enemies I don't know about?"

"Not that I'm aware of, but I'm not sure Brianna is an enemy. I mean, I don't trust her, but what does she have to gain by trying to get into my house during the night? Is she going to shoot me in my sleep for stealing you away from her? Or at least in her mind, that's what happened."

"I don't know. But, if it's okay with you, I'm going to sleep on your couch tonight." Abraham's stomach had been churning ever since Yvonne told him about the lock.

"You don't have to do that." She stared into his eyes, and even though she had given him an out, he could see relief in her expression.

"I know I don't have to, but I want to. I'm concerned about this." He finally walked to the couch and sat down.

Yvonne joined him. "Let's just enjoy today," she said. "It's Christmas, and it's been the best one I've ever had."

He leaned over and kissed her. "And it's not over yet."

"Thank you for telling Jake about my firewood holder that was falling apart." She gazed at the gift that now rested by the fireplace filled with wood.

"You're welcome, but Jake gets the credit. He did a great job building that thing. And it holds a lot more wood."

Abraham fought to hide the fear he felt. He couldn't stay on Yvonne's couch every night. He was going to worry continuously if Brianna didn't stop her craziness. Maybe he did need to consider that it could be someone else, but Yvonne hadn't been here long enough to have anyone want to harm her. He shivered to think it was a random stranger, someone who could really hurt her.

"Abraham . . ." She cupped his face in her hands and gazed into his eyes. "You've got to stop looking so worried, at least for tonight." She kissed him softly, and he had to admit that when her lips were against his, everything else became a blur.

"I have a gift for you." She nodded toward a box on the coffee table. "It's not much, but it's something I sort of made for you."

"Hmm . . . sort of? Sounds mysterious." He'd already set a card on her coffee table, knowing his gift would be inferior compared to anything she gave him, and he wished he had chosen differently.

"Open it." She gripped her fingers tightly together and grinned.

"Okay." It was a flat box about a foot long and an inch thick. When the package was unwrapped, he opened the flap on the box, and there sat a frame, which made him think of the picture Brianna had given him. He had thought it was too soon, but he would treasure a photo of him and Yvonne. Although he couldn't recall them ever taking a picture together.

She slammed her hand on top of his, stopping him from removing the tissue paper as her face turned red. "Now I'm feeling embarrassed." She shifted her eyes from his. "Maybe you can just open it at home later."

He tilted his head to one side. "I will love whatever it is. Don't be embarrassed."

She covered her face with her hands. "Ugh."

Abraham laughed, which felt good, considering all the worrying he'd done the past few hours. "What's wrong with you?"

"Ugh," she said again as she kept her palms over her face.

Abraham took out the frame, which held a beautifully hand-scripted note . . . or poem? He read it quietly to himself while Yvonne held her hands over her face, but she was peeking between her fingers with one eye.

To Abraham

AS SEASONS CHANGE

The whispers of fall prepare all things thriving for
    the stillness of winter by shedding the old in
    preparation for the new.
Winter cleanses the earth of all that was,
    regenerating the season with rest for the
    glorious spring growth to come.
Spring brings rain showers to nourish the beauty
    that will peak in time for summer.
Summer shines brightly and gifts us not only
    rainbows and butterflies, but hope that with
    each changing season, better ones will always
    follow.
Such is life, an imitation, when it comes to the
    changing of the seasons.
            TENDERLY, YVONNE

Abraham could barely breathe. He wanted to grab her, kiss her, tell her that he'd loved her since the moment he saw her. It would probably terrify her that he had such strong feelings so early into the relationship.

He eased her hands away from her face, then drew her mouth to his, which always invoked a dreamy intimacy he'd never had with anyone else—feelings of desire that went way beyond just his physical attraction to her. No matter his calling, he knew in this moment that he would never leave her.

"This is the best present I've ever received," he managed to say before he cradled her face and kissed her again.

Yvonne hadn't felt such passion from a kiss before, not even with Trevor, which made her feel a little guilty. She had loved Trevor with all her heart, and she'd feared another man would never match or surpass what they'd had together. Yvonne also knew that the stakes were growing where Abraham was concerned. She'd fallen hard for him in a short amount of time. Her heart would be shattered if he chose his faith over her. She wanted to be brave and leave it in God's hands, but right now she was in Abraham's arms, a place she didn't think she would ever want to leave. But she eased him away.

His eyes blazed with passion, and she was breathing as heavily as he was. But sleeping together was not an option, and she felt it best to slow things down a little.

"Sorry," he said as he blushed.

She shook her head. "Don't be. I was right there with you." She smiled, feeling like her face was also red.

"I need to tell you something." He took her face gently in his hands. "I've never wanted another woman the way I want you, and I don't mean just physically." He paused to brush his lips gently across hers before he went on. "I don't want to scare you off, but I felt something the first day I saw you in the bookstore. Somehow, I just knew our paths would cross again. It was such a bad time for you after that, but I still held out faith that I'd see you again someday."

Yvonne thought briefly about what Eva had told her, a version of what Abraham had just said. She was so touched, and she wanted to tell him how guilty she'd felt at Jake and Eva's wedding because she'd felt something, too, so soon after Trevor's death. But she bit her lip and avoided his gaze. She'd been foolish to let things get to this point.

"I know what you're thinking." He ran his fingers down one side of her cheek and waited until she looked at him again. "I'm not going to be baptized back into the Amish faith."

Her jaw dropped as she pulled away from him and shook her head. It should have been music to her ears, but she couldn't stay quiet. "It's too soon for you to make that type of decision. We've barely been seeing each other for any time at all."

"You're right." He stared into her eyes. "But with the possibility of baptism hanging over our heads, it will be a natural instinct for both of us to pull back on what I think we both feel. And my need to know you better is stronger than my pull to rejoin the Amish."

Yvonne suddenly felt like she was wrecking his life, taking him from his calling, and maybe even going against God.

But if this was truly the way he felt, her heart would no longer sit on a platter waiting to be crushed. "Abraham . . ." She sighed but held his gaze. "I want to get to know you better, too, and you aren't misinterpreting my feelings. But a calling from God isn't something to ignore."

"I know. But that isn't the only decision I've made." He tucked her hair behind her ears, smiling. "I don't want to be a cop anymore. I know that. The whole thing with Will and Maureen has stayed with me. Every time the muscle in my arm twitches or strains, I think about pulling the trigger and shooting Will. I was young when I joined the force, and just because I want to leave that kind of work, it doesn't mean I have to go back to my Amish roots."

"It almost sounds like a compromise." Yvonne swallowed hard, unwilling to mess up their Christmas but feeling the need to present both sides of the argument. "You can't compromise when it comes to God."

He kissed her gently, his lips brushing softly against hers again. "I'm not going anywhere unless you tell me to." He smiled as he raised an eyebrow.

Yvonne didn't have the strength to tell him to get out of her life. "Why don't we just table this conversation and enjoy our time together. Let's agree to push all worries aside for now." She wasn't sure that was possible.

"Deal." He smiled down at her before his eyes lost focus. "Your gift." He snapped a finger. "It's not as good as what you gave me, which I absolutely love. I had no idea you wrote poetry."

She laughed, and it felt good to tone down the seriousness of the conversation they'd slipped into. "I'm not sure I would call it poetry, but I have a notebook that I scribble in." She looked away from him. "But I did write that especially for you."

Blue disrupted them when he stood up and walked to the front door. Yvonne waited for him to bark, his sign that it was time to go out, but he just took up his prayer position in front of the door.

"I love it." Abraham set his gift on the coffee table and handed her the card he'd set there earlier. "This is your gift, although it's not as personal as yours, and now I'm thinking maybe I should have gotten you something else. Or made you something."

Yvonne's hands trembled as she opened the card, then read the message inside. "What?" She laughed. "This is way too much. I can't let you do this!"

"It's too late. I already paid for it. Mr. Reynolds didn't have a problem with it."

"Why would he? I'm just renting the house." She chuckled again, then shook her head. "This is too much."

"Look, Texas girl . . . I've never heard anyone talk about the weather as much as you, and I know you're worried about a cold winter in this house. The guy will be here next week to blow insulation into the walls." He held up a hand when she opened her mouth to protest again. "I got a great deal."

Yvonne blinked back tears. Telling him she loved him was on the tip of her tongue, but could she really be in love with a man so soon? "Thank you so much," she said in a shaky voice, incredibly touched. Like Christmas at Jake and Eva's, he had given her a practical gift, although he had surely spent way too much money. "I *have* been a little worried about the winter here." She wrapped her arms around him.

Blue started barking as he faced the door.

"He needs to go out," Yvonne said as she forced herself out of Abraham's arms, then sidled up to her dog. She pulled the door open without giving it a thought, and Blue rushed out of the house.

But it wasn't to go potty. There was someone in the front yard, her silhouette barely visible in the darkness as she darted off into the woods, shoulder-length hair bouncing against her back and Blue on her tail.

"Abraham!" Yvonne screamed. "Someone is outside." Then she prayed that Blue wouldn't harm or kill whoever he was chasing.

Abraham almost knocked Yvonne down as he rushed past her and ran to his truck. After he took his gun from the glove compartment, he sprinted toward the woods.

"It's a woman!" Yvonne yelled from the front porch. "Don't let Blue hurt her."

Abraham wasn't concerned about the dog hurting the intruder nearly as much as he was about someone hurting Yvonne, but when he heard someone cry out in the distance, his fears shifted for the moment. It was clearly a woman's scream combined with growling.

He ran as fast as he could, branches slapping against his face, no visible path to know where he was headed. Then he stopped cold when everything went quiet. No screaming, no growling. After listening for a few seconds, he took slow steps, hoping to hear something to lead him in the right direction.

The minutes passed as he searched, until he finally had to admit defeat. He hadn't found Brianna or Blue. He made his way back to the house in the darkness. Yvonne hadn't moved from the porch, and without a coat she stood there shivering.

"Where's Blue?" she asked tearfully. "Did you see the woman?" A tear rolled down her cheek. "Where is Blue?"

Abraham put an arm around her and ushered her inside and to the fireplace so they could both warm up.

"I heard screaming," she said in a fragile voice. "Then I didn't hear anything. Where's Blue?"

Abraham pulled her to him and kissed the top of her head as they both stood shaking in front of the fireplace. "I don't know, but this is going to end tonight."

He went to the coffee table where he'd set down his gun on the way to the fireplace. After he picked it up, he took it to her. "Do you know how to use this?"

Her fingers trembled as she took the weapon and shook her head.

"There's a bullet in the chamber." He pointed to a button on the side of the gun. "Just push the button to take it off safety."

Abraham kissed her. "I need a flashlight."

Yvonne went toward the kitchen, holding the gun about a foot out to her side as if touching it was burning her hand. He prayed she never had to shoot anyone, sure she would feel as messed up as he did about shooting Will. But he couldn't leave her alone with no protection.

She was still dangling the gun at her side and crying when she handed him a flashlight. "You can't go out there without your gun."

"I'll be fine. Lock the door behind me."

She did what he asked, but Abraham didn't have to go far. Blue came out of the woods, blood dripping from his face and one of his legs dragging behind him.

As Abraham rushed toward Blue, the animal locked eyes with him, then fell over.

Oh, dear God, no.

CHAPTER 21

I t was three in the morning as Yvonne and Abraham sat in the waiting room of the vet's office. They'd had to call three vets before they were able to reach someone, and Dr. Ridlen had graciously agreed to meet them at his office just outside of Montgomery. Blue had bitten Abraham when he carried him to his truck and laid him in the back seat, but the dog had lost consciousness soon thereafter. Yvonne had thought for sure her dog was dead, and she'd wept all the way to the vet's office.

"Is your arm okay?" Yvonne hadn't thought she had any more tears, but apparently she did. She swiped at her eyes as she stared at Abraham's torn white shirt that was speckled with blood.

"He barely nipped me." Abraham pulled back his ripped sleeve and showed her the bite mark. It looked like more than a nip to Yvonne, but it didn't look like it needed stiches. "He didn't mean to hurt me. He was just in pain and scared," he said.

Yvonne's best Christmas ever had turned into a nightmare. Her dog was in surgery, and they'd seen proof positive that it was a woman who was stalking Yvonne. Abraham had asked her repeatedly to describe what she saw. He was convinced it was Brianna. Yvonne couldn't be sure, and she still found it hard to believe Brianna was so bitter that she would try to cause them harm.

They both stood when Dr. Ridlen emerged from behind a closed door. "He's going to be okay. His back right leg is broken, and he has some lacerations on his face, but those mostly look like they came from branches in the woods. The broken leg was from a blow to the limb, although I couldn't tell you what he was hit with." The doctor ran a sleeve along his forehead where he was sweating. Yvonne was freezing despite Abraham telling her to get her coat as they walked out the door, which she still wore. "I'm going to keep him a couple of days. I didn't see evidence of any internal bleeding, but he does have a few stitches on his face, and I'd like to keep him a little sedated so he doesn't feel the pain as much. He's got a cone on, and he's sleeping soundly. He'll be fine until daylight, and I'll come back and check on him. My house is on the property. We're closed tomorrow—or actually, I guess it's today—but if you want to pay him a visit, just give me a call, and I can meet you at the office."

Abraham shook the doctor's hand while Yvonne dabbed at tears. "Thank you very much. We're sorry to get you out of bed, especially the day after Christmas, but we're very appreciative," Abraham said. All Yvonne could do was nod in agreement.

She fought more tears all the way back to her house. "I feel like I'm never going to feel safe here again." She sniffled. "But thank God Blue is going to be okay."

"You're going to feel safe. I'll make sure of it." Abraham pulled his truck into Yvonne's driveway. She wasn't sure how he was going to do that, but she was so tired she could barely keep her eyes open.

As soon as they got in the house, Abraham insisted she get some sleep. Yvonne didn't argue. She kissed him in front of the fireplace before she got into her bed, wishing he was lying next to her solely so she wouldn't be alone there. She reached her arm across to where Blue usually slept and thanked God again that her beloved pet would be okay.

Afraid he'd fall asleep, Abraham didn't lay down on the couch. But at some point, he'd given up the fight. He lifted his head from the back of the couch when the sun began to light up the room. It was freezing inside. It might not have been the most personal gift, but he was glad he'd gotten someone to come blow insulation into Yvonne's walls this week.

After he got a fire going, he splashed water on his face, went to the kitchen, and made a pot of coffee. Yvonne walked in yawning, still in the clothes she'd had on the day before.

"You should have stayed in bed and slept longer," he

said. "I hope you don't mind." He nodded to the coffee maker gurgling on the counter.

She shook her head, her eyes swollen and red. He pulled her into a hug and kissed her on the forehead. "I was going to call Brianna this morning, but then I remembered that I deleted her number and blocked her. I'm going to go see her shortly."

"Are you sure you want to do that? What if it wasn't her?" Yvonne sniffed. She'd been crying again this morning.

"I'll be able to tell if she's lying." Abraham wasn't sure about that since she'd lied to him before without him knowing. "But I don't want to take any chances. Let me take you somewhere while I'm gone. I don't like the idea of you staying here by yourself. What about Eva and Jake's house?"

Yvonne shook her head. "No, I don't want to worry them, especially Eva. I haven't said anything to her about all of this. And I want to get a shower and go see Blue in a little while."

"I'll take you to the vet when I get back. How's that?" Abraham tried to sound firm without appearing scared— which he was, for her.

Again she waggled her head. "No, I'll lock everything up. Like you said, it's probably Brianna, and you're heading that way, so I'll just feel better here after a shower."

"Honestly, I'm not real comfortable leaving you, but on the off chance it wasn't Brianna, I'm leaving my gun with you." He pointed to his weapon on the coffee table.

She eyed it for a couple of seconds. "I need to call Dr. Ridlen and see when a good time is to go see Blue."

She went to her bedroom and returned with her phone.

Based on hearing one side of the conversation, it sounded like Blue was doing okay and that Yvonne was going to meet Dr. Ridlen in about an hour at his office, after she showered.

Good. That would get her out of the house.

"He's a nice man," she said after the call ended. "I think he can be Blue's regular vet. He said he had just checked on Blue, and that he was sluggish but doing fine. I'll shower, then he said to knock on the door of the main house on the back of the property when I get there."

"That's good news." He poured them each a cup of coffee and handed her a mug. "You sure you're going to be okay while I go to Brianna's?"

"I'm sure." She frowned. "Is it okay if I hold out hope that it wasn't Brianna snooping around? I'd just hate to think that someone I know would scare me like that and hurt my dog."

"We'll know soon enough." He kissed her on the mouth before he left.

By the time he got to Brianna's, he was so angry he was shaking. He sat in his truck for a few minutes to try to calm down.

Brianna hadn't planned to be intimate with Bruce on their first night together, but he'd been impossible to refuse, and it had just happened. Maybe it was a blessing in disguise that things hadn't worked out with Abraham. She hadn't realized how much she'd missed being physical with a man.

"Good morning," he said as he pulled her close to him in the bed, seemingly ready to go another round.

Brianna snuggled against him, but a knock at the door startled her. She rolled her eyes. "Who could be pounding on my door this early in the morning?

"Want me to go see who it is?" Bruce leaned into his embrace as he kissed the tip of her nose.

"No. I'll go." She sighed. "You stay right here, and I'll be back as soon as I can."

He smiled, and Brianna slipped into her robe at the foot of the bed, then shuffled out to open her front door.

Abraham. "What are you doing here?" she asked as she folded her arms across her chest and faced off with her ex.

"Can I come in?" Abraham's face was red. He was mad about something, but she didn't want Bruce to hear an altercation between them.

She glanced over her shoulder before she turned back to Abraham. "This isn't a good time." She scowled. "So whatever you're all worked up about will have to wait."

"I think you know what I'm all worked up about." He shifted his weight and put a hand on his hip. "Want to tell me what you've been up to all night?"

She chuckled. "Uh . . . no. I don't believe it's any of your business." She held up a finger. "But as long as you're here, I have something to give you." She left the door cracked, went to the kitchen, and retrieved the only thing that she had of Abraham's from a drawer, then went back to the door.

"Here." She held out the key to his house. "I had a copy made when I was staying at your house. At the time, I thought we were moving in a direction where I would need a key." She shrugged. "Clearly that wasn't the case. Now, what are you doing here? Make it quick and keep your voice down."

Abraham stared at the key in his hand for a long few minutes before he eyed Brianna. Her auburn hair was tousled as she scowled at him. He was trying to figure out why she was fessing up about having a key to his house made, especially now. When he didn't say anything, she shrugged. "That's the last thing I have of yours."

A voice boomed from behind her. "Brianna, are you okay?"

Abraham recognized the voice before Bruce cozied up behind her wearing only a towel.

"Uh . . . Abraham, what are you doing here?" His face was as red as Brianna's nail polish.

"How long have you been here?" Abraham asked as he shook from the cold standing on Brianna's porch.

"I came in yesterday evening." Bruce shot him a questioning look. "Why? Is there a problem?"

Abraham shook his head. "Uh . . . no." Then he thought about Yvonne, alone at her house. It obviously hadn't been Brianna there last night. So who . . . ? "I have to go. Sorry to have bothered you."

He did an about face, and just before the door closed, he heard Brianna say, "I have no idea what he was doing here. I'm telling you, the guy is crazy."

Abraham shook his head as he got into his car. Bruce

would learn soon enough that Brianna was beautiful on the outside, but her temperament didn't always mirror that beauty on the inside. His coworker would probably dump her now that he'd obviously slept with her. Bruce was a super nice guy—with a lot of women on his roster. Abraham suspected the only reason he'd shown up at Brianna's house yesterday was to hop into bed with her.

Despite everything, Abraham would hate to see Brianna get hurt, especially now that he knew she wasn't their stalker.

He shivered at that thought and drove as fast as he could to get back to Yvonne. Whoever had been in the woods could still be there, or still have bad intentions and come back. His chest tightened as he pressed harder on the accelerator.

Yvonne shook from head to toe as tears spilled down her face. She'd never had anyone point a gun at her. She'd left the weapon on the coffee table where Abraham had put it, gone to the bathroom, and when she got back . . . she wasn't alone.

"Not feeling so brave without your stinking boyfriend or vicious dog to protect you, huh?" Maureen's face was a glowering mask of rage as her nostrils flared with fury. "Abe has ruined me and Will's life. And I don't have the money to pay a bail bondsman. Otherwise, he'd be here himself." Her lips thinned with more anger, and her sardonic expression made Yvonne weak in the knees.

The woman snapped her finger. "Oh, wait." A fake laugh

erupted. "Will can't hold a gun. He doesn't have much of a hand left. Abe blew his hand off, and now he's being charged with attempted murder of a police officer. That doesn't make much sense to me since Abraham shot him first."

Yvonne was sure the color had drained from her face. She was terrified that anything she said would further anger Maureen. Yvonne had never met the woman until now.

"And I hope I killed that stupid dog of yours! That animal is a monster. Even bit me on the leg." Her eyes darkened like angry thunderclouds. "Good thing I had a baseball bat with me."

Yvonne squeezed her eyes closed as she thought about Blue being hit with a bat. But Maureen was here for revenge, the extent of it unknown.

"You got anything to say?" Maureen was a small woman and younger than Yvonne. Her jeans and pink hoodie were splattered with blood, and she had a cut on her face, most likely from being slapped by branches, like Blue. Her tangled blonde hair hung like a mop around her face.

"I-I don't know what you want me to say." Yvonne could barely breathe, much less talk.

Maureen took a few steps toward her, her arm outstretched with the gun close enough to Yvonne that she could have grabbed it if she'd had the nerve to try.

"I'd like you to tell me which body part you'd like to give up." She raised one shoulder and dropped it slowly as her eyes blazed. "It seems only fair that you should lose a hand like my Will. Or a foot. Since you're Abe's main squeeze, seeing you bleed should make him hurt as much as I do. I might go to jail, but it will be worth it."

Yvonne opened her mouth to say something, but tears blinded her eyes, and her voice had abandoned her.

When the front door slammed open so hard that it fell off the hinges on one end, Yvonne screamed and fell to the floor. She covered her ears when Maureen shot in her direction, but Abraham was on her before she had a chance to fire the gun again. It didn't take much for him to wrestle it from her hand, spin her onto her stomach, then hold her against the wooden floor.

"Are you okay?" he asked Yvonne, who could only nod as compulsive sobs shook her. "Do you have any rope? Or better yet, zip ties?"

Yvonne somehow managed to make it to the kitchen, even though her legs felt like rubber. She returned with a short piece of rope. "This is all I could find," she said through her tears.

Abraham bound Maureen's hands as the woman thrashed and tried to get away. Abraham had slapped the gun out of her hand, and it rested near the fireplace.

He took his cell phone from the pocket of his coat and called dispatch. Abraham gave them Yvonne's address and the short version of what had happened. "Just send a car."

Maureen started to cry, but Abraham didn't have much sympathy. "I hope this has been worth it, Maureen. Now you'll be joining your husband in jail. Although I'm guessing you'll rarely see each other." He gently flipped her over, her hands bound behind her back. "He beat you all the time, Maureen. Why didn't you just take advantage of having a break from him?"

"He wouldn't have shot me, and you know it, Abe. You

took away the only man I've ever loved, and you ruined our lives." Maureen wept. "I wanted you to pay."

"By harming the only person I've ever loved? Why didn't you just come after me?" Abraham glared at her. "I got shot, too, Maureen. Don't you think that's revenge enough? I was trying to save your life."

Yvonne was still trembling, but she'd heard Abraham express how he felt about her loud and clear.

Maureen spit in Abraham's face, but even though his anger showed, he didn't react, except to say, "Did you go into my house when I wasn't there?"

"No." Maureen turned her head to the side.

Yvonne wondered if she was telling the truth. Maybe Brianna *had* snuck into Abraham's house after they'd broken up.

After the officer on duty had taken Maureen away to book her, Abraham pulled Yvonne into his arms as she whimpered and clung to his shirt with both hands. He rubbed her hair and just let her cry for a while before he eased her away and offered her a weak smile. "You're okay now. No one is going to hurt you."

Abraham's heart was still pounding against his chest. He'd taken a chance by handling things the way he did, but he knew that when he kicked the door in, it would turn Maureen's attention to him and point the gun away from Yvonne. It had been a risk that had worked. He had been lucky they hadn't heard his truck pulling into the driveway, and he'd heard women's voices as he came onto the porch.

He walked her to the couch, and they sat down. Abraham kept her in his arms until she finally stopped shaking. As he replayed the events in his mind, he recalled the way he had announced that Yvonne was the only woman he'd ever loved. Even though he wondered how she felt about that, this wasn't the time to ask.

"We're going to need to get you a new door," he said as he kissed her softly and pushed her hair away from her face.

She flashed him a timid smile. "I think that's the least of our worries."

He reached into his pocket and took out the key to his house. "Look what Brianna gave me. Apparently, she had a key made without me knowing."

"Why would she give it back now? And it wouldn't make sense to sneak in through the bathroom window if she had a key." Yvonne sniffled, but she was slowly calming down. "Maybe Maureen snuck in the window."

Abraham thought for a few minutes. "Or maybe no one did. You know, I'm not sure I'd ever checked the lock on that bathroom window. I never had a reason to. For all I know, it could have been open for months, or years. Maybe even since I bought the place. Maybe Brianna opened it to vent steam during her shower and forgot to lock it." He shrugged. "Possibly, I was just being paranoid when I felt like someone had been in the house. Or perhaps Maureen snuck in. Either way, both women are preoccupied. Maureen is going to jail, and I don't think we have to worry about Brianna, at least not until Bruce dumps her."

"What?" Yvonne's eyes widened, and Abraham filled her in on his visit to his ex-girlfriend's house. "Wow," she said. "She didn't waste any time, did she?" Then she slapped a hand over her mouth and laughed. "Guess we shouldn't be talking, huh?"

Abraham hugged her tighter and pressed his cheek to hers, glad she could find something to chuckle about. Maybe now she could feel the way he loved her even though he couldn't tell her.

"With everything going on, I forgot to mention that Eva had invited us to go to worship with them today. I'd been looking forward to that, but then . . . Blue was hurt, and . . ." She waved a hand around the living room. "And just everything else."

He kissed her on the forehead and guided her head onto his shoulder. "*Ya,* today is Second Christmas. That would have been nice to attend worship." He shifted his weight and twisted to face her, waiting until he had locked eyes with her. "I meant what I said, Yvonne. I want to change jobs, but I won't be rejoining the Amish."

She looked down, bit her lip, then looked back up at him. "Abraham, you had been considering it before you and I became closer, and whether you want to admit it or not, I've influenced your decision."

He thought about what she'd said. He didn't want to be dishonest with her. "You're right. My feelings for you have altered any possible plans I might have had to conform. But that's okay. I don't want to be without you."

"How do you know that? What if you change your

mind? You could regret it and grow to resent me." A tear slid down her face.

"I think you know how I feel about you." He was sure she'd heard him blurt it out.

She was quiet, and Abraham wondered if he had made a huge mistake. But at the time, his emotions had been running on overdrive.

"I hear my phone ringing in the bedroom." She slowly got up and shuffled to her room, but when she returned, there was a beautiful smile on her face.

"What is it?" Abraham couldn't help but smile.

"Eva is having the baby."

He stood up, went to the woman he loved, and hugged her. "I guess we better get to the hospital."

A nice ending to one of the worst days Abraham had ever had.

CHAPTER 22

The winter grew colder over the next few weeks. Abraham's insulation gift had been the best present she'd ever received. Montgomery, Indiana, was bitter in the winter.

Today, Yvonne sat bundled up in a sweatshirt and heavy coat she'd bought when she realized the jacket she'd brought from Texas wasn't going to cut it during the winter months. She also had on two pairs of socks beneath a heavier pair of boots she'd purchased. She'd slipped the hood off her head just as the worship service was beginning, and even though the house was warming up, she wasn't ready to shed her coat.

She and Abraham had been going to church every other Sunday through January and up to now, the middle of February. Even though she couldn't sit by Abraham at the worship service, since men sat on one side and the women on the other with the bishop and elders in the middle, she could see his handsome face across the room. Today's service was being held at Abraham's childhood home again, where his brother Leroy and his family lived. They hadn't been scheduled to host the church service since they'd done so back in December, but the family who was supposed to had two ill family members.

Over the past month and a half, Yvonne had met and spent time with Abraham's parents, siblings, and nieces and nephews. She'd also spent time with Eva when she wasn't at the bookstore. Jake's father's health had continued to worsen, so Jake was needed more than ever around the farm. Eva stayed busy with the baby and tending to her little family.

Jake's mother, Eva's mother, and Yvonne all playfully fought to sit by Eva during the worship service to share the holding of the baby during the three-hour celebration. Yvonne felt like they were all one big happy family. She was slowly becoming a part of Abraham's family as well. They'd warmed up to Yvonne, although there seemed to be an unspoken undertone that maybe Yvonne was the reason Abraham had not rejoined the church.

Yvonne felt blessed that they were both able to attend services every two weeks even though neither of them were Amish. Abraham understood everything that was said. Yvonne was slowly learning more Pennsylvania Dutch, but there was a lot of the dialect she still couldn't follow. Abraham translated for her later, and she looked forward to their discussions about the service, talks that sometimes lasted for hours. There was a closeness they shared that Yvonne didn't think they'd have if they hadn't been worshipping together. Not to say they wouldn't still be close, but there was an extra-special something they'd attained along the way, a gift of sorts.

She still heard from her Aunt Emma, but it was less and less, and that was okay. Her aunt had started playing bunco with a group of women and expanded her activities to include more social events since Yvonne had left. Yvonne was happy about that. Aunt Emma was even planning a trip to Europe with some of the ladies.

Mary Elizabeth was getting squirmy in Eva's arms. "Here, I'll take her," Yvonne whispered. She'd managed to get a spot next to her friend today.

As Yvonne cradled the baby, she looked across the room at Abraham, whose eyes captured hers. He smiled ear to ear every time Yvonne held the baby.

After the service and the meal, Eva tugged on Yvonne's arm and motioned for her to follow her to a back bedroom. Eva closed the door behind them.

"Is everything okay?" Yvonne asked in a whisper.

Eva sat on what appeared to be one of Leroy's daughter's beds. There were two faceless dolls on a double bed covered in a pastel-colored quilt.

"Everything is fine. I just never get a moment to myself, and we haven't had time to catch up." Eva blew upward, clearing a strand of hair that had fallen across her face. "*Mei mamm* and Jake's *mamm* will share the *boppli*, and I just need a few minutes away from everyone."

Yvonne sat beside Eva on the bed. "I can understand that."

"So . . ." Eva grinned. "Things are still going *gut* with you and Abraham?"

"Better than good." She smiled as she thought about all the happy times they'd had since the Maureen incident. "And Abraham loves his job working at the hardware store. I could see the relief just wash over him after he turned in his resignation at the station."

Eva shook her head. "I still can't believe all of that happened with Will and Maureen. It's sad."

"It is, but I still shiver every time I think about Maureen pointing that gun at me." Yvonne gave her head a quick shake. "I try not to think about it." She paused. "You know, I have a really good life. I love working at the bookstore. I love my dog. And I love . . ." She bit her bottom lip, then grinned.

"Abraham?" Eva smiled.

"Yes. I love him. We haven't officially said the words to each other. He slipped and said something during the Maureen ordeal, but it was in passing, and I'm not even sure he knows I heard him or remember. I felt like I was in shock at the time."

"Tomorrow is Valentine's Day. Maybe that would be a *gut* time to tell him." Eva's eyes lit up. "So romantic."

"Yeah, that's what I was thinking. I think I'm going to ask him to meet me at the bookstore tomorrow after work, then tell him there. We first met at the bookstore." She recalled the break-in at the store and how Abraham was the officer on duty that day. "That seems so long ago."

"Over a year and a half ago." Eva leaned back on her hands and smiled again.

"Do you do anything for Valentine's Day?" Yvonne had educated herself about the Amish, but she realized she didn't know about February 14.

"*Ya*, we do." She paused. "No outward displays of affection, fancy restaurants, or anything like that, but we make special cakes and cookies, things like that. Are you giving Abraham a gift?"

"Yes. I am." Yvonne's stomach swirled with excitement when she thought about what she was giving Abraham for Valentine's Day.

Eva lifted off her hands, sat taller, and stared at Eva. "*Ach*, are you going to tell me?"

"Nope."

Eva nudged her. "Ha ha. Now, what are you giving him?"

Yvonne put two fingers together and ran them along her lips like a zipper. "Can't tell you."

Her friend dramatically threw herself onto her back. "Ugh. The suspense!"

"I'll tell you after I give him his gift."

Eva sat up again. "It must be something really special."

"I think it is." Yvonne was nervous about the gift, but she was sure she'd chosen something he would like.

"*Ach*, one more thing before I report back to *mei* life, which I love but needed a short reprieve from. I haven't heard anyone say anything about Brianna. No one has seen her around town or anything. Someone even said her house is up for sale."

"Yep, it's true." Yvonne chuckled. "Evidently, Bruce was quite the player before he met Brianna. But Abraham said Bruce is insanely in love with her. He hasn't seen anyone else since he met her, and they are moving to Indianapolis together. Bruce took a job there." She laughed again. "There's someone for everyone, I guess."

"*Ya*, I guess so." Eva stood up. "I better go find *mei boppli* and make sure Jake's *mamm* and *mei mamm* aren't fighting over her." She rolled her eyes. "I say that with an abundance of *lieb*."

"I know." Yvonne hugged her friend. "Motherhood looks good on you."

"Jake already wants another *boppli*. Most of us have large families, but I spent so much time in bed, I'm hoping to wait just a little while longer."

"I picture what Abraham and my kids would look like sometimes," Yvonne said dreamily.

"You'd be a wonderful mother, and I'm happy you're thinking about such things with Abraham. You're going to melt his heart when you tell him you *lieb* him tomorrow. I wish I could be a fly on the wall." She started toward the bedroom door.

"I'll give you all the details." Yvonne followed her out, then wound her way through the crowd until she found Abraham.

***

"I'm ready to get out of here. What about you?" Abraham whispered in Yvonne's ear. "I think our dog misses us."

"*Our* dog, huh?" Yvonne grinned at him. "Wait until you see what I taught him since you were last at my house."

"That was only three days ago." Abraham chuckled, wishing he could spend every single day with her. But he had stayed late at work the past few days to help the owner with inventory at the hardware store. "He learned a lot during those three weeks at that school you took him to."

"He did. But I've taught him a few other things."

"Let's go before I kiss you right here in front of everyone."
Abraham inched closer to her.

"You wouldn't dare." She batted her eyes at him.

He shrugged. "I might. You better say your goodbyes, and I'll do the same." He glanced around the room.
"Hard to believe this is the house I grew up in. Not much
has changed, except there are three girls and only one boy
growing up here instead of just me, Leroy, and Daniel." He
chuckled. "I think *Mamm* always wanted a girl too. Now,
she's got three granddaughters."

Abraham and Yvonne made the rounds and told
everyone they were leaving. Blue greeted them at Yvonne's
house shortly thereafter. The dog had stopped growling
over a month ago when Abraham came to visit. Now he
just panted and waited for Abraham to scratch him behind
the ears. He had a small scar on one side of his face, but it
was barely visible, and thankfully the dog had made a full
recovery.

Yvonne unlocked the door—a new one Abraham had
gotten a deal on at the hardware store—and they rushed
into the house and out of the snow.

"More snow shoveling tomorrow, I guess." Yvonne
peeled her coat off, then her gloves.

Abraham laughed. "Not as beautiful and glamorous as
it was, is it?"

"Oh, it's still beautiful, just inconvenient sometimes."

He pulled her into his arms, kissing her as if he hadn't
seen her in a month. "I have something for you for Valentine's
Day tomorrow."

"Really?" she said, grinning. "I happen to have something for you too."

"What is it?" He playfully lifted his eyebrows up and down.

"I'm not telling," she said as she walked to the couch. "Remember how building a fire was always the very first thing I did when I walked into this house?" She sat and tapped a finger to her chin. "Then some super-nice guy paid to have insulation blown into my walls, and I am forever warm."

He slid onto the couch beside her, cupped her cheeks in his hand, and said, "I love you, Yvonne." He hadn't meant to say it right then, but the words slid off his tongue with ease. If he had read her right the past couple of months, she loved him too. But he needed to know for sure.

She gazed into his eyes, and he knew the words he had been waiting to hear were coming. "I love you, too, Abraham." After several long celebratory kisses, she batted her eyes at him. "Is that my Valentine's Day present? Telling me you love me?" She grinned. "Which I already knew."

He laughed. "Yeah, I figured you heard me that time it slipped out, but I wanted to be sure. But that wasn't my Valentine's Day gift to you." He paused. "Was that your gift to me? Because I can't imagine a better present than knowing you love me."

She shook her head. "Nope. That wasn't my gift to you either."

He laughed. "Well, I can't wait for tomorrow to get here, then."

"Can we exchange gifts at the bookstore when I close it for the day? That's where we first met."

"I remember that day well. I promise you it was love at first sight." He kissed her again. "But I didn't realize how much I could truly be in love with someone."

"I completely understand that. I feel the same way." After several more passionate kisses, she eased away, grinning.

"You have to see what Blue can do." She reached for a bag of dog treats on the coffee table. "See how he didn't even try to rip the bag open while I was gone?"

"Is that the new trick?"

She playfully slapped him on the arm. "No. Watch."

She called the dog over. "Sit and shake, Blue." The dog did both, and Yvonne gave him a biscuit. "Play dead." He rolled onto his back, and she rewarded him with another treat, then rubbed his belly. "Good boy." She turned to Abraham. "At the obedience school, that's pretty much what they taught—obedience. I wanted to teach him some fun tricks, and he learns easily."

Abraham watched her, mesmerized by her every movement. He didn't think that would ever change, and he hoped she liked his gift tomorrow.

"I guess I better go. I need my beauty rest for this big gift exchange tomorrow."

Monday morning, Yvonne told Blue bye, bundled up for the ridiculously cold weather, then picked up Abraham's gift. It wasn't something he would want to keep, but he would understand its meaning. *Maybe*. She smiled before she rushed out into the snow.

She couldn't imagine what he might be giving her, but she was sure he was clueless about her gift to him.

The day dragged on; there were only three brave women who battled the snow and came into the shop. She was glad to see Abraham show up about thirty minutes before closing time. Yvonne had two cinnamon candles lit that were left over from Christmas. As she peered out the window, Abraham scurried to the door, but Yvonne didn't see a present. Maybe it was something small in the pocket of his coat.

He rushed inside, bringing a whirlwind of snow with him. But he shed his coat quickly, hung it on the rack, and pulled her into his arms, a place she wanted to stay forever.

She held out her hand. "Give me my present."

Abraham laughed. "Present?" He scratched his chin. "Did I say I had gotten you a present?"

"Yes, kind sir, I believe you did."

He shrugged. "Okay, I guess I did. But you go first."

Yvonne's heart pitter-pattered as her excitement built. "No. You go first."

"Are you sure? It's a pretty big present." He raised his eyebrows and grinned.

She looked around him, then met eyes with him and smiled. "I don't see a present."

Then he dropped to one knee, and Yvonne almost fell to her own knees as she gasped and brought both hands to her mouth so she didn't scream when he produced a small box—the size that could hold a ring in it.

He was trembling, and Yvonne didn't think it was from the cold. Her heart was busy melting as he opened the box. "I love you, Yvonne. I've loved you since the day I saw you right here in this store." He hung his head before he looked back up at her. "I know it's only been a few months that we've officially been seeing each other, but this fall will be almost two years since I met the woman I knew I wanted to marry someday."

Yvonne lowered her hands from her mouth, took the box in her hands, and admired a beautiful white-gold band with a huge square-cut diamond. "It's the most beautiful ring I've ever seen." Her hands trembled as she felt the weight of its meaning in her hand. There was no doubt in her mind that she had chosen the perfect gift for Abraham, and her heart pounded with anticipation.

"Well? You're killing me here." He stared at her with puppy dog eyes. "Well?"

"Yes, I'll marry you, Abraham." She was still staring at the ring when he stood and started kissing her, gently cradling her cheeks in his hands as flashes of their future filled her mind with glimpses of the life they would share. She could have stayed in his arms forever, but all of a sudden he eased away.

"Ha!" he said as he pointed a finger at her. "Top that gift!" He blew on his fingers and stood taller. "Betcha can't."

She shrugged. "Hmm . . . I don't know." She pointed to the box on the counter wrapped in red and about the size of a shoebox. "Open it and see."

He ripped into the paper like a kid, and Yvonne's insides

churned and spiraled and spun again as she waited for him to lift the lid.

Abraham blinked with bafflement as he took out an Ausband, the Amish songbook. Then he lifted a dictionary—*The Pennsylvania German Dictionary* by C. Richard Beam. And lastly a prayer covering. "What is all this?"

Yvonne placed her hands on his shoulders and gazed into his eyes. "Don't you think I know how hard it was for you to choose me over your heritage? I see it in your eyes every time you look at your brother's children—the regret that your children won't be raised Amish. I see it in your eyes every two weeks at worship service. I know you love me, Abraham, but I also know that you gave up something very dear to be with me. I'm giving it back to you."

He stared at her with his mouth open.

"I've been studying Pennsylvania *Deitsch* and researching the history of the Amish. I met with the bishop and asked him if he could share the *Ordnung* with me. He explained to me that it was the unwritten rules of the Amish and that most people know them by heart. I took notes. And then I met with God, and I prayed hard about this. I want us to raise our children not just here in Montgomery but with the traditions, values, and beliefs of the Amish. I really want this, Abraham, and I'm not doing this just for you. I'm doing this for us because I believe that we will be happiest sharing our faith and love of God together, the way that you grew up. Except for my aunt, the only family I have is here. Eva and Jake are my family. You are my family."

"Yvonne, are you sure?" Abraham blinked his eyes, and she didn't hesitate when she nodded.

"Yes." She swallowed back a lump in her throat. Not because she had any doubts but because the emotion on her husband-to-be's face gave her such joy.

"Well, you've now made me the happiest man on earth . . . *twice* in one day."

She took the ring out of the box. "I know I won't be able to wear this, but until we are married, I'd like to wear it on a necklace tucked beneath my shirt and next to my heart." She paused, knowing what a ring like that must have cost. "Unless you'd like to take it back."

He shook his head. "Absolutely not. It is yours to keep forever."

She eyed what would have been her engagement ring under different circumstances, then slid it onto her ring finger. "It really is beautiful, Abraham." And it fit perfectly. She took it off, but not with any regret. It was simply a piece of jewelry.

But when it slipped from her hand and fell between a crack in the wood floor, she gasped and was quickly on her knees. "Oh, no!"

Abraham knelt beside her. "I see it. It's lodged just below the surface. There must be plywood or something underneath the floor."

"That crack has always been there. I notice it every time I sweep." She brought her face closer to the floor. "Of all the places to drop the ring. I'm so sorry! We have to find a way to get it out."

Abraham ran a hand through his hair, and even in this precarious moment, she tried to picture him with cropped bangs, suspenders, and a straw hat. It was a lovely image, and she smiled before refocusing on the problem at hand.

"We're going to have to pry this piece of wood up, but I'm not sure we won't break it. Should we call Jake?" Abraham sighed. "I hate to bother him, but . . ."

"No. Let's find something to pry the board up. He would definitely tell us to do that anyway."

Yvonne rushed to the back, first grabbing a flashlight from the counter, then returned with a screwdriver. "Will this work?"

"I think so." Abraham wedged it between the two boards, and sure enough, the board split when he lifted it up.

"Oh, no." But Yvonne was able to reach between the wood and grab the ring. But something else caught her eye, and once she had her ring safely in her hand, she reached for the small object that had been sitting beside the ring. Nothing else was there, just one worn-out coin. She wiped it on her jeans, then eyed the unfamiliar markings on both sides. With her eyes wide, she looked at Abraham. "Are you thinking what I'm thinking?"

"You bet I am. I've never seen anything like that." He met her gaze with his own wide eyes. "And *now*, we should probably call Jake."

Still kneeling on the floor with a busted board between them, Yvonne kissed Abraham, knowing they would live a wonderful life together. And if they had the chance to search for buried treasure beneath the floor of the bookstore? Well, that would be a fun bonus.

ACKNOWLEDGMENTS

Thank you to my readers for trusting me with your time. There are a lot of books out there to choose from, and I'm grateful each time mine is chosen. Much thanks, also, for continuing to walk alongside me as I strive to bring you stories that I hope entertain and inspire.

I'm thankful to my wonderful agent, Natasha Kern. My dear friend and assistant, Janet Murphy, is irreplaceable. And I'm blessed with a fabulous publishing team. I'm grateful for all of you!

Thank you to my wonderful street team, Wiseman's Warriors. You gals rock, and I'm so fortunate to have you all onboard.

To my husband, Patrick—what can I say? I'd be lost without you. I adore you. I respect you. And I love you with all my heart. I'm "always your Annie" . . . forever and ever.

Every breath is a gift, and as I continue to inhale the

blessings I've been given, I hope that in some small—or maybe big—way my stories touch lives and infuse faith, hope, and love into the hearts of my readers. Thank you, God, for allowing me to serve You via stories to tell.

DISCUSSION QUESTIONS

1. Brianna isn't always the most likable character, but if you look closely at her personality, what vulnerabilities do you see?
2. Blue is a character in his own right throughout the story. The book is even dedicated to my beloved dog, who passed quite a few years ago. Have you ever had a fur baby that didn't start out as "man or woman's best friend" but ultimately won over your heart the way Blue did with Yvonne?
3. Abraham is smitten with Yvonne from the beginning. How much does that push him to part ways with Brianna? Would Abraham have broken up with Brianna if Yvonne hadn't moved to Montgomery?
4. Yvonne truly overhauls her life, geographically and spiritually. What are some examples of Yvonne's spiritual journey, and how does she apply them in her life?
5. Maureen is clearly involved in an abusive relationship

and unwilling to press charges against Will. Have you known a person in such a situation, and did they eventually seek help and/or make the changes necessary to live a peaceful life?

6. If you had to choose a favorite character, who would it be and why?

7. There is a tangible item in every Beth Wiseman book, including *The Story of Love*. Do you know what the item is?

8. Yvonne and Abraham fit together in ways that he didn't with Brianna. What are some examples of this?

9. If you could become any character in the book and make modifications to the story, who would you be, and what would you change?

10. Yvonne and Abraham are set on paths that eventually merge. Did you see any crossroads where they might have ended up going in a different direction? Were their steps deliberate, inspired by their faith, or random? If random, how so? If by God's perfect timing, can you give an example?

11. Abraham is attracted to Yvonne and to Brianna. Even though the women are very different, they do have some similarities. Can you name something the women have in common?

12. At the end of the book, Yvonne and Abraham find an old coin. Can you speculate as to how this will tie into the next book in the series?

The Amish Bookstore Series

Available April 2023

The Amish Inn Series

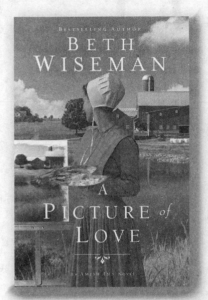

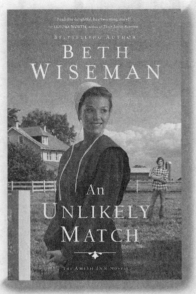

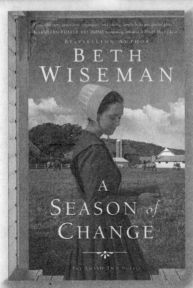

 ZONDERVAN®

AVAILABLE IN PRINT,
E-BOOK, AND AUDIO

The Amish Journey Series

Enjoy four celebratory Amish stories centered around a birthday, a baptism, a wedding, and the Christmas season from bestselling author Beth Wiseman!

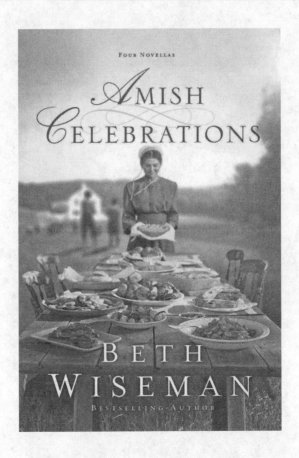

ABOUT THE AUTHOR

Bestselling and award-winning author Beth Wiseman has sold over two million books. She is the recipient of the coveted Holt Medallion, is a two-time Carol Award winner, and has won the Inspirational Reader's Choice Award three times. Her books have been on various bestseller lists, including CBA, ECPA, Christianbook, and *Publishers Weekly*. Beth and her husband are empty nesters enjoying country life in south-central Texas.

Visit her online at BethWiseman.com
Facebook: @AuthorBethWiseman
Twitter: @BethWiseman
Instagram: @bethwisemanauthor